Andrea, Don't forget to Change lanes!

THE MIDDLE ROAD

K.G. REUS~

CM LALLY

The Middle Road © 2019 K.G. Reuss, C.M. Lally

ACKNOWLEDGEMENTS

earest Reader

Thank you for taking a chance on *The Middle Road*! We'd also like to take a moment to thank everyone involved in this book—our families, pets, editor, cover designer, complete strangers who paved the way for Carter's story, and maybe one or two cocktails in the late hours of the night.

We wanted this book to be raw and emotionally charged. Carter's story was inspired by our own heartbreaking experiences and many nights in the back of an ambulance. Stories from patients recalling their most vivid, heartwarming memories about living their best lives (dancing on Broadway, falling in love in the rain) to their worst moments (losing a loved one, uncertain futures). It's their tears, anger, fear, *hope* that is the blood and bone of Carter George.

We sincerely hope Carter's story will give others the courage to fight whatever it is they're facing. You know that saying, "Live like you're dying"? Yeah. Do that. Every single day. Always.

Now, let's buckle up. It's going to be a rough ride, but we promise it will be *so* worth it at the end.

K.G & C.M.

"Every man dies. Not every man really lives." -William Wallace

ONE

CARTER

*K*_arma is a fucking bitch._

That's the thought that pops in my head the moment Doctor Aarons says the three little words that alter my life.

"Carter, did you hear what I said?" Doctor Aarons calls out to me, bringing me back to his office, his words from earlier still ringing in my ears.

I take in his wizened face, graying hair, the fine lines etched into his skin indicative of his age. An age I'll never be able to obtain.

You have cancer. It's terminal.

"Yeah. I'm dying," I grunt, feeling numb inside. I'm not even sure if my heart is still beating. Maybe I've already died, his words the nails in my coffin.

"There are multiple tumors visible on the scans. We can keep an eye on them, see if they're growing. But honestly, Carter, it's not good. I wish I had more answers for you." He surveys me carefully, clearly trying to be delicate in his wording.

There are only so many ways you can kindly tell someone they're dying. I get it. Sugar-coating it won't change a damn thing.

"I'm so sorry, Carter. We can begin treatment—"

"What's the point?" I snap at him, getting to my feet, my head aching. I sway slightly. Doctor Aarons reaches for me, but I flinch away, not wanting him to touch me. I don't need his help. Not that he can help me anyway. I'm a dead man walking. And only thirty-two years old.

The pounding in my head throbs tremendously, making me want to vomit. I swallow down the burning bile, unsure if it's just from the headache or the sickness from the news. Either way, this headache has been killing me for months. I guess that's the fucking understatement of the year.

I make my way to the door and pause, looking over my shoulder at him. "How long do I have?"

"Maybe six months. Tops," his voice is somber, his mouth turning down into a deep frown. The sympathy in his brown eyes kicks up the nausea rolling around in my gut. "Here." He steps forward and hands me a script for pain medication. "These will help."

"Will they cure me?" I ask softly, looking down at the small, white square of paper clutched in his hand.

The scribbled mess of his handwriting reflects the images of my life as they flash before me. I take note of his gold wedding band. I've never been married. Hell, I've never even fallen in love. I've been too busy amassing a real estate empire and tearing down companies which won't aide in the fight for my life that I've forgotten about marriage. Family. Love.

"No," he answers, patting me gently on the back.

"Then they won't help me." I turn to pull the door open.

"Carter, take the damn prescription. The headaches will only get worse. You're going to want them."

Snatching the script from his hand, I stuff it into my suit pocket. "My father died from the same disease. You know what the last thing he said to me was as he lie dying in his bed surrounded by all the stuff he'd accumulated over the years? All the money, the real estate, the enemies?"

Phil Aarons had been one of my father's friends. They'd gone to college together. He'd been the one to diagnose him with terminal brain cancer.

"What?" he asks, his eyes filled with more sympathy.

"He said, 'Don't make my mistakes.' It looks like I'm the spitting image of him, right down to dying in a high-rise that won't mean shit once I'm dust and ash. The only difference is I won't have anyone to hold my hand on the way out."

"Carter, there are support groups—"

"Fuck support groups." I tug the door open, letting it bang against the examination room wall. The models of different body systems tremble on the table, threatening to spill to the floor. I don't bother waiting for him to reply. I storm out of his office and out to the street.

I only make it as far as a parking meter before I hurl my guts out onto a New York City sidewalk and someone's parked Nissan. People dodge away from me as I continue to vomit onto the cracked sidewalk, my hand clutching the parking meter. The pain in my head soars to new levels, the noises and lights from the busy city making my vision blurry.

When the nausea passes enough for me to pull my phone from my pocket, I call Derek, my driver. When he answers, I'm quick in my needs. After all, time is of the essence.

"Come get me," I croak.

I don't wait for his response. I end the call and straighten up, leaning against the parking meter, sweat pouring from my face. Within minutes, Derek maneuvers the sleek, black SUV beside the Nissan. Staggering forward, I open the back door before he can come around and do it for me.

"You look bad," Derek comments as he stands at the opened door. My head rests against the cool leather of the front seat, perspiration dripping from my forehead. A car honks behind us, making me wince.

"I'm dying," I breathe out, closing my eyes.

"What?" there's panic in Derek's voice.

Derek is young. Twenty-five. I'd given him a job as my driver after he'd delivered many packages and correspondences to me on his bike as a messenger. I saw something in him. Perhaps, it was adventure, something I've always wanted. It reflects in his dark eyes whenever he looks around. It's a hungry look, a voracious craving for more than what life was currently providing. Maybe by driving me, he'd someday be able to afford that backpacking trip through Europe he's always going on about. But if I'm dead, Derek is out a job and an adventure.

I keep my eyes closed, desperate to make the pain go away. I reach into my pocket and pull out the script from Doctor Aarons. "I need this. Hurry."

Derek wastes no time taking the script from me and scurrying around to the driver's side of the car. The SUV jerks forward, my stomach rolling again, my head feeling like a drumline is using my skull as its percussion section.

Maybe death won't be so bad. Anything is better than the pain and hell I'm in.

"Derek, crank the air up, full blast." Within seconds, the cooler air reaches me, and I sink deeper into the seat, loosen my vomit-stained tie, and watch the masses of people go about their day in this city, doing whatever the fuck it is they do to fulfill their lives.

My life is as dark and depressing as the interior of the car. Black is supposed to be professional, elegant, and a sign of high wealth. What a joke for all the good it does me. All the riches of the world can't buy me a cure.

Derek swerves the SUV into a corner space outside of McCabe's Rx and runs in. They filled my father's scripts, and here we are, full-fucking-circle, getting mine filled. The twisted, witchy laugh of karma reverberates in my skull making me want to pound my head against the glass window.

An RV pulls up at the light and waits next to me. I glance over, and two little boys have their faces smashed against the windows, trying to see the height of the tall buildings. Large, luminous eyes take in the big city while tiny fingers point in a million different directions, attempting to get their mom to see everything they see.

In true Derek loyalty, he brings the pill bottle and a water right to my door, twisting the caps off both to try and please me. With my palm held out, he places two bright green capsules in my hand, and I pop them into my mouth with all the reverence of magic pills, chugging water to wash them down.

With a sigh, I sit back and close my eyes, squeezing them tighter when a blaring horn assaults the quiet of the car as Derek slides into the driver's seat. "Where to, Boss?" he asks quietly.

"Just follow that RV. I want to see what they see," I murmur, pointing to the big cream and brown colored contraption a few car lengths ahead of us. Derek does as I say, not saying a word about my strange request. Never once have I told him to follow another car, let alone an RV. His eyes slide over to me several times. *He thinks I've finally cracked.*

And I just may have.

Eventually, we follow the family across the Brooklyn Bridge and into Liberty Park. We park a few open spaces away, my gaze evaluating the value of the vehicle. The RV has more rust on it than an old tractor I saw once abandoned in a corn field. *Neglect. Wasteful neglect.*

This particular rust is older than both parents combined. Here are two people giving their children a lifetime of memories with the only means they have: a rusty, beat-up recreation vehicle and their time and effort inside an adventure.

Yesterday, I wouldn't have even paid the slightest attention to them. Today, I'm deeply moved by this loving family. Would my life have turned out differently had my parents given me more time and effort instead of possessions? For all of the things I own, the one thought that won't escape my mind is that my empty life is a result of neglect.

Damn it. I rub my forehead trying to erase the throb inside my skull. The ache is lessening, but it's still a dull roar. Like a bee is trapped inside it, buzzing and flitting around looking for a means of escape.

"Are you all right?" Derek moves the rearview mirror to take in my full face. Fresh worry lines wrinkle his forehead, no doubt a result of the poorly-timed delivery of my diagnosis from earlier.

"Yeah, take me home. I need rest."

～

I JOLT AWAKE WHEN THE ENGINE CUTS OFF AND DEREK OPENS MY DOOR. The quiet of the garage at my apartment building soothes my troubled mind. *Home.* Even the *whoosh* of the elevators rising to the penthouse suite washes away those three life-altering words from my memory for a while.

I head straight for my office and wait for my computer to boot up.

"I thought you were going to rest," Derek chastises as he plops down into the leather chair across from me.

"I am, after I send a few emails regarding tomorrow."

"And may I ask, what is tomorrow— besides Wednesday?"

"Tomorrow is the day I release my company into the hands of the CFO, I meet with my attorney to settle my affairs, and it's also the day you buy us a recreational vehicle fit to go across the country. We're going on an adventure."

"We are?" his voice rises with excitement and an unknown hesitation.

"Yes, we are," I assure him, turning all my focus to my email.

"This isn't going to be some Thelma & Louise trip that you're planning for…you know, the final scene." His eyebrows draw together in distress over the thought of it.

"I didn't plan on it ending that way, but if it does, I'm calling dibs on Thelma. If anyone's having hot sex on this trip, it's me."

DIARY

Day 1

I don't know why the hell I thought I'd start a diary. No. Let's call it a travel log. I guess maybe I thought it might help sort my thoughts. Perhaps, after I'm gone someone can auction it off and make a few dollars. The great Carter George's innermost thoughts before his death. Yeah, I can see it becoming a bestseller now.

To be honest, I don't know what I'm doing. I've never had a 'no return from here' situation. There's always been another deal that's usually bigger and better. This dying shit definitely doesn't have another deal after it unless I'm somehow able to barter with the devil once I get to his gates.

I remember watching my father go. It made me pray to a god that clearly doesn't exist that I'd go fast. Fuck, I don't want to suffer like my father did. People say he deserved the long, hard death he got. He was ruthless. He was a businessman, and I'd followed in his footsteps. By the way it's looking, I'll keep following them right to the grave. With one exception.

This road trip.

Dying has a way of fucking with your head. Maybe this really is karma for being the man I have been. I was my father's son, after all.

He worked himself to the bone, ignoring my mother and me. Then she bailed. She kissed me goodbye, hopped in a limo, and left without a word or consolatory hug. Nothing.

At first, I got phone calls from her a few times a year, which dwindled to a few times every other year, and became non-existent as I aged into adulthood. Hell, I haven't seen my mother since I graduated from college. Scratch that. She didn't show up to that.

Enough about that. Today I have to go to my board and explain what the hell is going on. They're going to be pissed, but it's not like I give a shit. I won't be here in six months, so it doesn't matter. It's not like I even have a legacy to pass the company on to. I lived the life of a perma-bachelor, never falling in love for more than an hour at a time. If I even had the time for that. I doubt I'd have stayed married for long anyway. None of it matters now though.

My story is going to start right after I meet with my board this morning. Then all that shit will be a past life.

I want to live, damnit. Maybe there's no cure, but I have six months left. I'm going to live the life I should've been living. Strange how your own looming funeral humbles you.

I've sent Derek out to get us an RV. I told him money wasn't an issue. I also had him get us some camping gear since I've never been. He seemed all too eager about it.

I have to go now. My meeting with the board is at 10:00 AM. I'll be back to finish this log tomorrow. I hope.

TWO

CARTER

"Good morning, Mr. George!" Abigail, my secretary, greets me as I walk through the lobby. Her large green eyes drink me in as they always do. I don't have any doubt she wants me to bend her over my desk and fuck her like a porn star, but the one thing I learned from my father was, "Don't fuck the help." It was engrained in my head that most women were gold diggers, and once they had the goods, they'd cut town, leaving you a broken man.

"Abigail," I grunt, moving past her and going into my office. The *click-clack* of her heels on the polished marble floor echoes behind me. Internally, I sigh because I know she wants to start the day off with my itinerary… or loads of questions about why I've canceled everything and called an emergency meeting of the board.

"Mr. George," she calls out as I sit at my desk and stare out the floor to ceiling windows, overlooking New York City. Truly a beautiful view. I've never really bothered to care before. "Did you want me to cancel all your meetings this week?" she asks from behind me.

I swivel back to find her frowning. I never cancel meetings.

"Yes, Abigail. All my meetings. In fact, cancel them all indefinitely." I press my lips into a firm line. Decision made.

Her eyes widen, her lips parting as she gawks at me.

"Um, Mr. George, you have a meeting with Senator Wilkins tomorrow. You've spent months trying to get this—"

"Abigail," I say with a sigh, rubbing my eyes as the muscles in my neck begin to tighten and my head starts to ache. "Cancel the damn meeting."

She pauses before coming to sit on the edge of my desk, putting her long legs in her short red skirt on display. It hasn't slipped past me what a beautiful woman she is. Hell, it was one of the reasons I'd hired her—something nice to look at. And I'd be a damned liar if I hadn't thought about wrapping her long, chestnut colored hair around my hand and pressing her naked body against my wall while I fucked her for all I was worth.

Her hand comes out and rests on mine, concern written in her eyes.

"What's wrong, Mr. George? Is there anything I can do to help?" She leans forward, her cleavage flashing me.

I have six months to live. I've never *once* screwed an employee. Well, not in the natural sense. And it isn't like I'll be around for the fallout. Reaching out, I brush the front of my fingers gently down her stocking-clad thigh. A visible shiver travels through her as she leans into my touch.

"Why don't you go close the door, Abigail," my voice is a soft, low command as my eyes meet her lust-filled ones. "Maybe we can find something for you to do."

The door clicks softly, and I'm hot on her stiletto heels, pressing her breasts against it before she knows what I'm about. She's wearing these black hose with a sexy seam sewn up the back, like hookers and strippers wear. My dick goes rigid every time she wears them. I trace that seam with my fingertips from the back of her knees all the way up under that fucking red siren skirt to grab her pert ass cheeks.

"Oh, Mr. George. I've waited forever for you to notice me," her voice is heavy with lust.

"Holy shit, Abigail. Are those garters?" I caress the smooth mounds of her ass cheeks, slowly inching forward to her sex until my fingers are wet, and my dick is pointing straight to the North Pole. I drop to my knees and shove my head under her skirt for a better inspection.

"Yes, sir. Do you like them?"

"*Fuck* yes. Now, what do we have here?" My knees nudge her legs wider apart for a better view of one soft, perfectly pink, and hairless pussy with a piercing. "Abigail, you're a naughty girl."

"Yes, sir. I am. It doesn't hurt if you want to touch…or lick it. Go ahead, Mr. George. You won't hurt me." The way her breathless voice addresses me has me ready to spill my load in my pants.

"Well…I haven't had breakfast yet, and they say it's the most important meal of the day." I snap her G-string in two with my fingers and run my tongue up the seam of her labial lips, flicking that diamond and sucking on her clit, putting a shine on it like it's on display with the Crowned Jewels.

Her climax comes quickly while juices that taste like pineapples drip down my chin. Pineapple happens to be my favorite fruit, so I eat like a man harvesting the best pineapple crop ever. I'm so involved in lapping her up, I'm oblivious to her hands pressing and pounding on the door with each orgasm that rakes through her.

By the time her legs stop quivering, I'm full-blown desperate to be inside her. My dick is aching and pushing on the zipper of my pants so hard, I swear it has teeth marks embedded on it.

"Abigail," I growl.

"Yes, Mr. George," she purrs like a kitten lying in the sun.

"My desk. Now," I command. She immediately steps around me and walks to the desk without another word. She flips her skirt up, flattening it neatly against the desk to avoid wrinkling it, and presses her chest against it, anchoring herself with her hands wrapped over the edge. Her face turns to meet mine. "I'm ready, Mr. George."

There's a knock on the door. "Is everything OK in there?" a female voice penetrates the locked door, causing Abigail to giggle.

"That's Lindsey," she whispers.

"Lindsey, everything is good. There was a bug. Go back to your desk." Abigail winks at me as her footsteps fade.

By the time I reach her, my hands have fumbled through unbuckling my belt and have undone my pants and zipper. I pull myself out of my briefs and stroke my dick a few times, pumping and priming it to ensure a good load.

Fuck. What about birth control? Do you really want to leave a kid without a father, or have a child who might die like you at a young age?

"Umm, Abigail, are you on something? You know, to prevent pregnancy?"

"Yes. I just had a new IUD placed last week."

That's all I need to hear before I kill my own mood. I thrust inside her, slamming her hips into the embossed leather desk pad.

A loud grunt escapes my throat as her pussy walls clench against my dick. *Jesus Christ, I'm done for.* I slam into her over and over, gripping her hips and swirling around hitting all the secret spots a woman has. She blabbers incoherently what sounds like "harder, deeper, faster...rougher." *Maybe.* I give up trying to make it out.

The lower part of my back tingles with my impending orgasm, so I slow down. A quick glance at the clock tells me I have thirty more minutes before my meeting. So, I tease her with the tip of my dick. After a few moments, she climaxes, soaking herself and the papers on my desk. Usually that shit would've pissed me off but not today.

My fingers lose their grip on her hips as her orgasm runs over the edge of my desk and onto my carpet. Wanting to see more, I roll her onto her back and watch as she opens her blouse and lets her tits spill from their cage.

I let out a groan of ecstasy as I push back into her, my hands fist around her luscious creamy mounds. "Fuck, Abigail. You've soaked everything. I'm going to have to finish here early just to clean this mess up."

I pound her until my balls leave red welts on her ass cheeks. When the tingle in my back travels up my spine, I explode like a rocket into her atmosphere. It's a full, throttle *kaboom* without the smoke and flames. *Damn, that's great pussy.*

Wouldn't you know it? That's karma getting another laugh in at my situation.

I STRAIGHTEN MY TIE AND STARE AT MYSELF IN THE MIRROR IN MY attached bathroom. My dark hair is a freshly tossed sexy mess. I haven't shaved, so I've amassed an impressive five o'clock shadow. Deep brown eyes stare dully back at me. Ugly, bruise-like circles surround them, a beacon screaming how sleep-deprived I've been. How stressed out I've been. How fucking close to death I am. *My little death halos.* I snort at the thought.

After splashing water on my face, I quickly towel off and leave my office, ready to face the board members on what could very well be my last day in my own company. Maybe a part of me hopes for a miracle, so I've decided not to totally let it go. I'm going to turn it over to my CFO for five months. After that, maybe I'll be able to gauge my health better.

Abigail is back at her desk when I walk out. She gives me a sexy smile, her cheeks reddening when her eyes rake over my body.

Whatever. I'm a one and done kind of man. But man, that pussy had been almost top shelf. Too bad for both of us. Again, karma was a real fucking bitch. I don't bother acknowledging her past a blank look.

"Carter, what's going on?" John Billings, my CFO greets me the moment I walk into the conference room. Concern is written all over his aging features, making his usually bright eyes appear larger.

"I'll explain if you'll have a seat, John," I say, patting him on the shoulder, back to being all business.

John Billings is another one of my father's old friends. He's probably been more of a father to me than my own father ever was. There's been more than one time in my life when I'd gone to John for advice instead of my own father when he was still alive. Father would've told me to crush my enemy by any means necessary. John would advise to simply think it through to find the best logical, beneficial approach without making a lot of waves. Overall, John is a decent guy. I trust him.

John surveys me before nodding gruffly and going to his spot among the eleven board members already seated. I move to stand in front of the room, facing them. All of them wear looks varying from confusion to concern. Some of the members I don't trust as far as I can throw them. And believe me, some of the pricks I'd like to toss from my office window. Money, greed, and time has turned a lot of them into snakes. But John will handle them. It's what he did.

"Gentlemen," I begin, clearing my throat. "I'm leaving."

"What?" John frowns, while the other members sit forward, all voicing their confusion.

"Where are you going?" David Sanders, one of the snakes, asks. "And what exactly does that mean?"

"I'm going on a trip that I may not come back from."

This statement is greeted by more confusion, so I hold my hand up to silence them. "I need time away for my own mental health and clarity. I'm going to be turning over everything to John to be dealt with in my absence. I don't wish to be bothered by anything. My phone will be off, and I'll be out of town."

"Jesus, Carter, for how long?" Richard Garber demands, the fear of what it means obviously scaring him a bit because his dark eyes look wild.

"Five months. Maybe longer," I reply, my voice not as strong as I hoped it would be.

Another murmur of confusion echoes through the room.

"Carter George doesn't leave his job behind to chase mental clarity," Bob Jones screeches, his eyes bulging, his overlapping stomach banging against the table as he sits forward quickly in his seat. "You take down men that do!" He pounds his pudgy fist on the table. "Don't you recall tearing apart Irving Davie's company after his wife passed away? You stripped the man of everything in only a matter of *hours*. You're a predator who strikes when prey is the weakest! You're not the prey. You've never been the prey!"

"Don't forget Cameron Unkel's company, Haspert Holdings. Unkel came looking for help, and Carter stole the company right from under his nose!" Brian Mathis adds, looking at the men in the room. Brian glances at me, shaking his head. "If I remember correctly, you screwed his wife *and* his sister right after you signed the papers."

Yeah, I'm a fucking snake. Probably the biggest one in the room. Those aren't even my worst atrocities in the business world. Karma finally caught up with my treacherous ass.

"Carter, what's going on?" John asks, his brows knit.

I shake my head and look down at my hands which are clutching the chair in front of me. I don't want to tell any of them. They'll probably overthrow me if they know what's really going on.

"I just need a break. That's all. I realized it's time to take one before the opportunity passes me by. My lawyers have drawn everything up. They're waiting outside." I can't stay around and answer questions or argue with them. I sweep from the room as it erupts in more questions. I haven't made it a few steps down the hall before John catches up to me.

"Carter, what the hell is going on?" he demands once more, stopping me. "There's no damn way you're walking away from this because you need a break. I want to know what happened."

"I'm my father's son," I reply, deadpan. "In *every* conceivable aspect."

"Your father wouldn't walk away from his empire, son," John's tone softens as he looks at me. "Only death could pull him away."

"Like I said, I'm my father's son."

"Carter, are you sick?" John's voice becomes hushed, his hand on my shoulder.

The backs of my eyes burn, my throat tightening. *What the hell is this? Am I struggling to not fucking cry? Jesus.* I haven't cried since I was five and fell off my bike. Father had come barreling out of the house my mother had loved so much, screaming at me to get up and not be weak. I remember the spit flying from his mouth, his hand striking me hard across the face. I'd fallen across my bike, breaking my arm in the process.

Tears were for the weak. And no son of his was weak. If I wanted to cry, he'd give me a reason to.

"No." I swallow hard, my voice wavering. "I just need a break, John. *Please*. Help me."

"Absolutely, Carter." John's eyes sweep over me again, the worry evident in every breath he takes. "What can I do?"

"Just keep my company safe. And take care of Linda. I always liked her," I say, speaking of his wife of forty years.

"Of course," John murmurs as I back away.

I can't bear to stand around and talk any longer. I need to get out of there. Wasting no more of my precious time, I walk out, not even bothering to return to my office.

"Derek?" I croak into my phone when he answers.

"Yeah, boss?"

"Are we ready yet?"

"Sure are. We can pick the RV up in an hour. I have all the stuff you asked for."

"Good. Come get me. I need to get the hell out of here." I drag my fingers through my hair.

"I'm already outside, boss."

I hit the *End* button on my phone and step outside. Derek is waiting for me just as he said, the passenger door already open. I step up to it and turn back to stare at the monstrous granite and stone building behind me.

It's probably the last time I'll ever look at it.

DIARY

Day 2

I don't know why I thought 6:00 AM was a good time to hit the road, but that's what I told Derek, so that's what I'm doing up at this ungodly hour. I've packed all of my casual clothing, which I'll admit isn't much, into two suitcases. Just goes to show how much of my life I've wasted in business suits. Anyway...

Today is the beginning of the end. Jesus Christ, how fucking morbid.

Today is the beginning of the end of me being a dick. There. That's better.

Here are the targeted goals for this trip:

Learn to be less of a dick and more open to new things. Meaning being less open to my usual hard-assedness, if that's even a word. Fuck it, it's my word, and if I live through this by some miracle, I'm going to trademark it for this journal's future publication.

Learn to appreciate the melting pot of this great nation with its diversity.

Learn to appreciate the wonder of small moments and the beauty within.

OK, that's enough platitudes for me at this hour.

Derek is here, and so is the beginning of the "Less Hard-Assed-ness" Tour.

THREE

CARTER

"*W*ow, Derek. It's roomy. Nice. I like it." I step from the interior and lean against the wall in the alley behind my apartment building to size-up the exterior of my new home on wheels. Having just finished the grand tour of the inside, I have to admit I'm pleased. It's luxurious.

"Well, you said recreational vehicle, but when I explained to the salesmen what we were doing, he showed me the tour buses. This is a Variomobil Signature 1200 tour bus. It's a medium wheelbase, so I can still drive it with my CDL- A license. And I already have my passenger endorsement from when I had to pick up clients from the airport. So, we're good to go. And check this out." We walk to the back, where he pulls a garage remote out of his pocket and clicks it. The back door lowers like something out of the future, and inside is my black Mercedes SL roadster, snug-as-a-bug.

"Derek, you are THE MAN." I high-five him for caring enough to bring my baby along.

"Thank you, sir. We need to hit the road now so we can miss morning traffic with this beast." He closes the back door, and the excitement builds up in me like I'm eight years old again going on my first plane ride.

"All right, but first." I pull a small bottle of Korbel out of my pocket and swing once, swing twice, swing three times and smash it against the back bumper, making sure I don't scratch it.

"What are we naming her, sir?"

"Why does it always have to be a woman? I think you called it before. I hereby christen you, the Beastmaster."

"I like it, sir."

"And stop calling me, sir. Call me Carter."

"Well, c'mon, Carter. We ain't got all day."

"Actually, we do. That's the beauty of it. We have all the time left in my world." He rolls his eyes at my melodramatics before opening the door.

We swing out of the alley quickly and roll through the nearly vacant streets of Fifth Avenue for a few blocks, passing the early morning joggers in Central Park. "Goodbye work-a-fucking-holics," I holler out to no one in particular before I slump down in the soft leather of the passenger seat and fall asleep.

I wake up near Allentown, PA with a horrendous headache and a grumbling stomach.

"Can we pull over? I need to eat and take some meds."

Derek pushes a button on the navigator screen and says, "Find pancakes." After a few seconds of searching, ten options appear, and he picks an International House of Pancakes close by. Once I make my way to the back bedroom and sort through my unpacked luggage for my toiletry bag, I find the dreaded bottle I need and walk back to the front. My God, pancakes sound divine.

SHELBY, OUR WAITRESS, SEATS US IN A BOOTH THEN POURS TWO OF THE smallest cups of coffee I think I've ever seen. The only saving grace is she leaves us both our own carafes.

"So, what's the itinerary for this trip? Do we have a final destination? Anything in particular you want to see or do?" Derek asks, pouring three creamers into his small mug and sipping it without spilling any. He reminds me of a giant drinking from a tiny teacup. I bite back the snicker before answering him.

"There's no itinerary. We drive without purpose or meaning. I don't want to do much planning on this trip. I just want to see what I see and experience whatever happens."

"OK. So we're hippies on a very luxurious caravan. I'm down with that."

"We're Lewis and Clark, exploring this great nation to find its hidden treasures." Derek spits out his coffee, splattering the table, amused at my historical comparison of our little adventure.

"I'm pretty sure neither Lewis nor Clark were Nigerian immigrants, but these are modern times. I'm happy my wanderlust soul is being catered too."

"It's not backpacking through Europe, but it's close enough," I remark, sipping my black coffee. *Good God, it needs creamer.* It tastes like tar. I add in two creamers, taste it, and add in two more. It isn't Starbucks, but it's caffeine, and it'll have to do.

A backpacking trip through Europe is now part of my will for Derek after I'm gone with a small stipend to boot. He's the closest thing I have to a best friend. He's my confidant. I mean, c'mon, the man has seen and heard me getting a blow-job in the backseat for Knick's tickets. He's witnessed me wheel and deal through some pretty ruthless situations. He's observed me slicing and dicing men's lives, leaving them and their families destitute. I'm pretty sure he thinks he's employed by the devil incarnate.

Our food arrives, and I swear, they're the best pancakes I've ever eaten.

Once we both have full bellies, we leave, piling into our home on wheels. Derek has a thing for loud rock music, and not the stuff blasting out of the local rock station. I mean full-on underground music with screaming guitars and band members who look like they're straight out of a nightmare with their elaborate makeup and stage presence. Cranking up something that screams at me makes me cringe. Derek assures me it'll get better. Trying to be more openminded, I listen to the songs of his favorite band as they squeal throughout the Beastmaster.

After three songs, I'm hooked. I air drum while Derek hollers at the top of his lungs. To passersby, we probably look like we're part of some rock band on the way to our next destination. Or like we're drug-crazed yuppies who've been snorting too much coke.

For the first time in my life though, I feel free. There's no looming deadline—unless we're talking my death—there's no work that needs to be done, no meetings to get to, no kiss-asses trying to get on my good side, and no media in my face asking for a story. Nothing. Just the prospect of life.

So, I grin like a fucking maniac as I air drum to my new favorite band.

DIARY

Day 3

I may have overdone it with the air drums. I ended up with a headache that required me to go to my room and lay down. I didn't wake up until just now. It's one in the damn morning. That has to be the longest nap I've ever taken in my life. Hell, I've never slept that long at night before, let alone from a nap.

I don't even know where the hell we are. I know we're not moving and some kind of lights filter in through my blinds. Maybe street lights? Derek is snoring in one of the bunks down the hall.

So far, I've had fun on this trip. I know. It's been a fucking day, and I slept through three-quarters of it. But I've never done that before.

I've also never wandered around in the middle of the night like some sort of runaway, but the idea is vastly becoming appealing to me as I sit here and lament my life in The Life and Times of the Ruthless Prick Carter George.

Fuck it. Y.O.L.O. Don't judge me for that word usage. I promise I'll never use it again.

FOUR

CARTER

I stumble out of the Beastmaster, taking care not to wake sleeping beauty who's snoring so loudly I contemplate putting him out of my misery. Derek has driven us to a grocery store parking lot and parked us in the back near the dumpster for Christ's sake.

I could've driven my baby out of the back garage, but decide I want to walk. I snap a photo of the store, so I'll remember the name, and make my way out to the front sidewalk. The street is well-lit, and there are still cars and people out. A stiff drink is definitely needed.

Walking down the road, I set my sights on a place that has multiple neon lights on the sign. It's too far away to read, but it's either a liquor store or a strip club, and I won't turn either down right now.

About halfway down the block, a young man sits on a bus bench playing some type of contraption that looks like a keyboard but sounds like a guitar. His hands are sliding left and right, making the instrument weep like a baby. It's fucking beautiful. He turns and looks in my direction, probably making sure I'm not going to rob him, and then starts bellowing out a song I've never heard before.

The rich baritone of his voice reminds me of the country music singer, Trace Adkins. Not that I run in those circles, but I heard him play once at a bar in the city while he was holed up waiting out a hurricane. It was an impromptu concert at a blues club my buddy owned. He sang three or four songs without any music, and I sat mesmerized at the way he could touch a crowd with song. The broad I had sitting on my lap was wiping tears from her eyes as he sang about making it to Arlington. *Yeah, just fucking beautiful.*

I walk around in front of him as I get closer and listen to him for the remainder of the song. His jeans are tattered at the legs, and his socks are mismatched. One of his Chucks has a hole in it by the big toe. Long hair hangs partly in and partly out of a ponytail near the nape of his neck, but his eyes are clear, his hands are steady, and his voice is strong. As he releases the last note and lets it hang in the air for emphasis, he nods to me with thanks for staying.

"Hey, uh, you do this every day out here?"

He nods his head at me.

"For money? I think they call it busking."

"No, sir. I just play for people to hear music. I don't play for money. There's no tip jar, and I don't own a hat. I don't have no money on me neither." His hands raise from the board and hold still in the air. He looks around nervously, like I'm either about to bust him for doing something illegal or rob him.

"I'm not a cop, man, and I'm not going to rob you. You're cool. I've just never heard anything more beautiful. What is that thing?" I gesture to the guitar box balanced on his lap.

"It's a steel guitar. I made her myself." His face beams with pride, but I roll my eyes. Another inanimate object assigned a female gender, but I'll give him this one because it certainly cries like a woman. I bet if he played it faster, it'd bitch and whine like one too.

"Are you some kind of music student from around here? And, by the way, where the hell are we?"

"You don't know where you're at? Are you all right, mister?" He looks at me like I'm crazy.

"Yeah, I'm fine, right now anyway. I rode in on a bus but slept most of the trip. So, no, I don't know where I'm at. Clue me in."

"You're in West by God Virginia. Just outside of Clarksburg. Where you heading?"

"Right now, I'm heading to those neon signs," I say, pointing the short distance down the street. "Then I'm going to find some food. You're welcome to join me as a tour guide. I promise, I don't bite, I won't ask for sexual favors, and I'm not a murderer."

He gives me a side-eyed look for a long moment, thinking about my offer, before he lifts the instrument off his lap and stands. "Yeah, I could stretch my legs for a while, but what are you going to the computer store for at this hour? It's closed and won't open until 9:00 AM."

"Fuck. That's a computer store? Never mind. I thought it was a liquor store."

"The only place that sells alcohol around here is the Walmart. It's just a few blocks away if you want to walk. It's open twenty-four hours."

"Well, then, lead the way, maestro. By the way, I'm Carter George." I hold out my hand to shake his.

"Luke Boyd. It's nice to meet you."

He places his instrument under the bench on the sparse grass and dirt and starts to walk away.

"Whoa, whoa, whoa. What are you doing? You can't leave that there. Somebody will steal it."

He shrugs. "Nah, everyone knows it's mine. It's fine. They won't take it, and if they do, I'll just build another one."

"So, you aren't emotionally attached to your woman? Jesus, I think if I could make something like that, that sounds like angels singin', it'd never leave my sight."

"I never thought about it that way, but she'll be fine. She's an independent woman." He snorts, laughing at his own joke.

I shrug my shoulders and follow his lead, leaving her behind. I've never met one of those women. I guess there's a first time for everything.

We make small talk while walking the few blocks to the Walmart Supercenter. He's a good kid with brains and a dream and apparently a sense of adventure. There is a fucking highway that cuts across the way. I've never in my life walked on a highway. It makes me realize how deer feel.

He jumps over the guardrail like a rabbit, while I have to sit on the motherfucker and throw my legs over. Youth. Damn, I wish I had it again. It's not that I'm old. Thirty-two didn't seem old a few weeks ago. My, how a death sentence changes a man. I'd do so many things differently. *Fuck, who am I kidding?* I'd do it all differently.

Isn't it funny how life throws you curveballs?

IN CLARKSBURG, WEST VIRGINIA IN THE EARLY MORNING HOURS, I sit in the middle of a swing in the garden department at Walmart on some fake grass, drinking rum and coke from a McDonald's cup I found just sitting on the shelf. We've been sitting here shooting the shit and getting to know each other. I have a new friend, and he doesn't even own a car or a building, much less a city block. *Isn't life grand?*

Luke starts yawning after a bit, and I take that as my hint to head back. Some people can only handle so much excitement.

"So when are you going to venture out for that dream you have?"

"Oh, I don't know. When I can save some money for a bus ticket to Nashville, I guess. I only get paid once a month. Extra pocket change is a little hard to come by after taxes and bills, ya know?"

"I'd figure so if you only get paid once a month. Damn, that's shitty. How do people survive that way? The company is making interest off the money you've earned while they hold onto it for you. That's not a good business practice if they want to keep good employees, but I guess if you want to keep your job, they have a hold on you. Fucking sucks."

"Yep, explains why they strike a lot but don't get anywhere."

We jump back over the guardrail, and I promise myself to never do that again. I'm all for adventure, but not when it comes to jumping over something that could slice my nuts off. I reach down and adjust them at the thought of putting them in danger like that.

"Luke, do you have family nearby?"

"No. It's just me. My parents passed away last year. They had me late in life," he explains when he sees the confused look on my face. "Sickness took 'em both. The winters get cold here, and the house is old and drafty. They got pneumonia and never recovered from it. It's just me living there now, taking care of the dog."

Jesus Christ. He is only twenty-one and already without his parents. What a fucked-up world we lived in. I feel for the kid. He has an amazing talent with his homemade steel guitar, but no one to make sure he reaches his potential. I can't stand the thought of his life without his dream coming true.

"Let me ask you something. What would you do if you woke up in the morning and found a bus ticket to Nashville?"

"Nothing, cause I can't take the dog on the bus. They won't let me. I've already asked."

What the fuck? He'd sacrifice his dreams because he can't take a dog on the bus. I don't know if that says he isn't serious about his dream or if he's that loyal to the animal.

"Really? You wouldn't go because you can't take the dog with you?"

"I can't let her starve. I don't have anyone to feed her, and I can't just let her run wild. A coyote would get her. She's all I have left, and I'll be damned if I put her in a shelter to be killed. She's just a pup."

We arrive back at the bus bench, and his woman is right where he left her. He picks her up, wipes a little bit of dirt off her backside and swivels around to face me. "Well, Carter, it's been fun being your tour guide through Clarksburg. Are you sleeping over at the bus station until your next one leaves? 'Cause I've got a comfy couch if you need a place to lie down for a while and rest."

"I'll be fine. Don't you worry about Carter George. I'm a New Yorker," I emphasize *Yorker* pretty heavily with my accent to make it sound like Yorkah. "We can make it anywhere...or so the song goes."

I pause for a moment, an idea brewing in my mind.

"Why don't you come with us?"

Luke raises his eyebrows in surprise. "What?"

"We're on a road to wherever. That wherever could run straight through Nashville. You can bring your dog. There's plenty of room for both of you." I shrug.

"You'd do that? For me?"

"Yeah." I nod my head slowly, a smile curling my lips up. "I would. I want to. What do you say? You in?"

He looks dumbfounded as he stares back at me, shifting his weight from foot to foot. "Can I think about it?"

"Absolutely," I say. "We're the big black RV parked down by the Piggly Wiggly. You can't miss us. We're leaving in the morning though so think fast."

He grins at me. "All right. If I'm at your door in the morning, you'll know my answer. If you don't see me, safe travels, my friend." He waves goodbye and walks up the sidewalk right behind the bus bench.

Well shit, he was home this whole time. He opens the door and is greeted by a big, red dog that looks to be an Irish Setter. The dog jumps up on him, placing its front paws on his shoulders, and he hugs it before shutting the door. Loyalty and love. That's all we need in this world.

I take a look at the run-down house for a moment. Most of the shutters are missing. There's only one green one hanging from the second-floor window. The front porch has a deep bow in the front from years of water damage and rot. It's amazing it hasn't caved in already. The stone steps are cracked, and bits of the corners have chipped away, making them unstable. The siding has mold growing on it, except for the pieces that are cracked and broken.

He put his whole damn paycheck into living here, and he's never thought to be dissatisfied with life. He's happy to come out every night and play his music for whoever will listen.

The only thing I know for sure is I'm a spoiled prick. But I'm a spoiled prick with a lot of fucking money to help people. I make my way to Derek and the Beastmaster mulling over my options.

DIARY

Day 4

Day 4? Jesus. It's almost been a week already. How did time fly so fast? Normally I struggle to make it Monday to Friday. I should've travelled more often.

I decided to offer Luke a trip to Nashville, or further if he wants. He'll probably want to bring the dog. I don't care. I've never had a pet. How difficult could it be?

We've got two extra sleeping bunks, so it should work out just fine. I can't wait to pull over every night and listen to some music before going to bed. I wonder if he writes too or just covers other people's songs. Man, I'd love to hear that contraption play some heavy metal. Maybe he'll take requests.

Stay-tuned for Luke's answer. Jeez, I'm bouncing in my seat. Is this how Oprah and Ellen feel when they give shit away?

And to think, I used to only get this excited when I saw more than six digits in between the $ and the decimal point of a deal. It feels pretty fucking good, to be honest.

All philanthropy aside, I still feel like shit. The medication dulls the pain but doesn't erase it. Sometimes I wonder if I'd be better off if I just. . . well, that's just fucking morbid of me. Deep breaths, not deep holes, right?

I'm not done here. I've got shit to do in this world. Just fucking blows ass that I'm on borrowed time.

Guess you never really know when it's time to check out. I'm just praying that it won't be anytime soon. I'd like to have at least made it across the country and back again before it happens. I can't imagine Derek having to deal with my dead ass.

There I go again being morbid.

It's too early for this shit.

FIVE

CARTER

I push my pills into a pile on the table then stack them up like Legos. Derek is still snoring down the hall, and I'm on my third cup of coffee already. I've found that an overload of caffeine has been helping to stave off these shitty ass headaches. Or maybe I'm just being fucking optimistic, a placebo for my slowly weakening mind. A loud, choking snort causes me to snap my head in the direction of where Derek is sleeping. *Christ, am I going to have to go give him mouth-to-mouth?* A moment later, the snores go on as normally as they possibly can.

I'm truly surprised the man gets any sleep at all. Lord knows, it's a struggle for me when he's just a few feet away. I swallow down my handful of pills for breakfast.

"Surprised the fuckers haven't choked me to death," I mutter, chasing the chalkiness with my coffee.

I rise to my feet, thinking I'll get a breath of fresh air and try to clear the sounds of Derek's death rattle from my head when there's a knock at the door.

I pull open the door to find Luke staring up at me, his dog wagging her tail beside him, his woman tucked beneath his arm where all women fit snuggly.

"Hey," I greet him, my grin spreading from ear to ear. "I was hoping it was you and not the damn police coming to see if we were slaughtering wild animals in here."

Derek gives a loud snoring splutter in answer.

Luke raises an eyebrow at me as I beckon him and his dog inside.

"He sounds like my grandpop's old '87 Mercury Grand Marquis used to after the muffler fell off. He'd gun it at takeoff just to piss Grams off." Luke chuckles at the memory as he surveys our palace. I smirk back. It seems like an accurate description of what Derek sounds like.

I couldn't fault Derek for sleeping so soundly knowing how long I slept yesterday. Must be the clean air and the open road. I just wish he'd do it more quietly.

"So, you're coming with?"

"I figured it was now or never. Figured Molly here ain't never been away on an adventure either. You came at the perfect time."

Molly licks my hand and wags her tail as if she's thanking me too. I'm sold on her. I think we will be good friends.

"I'm glad you're here. Truly," I say, patting Molly on the head.

I peek out the window and gauge the day. It's just after 8:00 AM, and it looks like the grocery store is bustling. I need donuts to help wash down the meds.

Yeah, big round chocolate ones with lots of icing. Maybe even some of those fancy ones with crumbled cookies in the icing. My mouth waters.

Seems like a great way to start the day.

"You like donuts, Luke?"

"I love donuts. Especially the ones with that creme center." Luke licks his lips as he rubs his stomach. Molly gives a whine. Apparently, she likes them too. That settles it. We definitely need some donuts.

"I'm going to run over to the store and grab some if you want to come with."

Luke frowns down at Molly. "Is it OK if I leave Molly here?"

"That depends." I glance at Molly. "She going to steal the RV?"

Luke laughs. "Nah, but she might crawl into bed with the phantom snorer back there." He jerks his thumb in the direction of Derek's tremulous snores.

"Then I'm sad we're going to miss it." A smirk tugs at my lips as I think about how Derek will react to a bunk mate. Without another word, we depart, but not before I place a good scratch on Molly's fluffy head.

We walk quietly across the parking lot for a few moments before Luke clears his throat. "Mind if I ask what's going on with you?"

I lift my eyebrows in question as I glance at him.

"I saw all the pill bottles on the table," he explains, not bothering to look ashamed that he had a glance.

I can't blame him. He's loading his life into an RV and leaving everything he's ever known behind. In his shoes, I'd want to know who the hell I was traveling with.

"Plus, you strike me as someone who's going through some shit."

"Aren't we all?" I give him a half-assed smirk.

He nods thoughtfully. Luke is a good guy. And since there isn't a reason in the world to keep him in the dark, I speak, "I have cancer." It hurts to say it. Like the fucking words choke me as they pour out of my mouth. I stop walking and plant my hands on my knees, drawing in a deep, shaking breath. I'd never said those words aloud before.

I have cancer. I'm dying. Fucking dying! Thirty-two years old and on my way out.

Luke stops with me and instead of looking like he's embarrassed at my quiet meltdown, he tugs me in for a hug. It's awkward, for sure, but I find comfort in having someone give a damn enough to do it. I haven't been hugged—*really* hugged—since I was a kid. My mom gave the best hugs. I miss those 'squeeze-the-stuffing-out-of-you hugs'. *Fuck. I should call her.*

"I ain't gonna tell you that it's going to be all right in the end, because chances are it ain't," Luke says as we pull away from one another. "I will tell you this though, for now, it *is* going to be all right. We're going to have an adventure, my new friend. We're going to drink beer and eat fucking donuts, and bitch about how women play with our hearts. Then we'll all go to sleep. Maybe we'll do it for quite a few nights. Maybe not. But we're going to go to sleep every night knowing we conquered the world that day. You with me?"

"I'm fucking with you," I say, giving him a watery smile.

He grins and tips his head in the direction of the store. "We best get our donuts. The old biddies get out and about and they take all the good ones."

"Plus, we look like a couple of fucking lunatics out here hugging it out in the parking." I chuckle as we start walking again.

"Ain't the worst thing I've ever done in a parking lot," he laughs loudly, the sound deep and rich.

"Fuck, me either, brother."

He gives me a fist bump as we enter the store.

He seems to know his way around the place and leads us straight to the donuts. I grab a box, and he proceeds to fill it with a dozen different kinds, all mouth-watering.

"You know, I don't think dogs can have donuts," I muse as we walk through the produce section with our donut haul. "I think I read that somewhere."

"Ain't too much out there Molly won't eat."

"Well, just to be safe, let's get her some treats and regular dog food."

Luke shrugs and leads me to the pet aisle where I gather an armload of dog toys, a bed, food and treats.

He lets out a low whistle. "Damn dog ain't gonna wanna leave you."

"Not many bitches do." I give him a wink.

Luke snorts at my joke and follows me to the register. I quickly pay for everything, even though he attempts to help. Once we're back at the RV, we find Derek is awake and sitting at the table with Molly beside him. He's petting her, and she looks like the happiest dog in the world.

"There you are." Derek glances up at me as Molly licks his hand.

"Had to get some donuts," I say, placing the package on the table. Luke and I sit down and each choose a donut. I go with the Boston cream and let out a contented sigh as I chew on it. It's one of the best damn donuts I've ever had.

Luke and Derek look equally satisfied with their donuts as Molly cocks her head at us, clearly annoyed she isn't enjoying her own donut.

"Hand me that bag," I instruct Derek. He grabs the bag on the couch and comes back. I rifle around inside and pull out a big ass dog bone and hand it to Molly. We all laugh as she takes it and rushes back to Derek's bunk.

"Derek, I didn't introduce you yet, but this is Luke Boyd and that beauty in your bed getting slobber on your pillowcase is Molly. They're going with us to Nashville."

"We're going to Nashville?" He bites into his donut and stares at me, waiting for me to answer.

"Yeah, you know, I feel like it's where we need to be heading. Luke here was just the push I needed."

"Well, yeehaw, let's do this." Derek gets to his feet and wipes his hands.

I grin at my two friends.

"Yeehaw! Let's go."

SIX

CARTER

*A*s we cruise along the highway, I look out the massive front window at the mountains, my eyes watering. Then it hits me. *This* is why people get teary-eyed when they sing "America the Beautiful". No wonder Luke's *girlfriend* plays such beautiful music here; it's a reflection of her surroundings. We've got to be close to Heaven at this elevation.

I've never really thought about God. I mean, yeah sure, I know who He is at least. I actually get mistaken for him in the throes of passion all the time, but that's not an appropriate thought at the moment. So anyway, God wasn't mentioned much in my home growing up—unless my parents were arguing or my dad was complaining about a bad deal, but when Luke called this state "West 'by-God' Virginia" He's kind of been on my mind.

God, I mean, not Luke, although he's been on my mind too. I've been thinking about Heaven and God, and angels. *A lot.*

Derek keeps looking at me sideways every so often like he's dying to say something about me wiping my eyes, but he doesn't. Smart man. He leaves me alone as we cross the border from this inspiring state and ride along the Virginia and Kentucky border.

I glance back over my shoulder. Luke's legs are stretched out on

43

the bench of the kitchenette table while he reads. Molly rests at his feet like the loyal lady she is.

"Whatcha reading?" I holler back at him, but my voice echoes through the cab and bounces off the massive windows sending a shooting pain right through the back of my eyes like a sonic boom. "Damnation! Motherfucker." I grab my head and lean forward as far as the seatbelt will allow, massaging my temples and trying not to choke on the damn belt.

"Are you all right, Carter?" Derek doesn't know what to do. He's got one hand on the wheel and the other reaches for me. I motion for him to keep going, but he ignores me. "Maybe I should stop for a bit." The bus slows down as we near an exit at the Cumberland Gap Mountain Pass.

"Don't stop. Just drive," I hiss, the searing pain making me want to wretch.

"I'm pulling over—"

"I told you to just fucking drive, Derek!"

"Shut your ass," Derek snaps back with a growl, his knuckles white on the steering wheel. "I'm the goddamn driver, not you, so I decide if we pull over."

"And I'm the goddamn driver's boss, so I say keep driving," I snarl, clutching my head.

"You're going to be roadkill in a minute if you don't shut the hell up." Derek eases the RV off the road and puts it in park. He disappears into the back only to return a moment later with some pain medication and a bottle of water.

"Thanks," I mumble, taking them from him. I swallow down the pills and catch a smirk on Derek's face as he watches me from the driver's seat.

"Just drive."

"Whatever you say, *boss*." He shakes his head and puts the RV back into drive and pulls onto the highway.

"Everything OK?" Luke asks, popping his head between the seats.

"He's fine. Just having a meltdown."

I roll my eyes. "I'm fine. Just a headache."

Luke glances between us before moving back to his seat, shaking his head. I'm sure seeing two New Yorkers verbally battling one another had to be enjoyable to watch. He's probably wondering what the hell he got himself into climbing into the RV.

Later, we end up pulling over in a rest area so Luke can take Molly out for a doggy pit-stop. He straps on the new leash I bought her and exits the bus to give us some privacy or some quiet time for his own sanity. He's got to be questioning his decision-making process after that scene earlier.

Derek hovers over me waiting for some direction from me, any direction. His eyes are wide with fright when I look up.

"Don't worry, man. This isn't the end. Just bring me my pills."

He scurries off to the table and brings me the whole bottle, twisting the adult-proof cap off for me in my aggravated state.

"Go lie down. You don't need to keep me company up front," he commands.

"I'm good, damn it. I don't want to miss this adventure, not one fucking second of it. I'm a grown-ass man, not a preschooler who needs a fucking nap," I snap at him.

He takes a step back from me, not used to feeling the brunt force of my asshole ways.

"Well, you sure are grouchy like a kid who needs a nap or a man that needs to get laid."

He grabs a bottle of water from the fridge and pulls his baseball cap down lower on his head before walking to the door.

"All right then. Go for a walk and get some fresh air. Or better yet, go find some pussy. Just don't fucking scare me like that again," he calls over his shoulder as he throws the door open and kicks it when it bounces back on him. He mutters and curses while he walks away, making me feel bad.

I MEET UP WITH LUKE, AND WE PLAY CHASE WITH MOLLY FOR AN hour. Some little kids join in and by the time we make it back to the bus, my headache is gone, and my mood is much better. See, I knew bringing her along would be a good addition to the trip. She's turning out to be one of those therapy dogs without any training.

Derek is still really pissed at me, and even though I give him one of my best apologies ever—hell probably my only apology, or at least in a long, long time—he continues to be moody.

I'm a little rusty. He needs to give a dying man a break. But it's OK because that lightning bolt of pain scared the shit out of me too. I can't be mad at him for yelling. I decide to give him space and time, so I go into my room to make some calls.

A few hours later, I come out with my notebook tucked under my arm. My notes are scribbled messily in it since I'm used to having a secretary do that for me, but the pages are full of a mighty fuckin' good plan of action for Mr. Luke.

I take a seat next to Luke, who's reading again. "Whatcha reading? You never told me before."

"It's called *How Music Works* by David Byrne."

"Oh, yeah. And how does it work?" I lean sideways to take a peek at the cover. It's solid black and tells me nothing about what's inside.

"It's a novel about one man's musical journey from personal enjoyment before records to the age of the internet."

"Really? Is it any good?"

"It's pretty deep, but I understand exactly what he's sayin'." He places his bookmark between the pages and closes it. "Basically, it's that music is an individual, soul-searching journey."

Yeah, and so is your health.

I set my notepad down on the table, and his eyes widen in either fear or amazement at the jotted chicken-scratch, arrows, and circles with names and numbers written all over the margins.

"What is all of that?" His fingers complete an air circle over the page.

"That, my friend, is a plan and some gigs for you once we get to Nashville." I tap the notebook several times with my index finger for emphasis.

"And what is this?" He points to a heavily traced doodle in the corner.

"Oh, that's me doodling a bunch of grapes while waiting impatiently to some really bad hold music. Ignore that shit." I click my pen and color it all in as one massive ink blot while he laughs and points to where I missed a grape. "Now listen, I got you a guaranteed five-minute spot at the Douglas Corner Café on Tuesday. That's open-mic night, and if we can make it over to another hotel down the street before 10:00 pm, we may be able to get you another spot."

"Holy shit, Carter. Two in one night? I don't know what to say." He sits back in his seat.

"Well I do. Tell me you can write music too."

"I've dabbled in it. I may have a few songs in my soul."

"I'm gonna puke, Carter," Luke says, holding his steel girlfriend tight to his chest as we stand by the side of the stage in a hotspot called the Basement.

"You're not going to puke. That's just your nerves." I turn to face him and grab his shoulders tight, shaking him slightly. "Listen to me. Do you want this dream to come true?"

"Yes," he says calmly, but nods his head excitedly.

"Can we get your emotions all on the same page here? I'm not feeling your excitement."

"That's because I feel sick most of all."

"C'mon, Luke. Do you want this more than anything in your whole existence?"

"Hell yes!" he shouts in my face, but not loud enough to drown out the jukebox.

"You've got ten minutes before the next set starts to shake these nerves and talk yourself into showing all these people here that living without Luke Boyd music in their life is akin to dying. Trust me, I know. Now I'm going to go find a seat and enjoy the show. Do whatever you need to do to rev yourself up because pep talks are not in my skill set."

Luke nods his head and walks to the far corner of the stage, turning his back to me and the crowd. I know he's scared shitless. Fuck, I'm feeling a little nervous for him, and all I'm doing is watching. He's got to do this for himself; I can't perform for him. I can only provide the opportunity.

It isn't too crowded tonight with the heavy downpour of rain outside, but there still aren't any open booths, so I head to the bar.

I slide onto the last stool next to a row of booths, hoping I'll get lucky enough to snag one if I loiter nearby. Right behind me, a man jabbers on about "priceless contracts, no better deals, and sky-rocketing royalties" like he's trying to convince someone to sell their soul to the devil. *Jesus Christ, what a liar.* I can smell the bullshit coming from his lips before he even opens them.

"Excuse us for a second," his oily voice says, and the booth goes silent.

"You're hurting me. Don't squeeze me that hard, Richie," comes from a woman's voice, her pain audible through gritted teeth.

I set my beer down to say something to Richie, the piece of trash, when she stumbles out of the booth and catches the end of the table with her hands to keep herself from falling on the dirty floor.

She stands straight and tall, adjusting her silver dress which had ridden while she sat, pushing it back down her long legs. It clings to her slim body as she brushes it off. She fakes an inspection of her shoes like they caused her to trip. "Go get us two more beers, Teddy. Long necks," he says, dismissing her. As she turns toward the bar, I catch her rolling her eyes.

Large, round green eyes flash at mine for one second before she slides in between my stool and the next one. She holds up two fingers like she's hailing a taxi, "Mike, I need two beers," she hollers at the bartender on the other side. "For dumb and dumber" she mutters under her breath. I snort out loud at her comment.

She turns to me, looking me up and down with her cat-like eyes, before turning back to the bartender coming her way. Apparently, she's passed judgment and finds me lacking. He places two bottles in front of her.

"Shit, Mike. They're for Richie."

"I got it," he says, annoyed, stopping himself from twisting the caps. He takes them away and comes back with two longnecks, pops the caps off for her, and slides them her way.

"Thanks, Mike."

Her full beaming smile makes my heart jump in my chest. She turns in my direction, sliding sideways from between the two stools with the beers held high so they don't get bumped and spill. Her elbow brushes my shoulder, and a burst of tingling heat rushes up my spine. I swing my stool around to watch the show, praying to God she pours one of those all over him.

Instead, she slams the beers down on the table in anger, and pastes on an overly happy, fake smile. "Here are your drinks. I poisoned one of them, but I can't remember which one." She taps a perfectly mani-cured finger against her lips sardonically, then switches the beers around on the table, and shrugs her shoulders. "Good luck," she says and walks away, the back of her dress flouncing with the sway of her ass.

I burst out laughing. The deep timbre of my voice makes the man sitting next to me jump, but I don't care. I like her. She's got brass balls.

"Hello. Hello." A man in a cowboy hat stands center stage and taps the mic to get everyone's attention. "Are we ready for more talented ladies and gents this evening?" The crowd cheers and whistles loudly. "We've got an amazing second-set line-up for you this evening. Can we raise our hands and hats for Mr. Luke Boyd?"

Luke walks onto the stage and takes a seat in the chair, next to the piano player and nods to him in greeting. He lays his musical contrap-tion across his legs. Never looking out at the crowd, the piano player starts the song Luke's been practicing, "Stars in Alabama" by Jamey Johnson. A few seconds into the piano intro, Luke starts singing, and I stand up in surprise, knocking the bar stool over. He's played this song a hundred times over the last few days and not once did he sing it.

Holy fuck! He's blowing my mind. The chorus arrives, and he slides his fingers nimbly across his girlfriend's body making her purr like a kitten stretched out in the summer sun.

Fucking beautiful.

I'm so excited. I edge closer to the stage. My whole body is vibrating with the notes he's releasing. I can't believe Derek is missing this.

The lights dim to the somberness of the song while couples hold hands and sway back and forth, listening to Luke's sad longing for home and his mama.

The song ends, and the crowd goes wild as the lights turn back up.

"Fucking beautiful, man," I yell out over the crowd.

Luke stands and takes a bow, still never looking out at the crowd.

I meet him by the edge of the stage and slap his back with congratulations. "Man, that blew my mind. You never told me you could sing like that. It was nothing compared to the night I met you. You've been holding back. You were awesome up there."

"Nah, I'm not any good. I'm just a steel guitar player."

"That's right, Luke. Stay humble. I can appreciate that."

It takes us a moment to walk back to the bar with everyone stopping and congratulating him on a song well sung. He's got a smile on his face a mile wide, and if he never makes it big, he's got this moment to show he tried.

"C'mon, Luke. Let's pack her up and get over to Hotel Indigo for their open-mic night. We need to ride this hot streak while there's still heat left in it."

"Then let's go."

SEVEN

CARTER

*L*uke purrs out another two songs at the Hotel Indigo to a massive round of applause. Call me biased, but the claps he received were much louder than the five people who took the stage before him. A few people approach him afterwards, handing him business cards about singing and playing at other locations.

My heart has this funny little twinge in it watching him mix and mingle with people, making his dreams come true. Luke Boyd is charismatic, and suddenly, I know he's going to do well in this town.

We head back to where the bus is parked on a side street around 2:00 AM. Rain is coming down in buckets, but it's not hard enough to drown out a couple fighting in the back parking lot. We round the corner and see a man and woman arguing beside a car. The back door gapes open, revealing a third woman inside, half-dressed. The man's shirt is untucked and buttoned crooked. His arms flail about as he raises his voice at the woman. It doesn't take a genius to figure out what happened here.

We intend to mind our own business until the man starts calling her names and airing out their dirty laundry for the whole world to hear. I'm not sure how that solves the problem of *his* cheating ways, but he's serving up some pretty low-blows verbally about her cold heart and lack of services in the bedroom.

We reach the street corner. When I hear the word "cunt", I can't stand it anymore. I hate that word, probably because I heard it one too many times from my dad about my mother. I turn around and head over to where they are, placing myself in the center of their scene.

"It's quite obvious what's going on here. There's no reason to call her names and embarrass yourself publicly like this. Just take your side-piece and go." I glance sideways at the woman I'm protecting and see it's the woman from the Basement with the silver dress and balls the size of Texas. *Why is she with this piece of shit?*

"Don't get involved in this, man. Just take your Guido ass back to New York or New Jersey or wherever you came from and stay out of this," he says.

What a fucking moron.

"C'mon, Teddy. Let's go." He grabs for her arm, but she steps back from his reach.

"I'm not going anywhere with you," she growls from behind me.

"If you don't come with me, you can kiss your singing career good-bye. I'll make sure you never sing in this town again."

"Well, it's not like it was going that far when you were helping me sing. So, I've lost nothing, you rat weasel. You're nobody in this town, Richie."

He lunges at her, and she goes at him with me in the middle as a buffer. Luke jumps Richie from behind and drags him off us both. He squirms out of Luke's hold and pulls his car keys out of his pocket.

"Fuck this, you dumb bitch." He looks at the chick in the backseat and tells her to get up front, and she scurries to obey.

"Hey, honey," Teddy leans down to yell at the woman in the front seat, "when he gets you into bed, he likes to fuck from behind, which is nice because you won't have to see his face. Just keep in mind, you have to bend forward and down real low because his dick is so tiny, it doesn't really reach. Just moan a lot and scream out God's name. He'll come soon enough, and you can go to sleep." She winks at her, before

Richie flips his middle finger at her and speeds out of the parking lot, splashing muddy water on us as he goes.

"You got somewhere to go?"

She looks at me and blinks, her magnificent green eyes are round and filled with worry. Then she looks at Luke and takes a few steps backward.

"We won't hurt you. We just want to make sure you're going to be OK. Can we take you somewhere?"

"I'll find someplace to go. Shit," she says, looking down at her sopping wet dress and shoes which are now covered in mud.

"What do you need? Some clothes, some money, what?" Luke asks, pulling out his wallet and waiting for her to speak.

"I won't take your money, so put it away." She turns and starts to walk toward the main street.

"If you need anything, just come to the big black RV with the silver flames painted on the side," I yell, hoping she hears me.

She raises her hand in acknowledgement but keeps walking.

"Some people would rather choke on their troubles than ask for help. I don't get it."

"Don't worry about her, Carter. You did everything you could. Let's go eat. I'm starving."

I HAVEN'T BEEN ABLE TO SLEEP FOR THREE DAYS. I'D LIKE TO SAY IT'S the excitement of watching Luke's dreams come true, or that my medication is letting me enjoy my adventure, but weirdly, there's a homeless, silver lioness somewhere in this city, and I can't erase her from my mind.

Teddy.

I've never once worried about a chick. I never chase them down. I've never cared because there's always another one two feet away willing to suck my cock for the chance at the non-existent diamond I'd never put on her finger.

But Teddy... There's something about her that's doing laps in my mind.

I'm worried about her. It's a gut-wrenching feeling that something isn't right, and I have no control over it. Knowing she's out there and I have no idea where—or even worse, where he is or what he's done to her—is fucking with my head. And I didn't think anything could do that, outside of the tumor feasting on it.

She could be anywhere. I pick up my phone and type "Teddy Nashville" into Google. How many Teddy's could there be. It's an old name. Hell, I have no idea how to find her, and my search only leads me to some dude who's definitely not the silver angel I'm looking for.

I catch a glimpse of my reflection in the phone as I close the search engine. The dark circles and eye bags are getting monstrous. I open my camera app and turn it around to see my face. Studying it, I swear I have a few more wrinkles than last week. *Fuck*. I might be trying to turn over a new leaf, but I still want to look good when they place my stiff body in the impeccable, new William Westmancott bespoke suit I plan to wear as I'm leaving this world.

A heavy rain starts to pound down on the RV.

A sudden knock on my bedroom door draws my attention. "Yeah," I reply half-heartedly.

Derek slides the door open and stares at me for a moment. "We were going to head out for some breakfast, but with this rain, I think maybe we can hold off for a while. It might pass, but I know you need to take your medicine. You look like shit. How're you feeling?"

"I'm fine. My stomach is a little upset right now." I push the curtain back, holding it with my hand, and look up at the sky. Big, thick clouds of gloom have spread across the city. "I don't think this is going to roll out of here anytime soon. Welcome to spring."

Right before I let the curtain fall back, I see her. *Teddy*. She's standing at the front of the church lot we're parked in. I get to my knees on the bed as fast as I can and slide the curtain all the way to the end of the rod for a better look.

Yep. It's her.

Pushing Derek out of my way, I throw the door open and run frantically toward her in my socks.

"Teddy. Teddy," I holler, waving my hand at her. *Jesus, why did we have to park in the farthest corner of the lot?* It's not like I'm out of shape. Hell, before I got sick, I worked out every day. I was a solid wall of muscle. But this fucking cancer is killing me.

Teddy starts to turn, looking left and right, probably to decide which way she should run.

"Don't leave. Wait."

She turns back to me and stands still with her arms crossed waiting, as the rain soaks her hair and clothes. When I reach her, I have to bend over and catch my breath. I raise my finger to let her know I need another minute. I stand up straight, but my hand flies to my chest as a bad spasm wracks it.

"Jesus Christ, don't die on me here. Take your time."

My eyes flash to hers. *Does she know I'm dying? Do I look that sickly and bad?*

"Are you all right? I've been worried sick about you," I wheeze in between the words as I speak.

Her brow wrinkles in confusion. "*Me?* Why? You don't know me."

"No, but I know what that piece of gutter trash you were living with can do to women, and I was worried, OK? He should be putting you on that stage instead of trying to get it on with the new talent."

"Are you a talent agent? You know, for that guy who plays the steel guitar," her voice takes on a higher pitch, and her eyes sparkle.

"Hell no. I just like the way he plays and offered to give him a ride to Nashville."

"Oh, I thought maybe you were a talent agent," she says, her shoulders droop and any excitement that was in her eyes before fades quickly. "Well, as you can see, I'm fine so you don't have to worry anymore." She turns and starts to walk away.

"You got a place to stay and some food? A job to help you out, maybe?" I ask.

Though her back is to me, I see her body go stiff.

The rain pelts down on both of us. She turns her head slightly and asks over her shoulder, "What do you care?"

"I'm just trying to do some good deeds on this planet. Pay it forward or something like that. How can I help you?"

"If you aren't a talent agent, then you can't help me." She shoves her hands underneath her soaked sweatshirt to keep them warm and walks away slowly.

"Like I said before, you need anything, you come to the black RV," I holler at her back as she crosses the street and disappears into the alley.

She doesn't raise her hand this time to acknowledge me or anything. Some people are just too damn stubborn for their own good. I make my way back across the parking lot in my sopping wet socks, cursing every now and again when I step on a pebble.

DIARY

Day 11

Sorry I haven't journaled in a few days. The road adventure kind of came to a standstill the minute we pulled into Nashville, while other adventures have taken off. I'm not sure which ones I should detail here, but after thinking about it, I say "fuck it". You're going to hear about them all moving forward, but I'll start with the most recent developments.

After chasing down Teddy in the middle of a storm, then choking down some breakfast, I got a call from Rising Star Records. It seems they want to meet with Luke, so I set it up for tomorrow morning. They offered to send a car, but I think we'll show up stylin' in my Benz, so they know where to start the bidding. I won't let them undervalue his talent.

I want to get him started on the right track, but I also want to get on with my own adventures. This town has been great for a few days, but I'm ready to leave.

On the Teddy front, well, I don't know what to say. There's something there my brain won't let go of. I've never helped a damsel in distress before. I'm not even sure she's in distress because she won't tell me anything. Most women I know tell me their whole fucking story in one night. This chick's like a clam. I'm going to have to pry the pearl out of her because she won't give it up easily.

But just like Luke, fate seems to have placed her on this adventure, and I need to make sure we all make it through. If I ever see her again, that is. God knows she's a constant on my mind. With every ounce of hope I have left, I pray I get one more chance to see her.

EIGHT

CARTER

"*I* feel like a horse's ass in this outfit, Carter," Luke whines at me.

With a roll of my eyes, I step away and survey how he looks in one of my suits and a tie. We are pretty damn close in size.

But he's right. He does look unnatural.

"Fine," I relent, frowning. "Wear whatever makes you comfortable, Luke."

"Thank you, sweet baby Jesus," he says, tugging the silk Armani tie off and chucking it aside. I snatch it up and place it back in the drawer, wondering how the hell he's made it so far not knowing how to care for a tie. Knowing he needs some privacy, I move to the living area of the Beastmaster and flop down next to Molly.

"He's worse than a damn woman," Derek says, jerking a thumb in the direction of my room where Luke is probably tugging a red, plaid shirt over his head.

I laugh with him, wincing as my head throbs. I clutch at it, wanting to rock back and forth in the fetal position until the pain passes.

"Fuck," I hiss, my eyes watering.

"Carter, you OK?" Derek is on his feet, standing over me, his hand

59

on my shoulder. My breath is deep and ragged for a moment before I get my shit together, and the pain subsides.

"Yeah," I say after a moment, shaking my head, my hands twitching. That was a real bitch. I frown at my fingers, a strange tingling in them.

"You sure? You look like something's wrong," Derek pressed, concern written all over his face.

"I have a fucking brain tumor and six months to live. Of course, something's wrong," I mutter.

"No need to be a dick about it," Derek volleys back, rolling his eyes at me. I let out a soft chuckle at him. I've got to hand it to him, he doesn't put up with my shit. With Derek on my case, I know I can't sit around feeling sorry for myself.

Before I can retort because calling him an ass feels right in that moment, Luke comes out of the bedroom looking as country as a fucking sack of potatoes.

"I'm surprised you didn't go with the red plaid," I say, nodding at him.

He grins, his eyes twinkling. "Blue plaid seemed more formal."

"Is that a Chevy belt buckle?" Derek asks, a dark eyebrow raised.

"Sure is," Luke proclaims, lifting his girl into his arms. It's hard to suppress my laughter, so I clap him on the shoulder.

"You ready to do this?"

"No," he breathes out. "But yeah. It's now or never."

"Then let's go change some lives, Luke Boyd."

GLEN ANDREWS, OWNER OF RISING STAR RECORDS, STARES wordlessly at Luke as he finishes crooning an original he's been working on. The blissful sounds of honky-tonk heaven and the good life are still hanging in the air around us.

Glen doesn't need to say a word. His answer is in his eyes. I think it's important to look into someone's eyes to learn all I need to know. And Glen Andrews's eyes have dollar signs dancing in them.

"You are truly incredible, Mr. Boyd. We'd love to work with you."

Luke's eyes are the size of saucers as he glances between me and Glen.

"Are you shittin' me?" he chokes out, causing me to snort, but I cover it with a cough.

Glen grins at him and offers him a nod. "I'm absolutely serious, Mr. Boyd. We could make you a star. Although, with talent like that, I'd say you're already one. You just need the backing. Do you have an agent?"

"Uh," Luke looks over at me, his Adam's apple bobbing.

"I'm representing Mr. Boyd until other arrangements are made," I say. Relief washes over Luke's face at my words.

"Carter George." Glen drums his fingers on his desk. "I didn't ask before, but are you the same real estate tycoon Carter George out of New York? The *billionaire*?"

If I thought Luke's eyes were wide before, they're nothing compared to the size they are now after hearing Glen's words.

"This isn't a dick measuring contest," I say.

Glen chuckles at me and nods. "I thought it was you. You're a ruthless man, Mr. George."

"We're both in the business of making dreams come true, Glen," I say with a wide smile. "Most of the time, they're my dreams I'm concerned with, but I know talent when I see it. Luke deserves to be given a chance. I'm here to ensure he gets it."

Glen looks to Luke. "How the hell did *you*, a country boy from nowhere West Virginia, meet up with the likes of Mr. George?"

"Fate," Luke answers, cradling his guitar. "And Wal-Mart."

Glen lets out a laugh. The man isn't a bad guy. He's fair and to the point. I like that about him.

"So, what's the deal going to be, Glen? You going to hook my friend Luke up with that contract?"

"You know what," Glen says, shuffling some papers. "I think I am."

Luke jumps into the air, whooping his joy with tears streaming down his face. Before I react, his arms are around me, and he's clinging to me.

"Thank you," he chokes out into my neck as he hugs me tighter.

I give him a quick hug, laughing as he pulls away. I've never seen such joy in my life. It lights my heart up. Glen is grinning just as widely as we are.

"Do I even need to ask if you're interested in signing with us?" Glen asks, a twinkle in his dark eyes.

"Oh, I'm interested," Luke says, finally settling down.

"I think it's time to talk numbers." I've gone from excited fairy fucking godmother to cutthroat businessman.

"Let's talk numbers." Glen sits back in his seat as I lean forward in mine.

If I wanted to, I could own his record company in thirty seconds. We both know who's really in charge.

But I smile and give the man a chance to wow me.

"Carter George, did my mama send you down from heaven to do this?" Luke asks in a choked-up voice as we sit in the Beastmaster later that night, celebrating the incredible deal I'd just gotten for Luke. There were so many zeros Luke had to ask me how much money it really was.

I give Luke a smile, my heart warming knowing I've helped him. Whenever I'd tear down a company, I was filled with an emptiness. I'd drink to it and fuck my way to feeling good. But now, in this moment, my heart is full. I'm happy. It's a feeling I'm not familiar with so I sit with a glass of whiskey in my hand, a shit-eating grin on my face, and enjoy Luke's excitement.

"Carter can talk his way into anything," Derek proclaims, grabbing his glass. "He's your man for all trade deals."

"A man I'll be forever grateful to," Luke says, raising his glass in my name. "To Carter George."

Derek follows suit, saying my name, and my fucking eyes get misty.

"Don't cry, ya big baby," Derek teases. I flip him off with one hand while I dry my eyes with the other.

The laughter dies down for a moment, and I'm able to pull myself together. Luke has grown quiet.

"You OK?" I ask him as he stares into his drink.

"I don't think I can do this."

"What?" Derek and I say in unison.

"Why can't you? It's your dream—" I start, but he shakes his head and looks to Molly who's enjoying a new chew toy. Sensing his eyes on her, she cocks her head, her tongue lolling out.

"I can't leave Molly. I don't have a home for her. It's the same situation as it was back home. It'll be too busy for me to care for her the way I should. I can't just up and walk out on her."

I look between Molly and Luke. I don't even need to think twice about it. "We'll keep her for you. When you're ready, you'll know where to find her. Right, Derek?"

Derek grins, nodding his head.

"See? It's settled. Molly stays with us, and you go make those dreams happen."

It's Luke's turn to get misty-eyed. "Are you serious?"

"Do you even need to ask that?"

"Thank you, Carter." He moves to me and wraps me in a one-armed hug. "Thank you."

I give his back a pat. "What are friends for?"

We break apart, and I discretely wipe at my eyes again. Friends. *Real* friends. It's certainly nice to be able to say I'm starting to actually make some. The rest of the evening is spent in laughter and comfort with my two friends. It's the last night we'll be together like this. I sit back and watch as the guys chuckle and talk about their exes. Luke jots notes in his notebook, no doubt a song brewing in his heart over our tales. I chime in every now and then with a story of my own, stories that seem unbelievable but are absolutely true.

The feeling hits me hard. I've never actually *loved* like my friends have. I've screwed many women, but *love*? Hell, I don't even know if I love my own mother.

My eyes drift across the dark church parking lot, my mind on the green-eyed angel I'd only briefly exchanged words with. Wherever she is, I hope she's safe. Not knowing is eating me up inside. Since it's our last night here before we bid Luke farewell, my heart is heavy. There's something about Teddy that has me feeling things like butterflies and...*hope*?

I'm not sure what the feeling is.

But damn, what I wouldn't give to find out.

NINE

CARTER

*A*fter setting Luke up in a hotel for a few nights and leaving him some cash to survive on until everything comes through from the record company, we bid him farewell amid hugs and manly tears. We exchange numbers, so at least we'll be able to keep in touch.

"That was awesome," Derek says as we pull away from the Hermitage Hotel where we left Luke. "You're a good guy, Carter."

"Not really." I smile sadly as we pass through the city. "But I'm working on it."

Derek shoots a grin at me before focusing on the road. My mind wanders to Teddy, my eyes scouring the passersby, wondering where she is. I frown as fat raindrops begin pelting the window of the Beastmaster.

Derek turns the wipers on high and leans forward in his seat a little more. As we travel out of Nashville, the rain starts pounding harder, making it near impossible to see.

"Shit," Derek hisses as we slow down.

We're getting close to the highway. In front of us is a woman in a short white sundress and brown cowboy boots with a guitar case slung over a shoulder and a suitcase in the other hand. She's walking with her head down. As we drive closer to her, I turn so I can see her, knowing that walk even though I've only seen it a handful of times. The way her ass moves in a dress has been carved into my mind for eternity.

Teddy.

"Pull over!" I shout at Derek.

He looks at me like I'm a crazy man but does as I say. I rush to the door and throw it open just as Teddy nears us.

"Teddy!" I shout into the wet, gray world, a veil of rain cascading down between us. Her head snaps up, and she looks in my direction. She hesitates for just a moment before she approaches the Beastmaster and peers up at me, her dark hair and clothes drenched, mascara running down her cheeks.

"Need a ride?" I ask, reaching my hand out for her to take. She studies it for a moment before her lips part, uncertainty in her eyes.

"I'll take you wherever you want to go," I continue, silently begging her to take my hand. "Where you headed?"

"Anywhere but here," she says in that sweet voice of hers, sending goosebumps straight to my heart, causing it to jolt in my chest.

"You're in luck, sweetheart. We're on our way to Nowhere, USA, and we have room for one more." I take a step down so we're closer, my hand still extended.

A tiny smile quirks up on her plump lips before she places her hand in mine. I tug her up the step. We're so close I can feel the chill from the rain on her.

"Sounds like you're heading in the right direction," she says, shivering.

I grin and lead up her up into the Beastmaster. Then I take her bag and guitar from her.

"That's the plan." Derek throws some kitchen towels down on the floor to soak up the rain dripping from her clothes, while I get some towels from the bathroom for her hair. Molly barks at Teddy, not comfortable yet with the new stranger in her space.

"Come back here and change out of those clothes. We have an extra bedroom you can use," I say, waving for her to come to the back of the bus. She walks warily toward me, her eyes shifting left and right, looking for God only knows what.

"Come on. We're not going to kidnap or murder you. I promise. We're just on a vacation, going across the country to see the sights. We mean no harm."

I slide the door back into the pocket wall and flip on the light to the room. She finally arrives, craning her neck around the corner to look into the empty room. Her gaze takes in a loft bunk with a built-in desk underneath it, a chest of drawers, and a mirror.

"It's pretty sparse, but you can unpack your things and make yourself at home. Luke stayed in here. The sheets were washed yesterday, after we left him at the Hermitage Hotel."

"I don't have much. Richie burned most of my stuff when he kicked me out. This is all I've got."

I toss her bag on the bunk. She takes the towel from my hand, patting her hair and dress. Then she kicks her boots off, the carpet soaking up the rain that spills from them.

I stare, mesmerized as perfectly, pedicured purple toes wiggle into the gray carpet. I've never had a foot fetish, but I may have one now. My dick tightens in my pants, and I turn away. My hand finds the door pull.

"I'll leave you to change and dry off. There's a washer/dryer combo in the bathroom if you need them. Bathroom is right across the hall here." I flip that light on, so she knows I'm not lying. Her neck stretches and looks over my shoulder until she sees the shower reflected in the mirror.

A small "thanks" escapes her lips as she grabs for the door and tugs it closed. I wait to hear the lock grip the wall latch before stepping away.

I stride back to the front of the bus and take a seat next to Derek, feeling lighter than I have in weeks. Not that I've known her for weeks, but for some reason, all my focus goes to her, making my own problems seem less. She's here, and she's okay. That's all I need to know. For now.

Derek studies the weather map. "This rain is coming in from the north. Do you want to head west through Texas or make our way up north to Route 66? Either is fine with me."

He hands me his phone, and I enlarge and decrease the map, moving it around on the screen, weighing my options. "Let's head towards New Orleans. I've never been there, believe it or not. I'd like to experience Bourbon Street."

"NOLA, get ready, 'cause here we come," Derek high-fives me for my spectacular decision-making skills, and plugs our new route into the GPS. He flips the blinker and guides us back onto the road. When movement comes from the back of the bus, he looks over at me. "New person, new adventure?"

"God, I hope so." I settle into the massive captain's chair, kick my feet up onto the dashboard, and enjoy the big picture view as we leave Church Street and head onto I-40.

The soft swaying of the bus lulls me to sleep within a few minutes.

"CARTER, WAKE UP." DEREK TAPS MY SHOULDER SOFTLY. I OPEN MY eyes and see nothing but fenced in hanging flowers and an expanse of bright red geraniums with bumble bees buzzing. This can't be New Orleans. It's supposed to be swampy and muggy. Although, I can feel the heat coming through the windows.

"Where are we?" I sit up straight in the chair and rub the sleep from my eyes.

We're in some kind of parking lot. I lower my legs from the dash-board, and that pins-and-needles feeling shoots through them to my feet.

"Ouch, damn it." I shake my legs, trying to get the blood to flow to them faster. *Why in the hell did I think falling asleep like that would be comfortable?*

"We're hungry, and we're out of snacks. And there's a bonus because we're at your favorite shopping place... Walmart Supercenter."

I groan, not knowing how one trip constitutes it being my favorite place.

He bends low and whispers into my ear, "Plus, it's time to take your meds, or you're going to be miserable later. C'mon, go take your meds, then we'll run inside to get some food. We'll be outside waiting for you."

We? Who the fuck is we?

I stand up and bounce on the balls of my feet, testing them to make sure they're going to hold me when I look up to see the other half of the *'we'* Derek is talking about. She's sitting in the living area, petting Molly. *Teddy.* She wasn't a figment of my imagination. She really got on the bus.

I straighten my shirt and run my fingers through my hair, pushing down on its long length to flatten it. I blow my own breath into the palm of my hand and smell it while she isn't looking. *Great. I need to brush my teeth too.*

I fill a cup of water and take it back to my room, swallowing down my pills as fast as I can. One of the caps gets stuck. I twist and turn it without much success, until I finally twist it so hard, I force it back into the right grooves. But now I have an indentation of the cap in my palm. *Jesus Christ. Why do they make these things so hard for sick people?*

After hiding my pills away, I head into the bathroom and brush my teeth quickly, while checking out my hair in the mirror. Yep, it's time for a haircut too. Maybe in NOLA, and maybe, *just maybe*, I'll get a new look for Carter 2.0. The possibilities are endless it seems.

I swing the door open to a partly cloudy day, and Molly runs out. *Shit.* She's not on her leash, and I freak the fuck out, running after her and hollering her name, "Molly. Molly!"

Derek starts chasing after her too, running in circles between the parked cars. She's fucking with him, thinking he's playing, and I burst out laughing.

Of this funny little side-show we have going on, the only sensible one is Teddy. She goes back inside the RV and grabs Molly's obscenely large chew bone and leash. She stands on the top step like the Queen Dogmaster she truly is and whistles one of those high-decibel ear-piercing screeches that makes me want to cover my ears. I swear, everyone in the whole parking lot stops whatever they're doing and looks at her. She hoists the dog bone high in the air and waves it like a flag while hollering in the sweetest voice I've ever heard, "Molly. C'mere pretty girl. Molly, I've got your bone. C'mon, Molly." She wiggles her ass, doing a little dance with the bone, slaps her thighs with her hands then claps them to gain her attention while repeating her name over and over.

I almost wish my name was Molly, because I'd run toward that booty shake too.

And I'll be damned. Molly finally spots her bone in the air and runs full throttle at Teddy to get to it. Teddy throws the bone inside the RV just as Molly reaches her, and quickly slams the door shut. *Whew! Crisis averted.*

Teddy starts strutting toward us, brushing the bone dust from her hands with a smug smile on her face.

My God, she's gorgeous. The wind whips her hair up and off her slender shoulders, while the sun shines brightly on her green eyes, making them sparkle. She's proud of herself, and I think I just fell in love. My heart is beating a thousand miles a minute, and it has nothing to do with the dog chase. The sweet vixen walking in slow motion toward me just stole my heart.

I look over at Derek, and his mouth is open as he takes in the same view. I lean over and whisper into his ear, "Dibs."

"Aww, fuuuck," is all he says before turning and grabbing a cart from the corral.

TEN

TEDDY

I'm not sure what I've gotten myself into with these lunatics. They can't even control their own dog. The art of distraction is like Doggy 101, so why don't they know this rule?

They seem nice, but then again my character judging skills have declined since I moved to Nashville.

I remember when I thought Richie was a nice guy too. *Asshole.*

Manipulative, abusive asshole, if I'm being accurate.

Derek, the driver, seems quiet and defers to Carter a lot. Derek keeps checking his watch. He must be the organized one of the two, and it's Derek's responsibility to make sure they stick to their destination schedule.

Which makes me think Carter isn't organized, or he isn't great with responsibility. Either way, they're both pretty smokin' hot, and I've won the lottery for great views to look at on this trip.

They both throw food into the cart like money is no object. Name brand this, name brand that. Had I known I'd be grocery shopping today, I would've packed my coupons.

"You know, the Great Value corn chips taste the same as name brand and cost a $1.49 less," I say, fighting the urge to replace them. I lift up the aisle tag hanging under the chips and look at the SALE going on. "Or even better, you can get two of the Great Value bags for only ten cents more than one of these." I pick up the bag of chips from the cart and shake it, enticing them with the offer of a better deal.

Carter takes it from my hand, stuffing it back into its spot on the shelf, and tosses two Great Value corn chips bags into the cart, before zooming down the rest of the aisle popping wheelies with the cart. He hands the cart off to Derek to take his turn.

Boys. Show-offs...if only I had my own cart.

"Damn, I could use you in the boardroom when I have a deal going on," Carter says smiling as he casually walks back toward me. "Feel free to add some food into the cart for yourself."

"I don't think they have price tags or *buy two for the price of one* deals in a boardroom. I wouldn't know the first thing about *that* kind of negotiation. What do you do in a boardroom?" I glance at him.

He walks beside me, matching his steps to mine. We turn down the next long row filled with baking items and other sweet products. His arm swings up to point at something and accidentally grazes mine. One brief touch sends a thousand-watt spark through me, heating me.

"Wow. Have you ever seen a can of pudding that big? That would feed a small army of children," he says, extending his hand to turn the can so he can read the nutrition label. "Yep, twenty-four servings. Just imagine the sugar high you'd get from that."

"I think it's meant to make pudding pies. See?" I point to the pie crusts sitting next to the large can on the shelf. "That's why they're together in this aisle."

His plump lips mouth the word '*oh*'.

"You're the practical type. You stay in the middle lane, don't you?" One dark brow rises up in question.

"I don't know what you mean." I walk over to the bags of nuts hanging on pegs and grab a few packs of natural almonds.

"You know, you play it safe, staying in the middle of the road in case you need to go left or right to get to where you want to go."

His intensely white smile is making my stomach do flip flops, so I walk in front of him. He walks closely behind, breathing in my ear. "The slow lane is boring and frustrating. There life just hums along at the same speed, but the fast lane is scary and dangerous, causing anxiety over whether or not you made the right decision. So you stay in the middle where it's practical and safe, going the right speed for any and all of life's decisions," he continues with his analysis of my life.

"There's nothing wrong with the middle road." I turn and bump into his chest, splaying my fingers across the hard cage of his ribs. "I think most people stay in the middle, to use your analogy." I pull my hands off him with the quickness of being burned.

"I disagree. I think most people change lanes according to what they're willing to risk for whatever it is they want."

"Is there a point to this conversation?" I turn and continue walking, gripping my bags of almonds. If I budget them correctly, I can snack on them for a few days and not spend too much of my money. Derek comes around the corner with the cart and stops next to me. He's piled it high with bread, pasta, dairy products, and manly, fresh meat...otherwise known as ribs and steak.

"No, no point. Just trying to get to know the stranger sleeping in my RV." He walks back to the massive cans of pudding and grabs one, while extending an arm out and picking up a pie crust to go with it. He adds it to the top of the cart. "I need to make sure you aren't going to kill us while we sleep." He and Derek both look at me questioningly.

"I haven't decided about that yet," I say matter-of-factly, sauntering between them and moving into the next aisle. I stand there at the entrance for a moment, giggling out of sight, waiting for them to either follow me or bail on me. Nothing would surprise me at this point. All of a sudden, I hear laughing, so I peek around the corner. They're smelling big bags of different flavored marshmallows and passing them back and forth to each other. *Boys.*

They are juvenile boys—boys with men's firm asses that round out their jeans. That's the view I'm facing when I stroll back up to them. If we were close friends, I'd swat them both on their perfection and cause a stinger to burn.

Carter holds the toasted coconut marshmallow bag up to my nose and shakes it teasingly, so I lean in and inhale. "Mmmm. That actually smells good." With my endorsement, he dumps it into the cart. I have no idea what we'll eat them with, but I guess we'll improvise.

"C'mon. Let's hit the produce department and call it a day," Derek announces, and turns the cart in that direction.

"Teddy," Carter says, his hand sweeping over the cart. "Please put some food in the cart for yourself to eat. It's on me." He reaches forward and takes the tiny bags of almonds from my tight hold and adds them to the growing mass.

WE SETTLE BACK INTO THE RV AND STORE THE GROCERIES AWAY. Derek and Carter work efficiently together, moving and dodging around each other while I keep Molly out of the way. I mentally note where things go so I don't piss off my hosts and get kicked to the curb. I'm determined to not *ever* let that happen again.

I have no idea what I was thinking when I agreed to move in with Richie. He's a smooth talker and paints a beautiful picture of how fabulous country music stardom can be. I was all too eager to step onto his cloud nine and float along in the dream, until I realized it's always been just that—all talk and a painted picture from a dream. *Stupid me. Naïve me.*

Never again.

My father would be majorly disappointed in the life I'm living right now. I can hear him now, "I told you to say in medical school." It's a good thing he's not taking my calls. I've been ex-communicated, cut-off, disinherited…officially ousted from the Bruce family.

"Teddy. Hello, are you there?" Derek snaps his fingers and waves his hands in front of my eyes to gain my attention.

"Yeah, sorry. What's up?"

"Would you like to join us at the table for a little scheduling pow-wow?"

I look over at the table, and Carter has a whiteboard and marker laid out in front of him. He's busy erasing something on it with a clean cloth.

"Umm, sure."

I slide into the far side of the bench seat on the opposite side of Carter. Derek boxes me in.

"Here, Derek," Carter says, pushing the board toward Derek and handing him the marker. "You write neater than my chicken scratch. Add Teddy's name to it. Then we'll hash out meals and laundry."

"You *can* cook and do laundry, can't you?" They both look up at me, waiting. Derek's face is passive while Carter beams a welcoming smile.

"Yes, I-I can cook. Am I..." I swallow down the knot that's suddenly tightening my throat. "Am I expected to wash your laundry and you w-wash mine?" My words tumble and trip out of my mouth like a dog in skates. *Jesus, I sound like an idiot.*

"Oh, God no." Carter's eyes crinkle in amusement and he winks at me when my shoulders relax. "We do our own laundry, but we schedule the day, so we aren't wasting precious water and waiting on someone else's clothes to wash or be folded. It helps since Derek spends most of his time driving and can't change his loads out."

"So, at least one day of the week, we don't travel. Sometimes it's more than that, like in Nashville, but we're winging it on this vacation and seeing how it goes. So far, it's worked out well," Derek advises, shrugging his shoulders like the concept amazes him.

He sets the whiteboard down on the table, and I see my name neatly written in the previously-empty bracket. Derek has school teacher writing. I wonder if that's his profession. The top columns are labeled with the days of the week, and then it's split into two sections, also neatly labeled *Cooking* and *Laundry*. A listing of our names separates each section. Yep, organized and partitioned just like a school teacher divvying out classroom chores.

"I don't care how we do it, but I don't want Friday." Carter picks up the pen and puts a big X on Tuesday for laundry and cooking. "I had that last go 'round, and it sucked. I don't want to be starting my weekend off with laundry and chores."

He passes the marker to me, and I stare at the board blankly. I've never had to do this...not even in the sorority house in college. "Umm,

I'll take Friday. I like doing laundry." I pass the marker to Derek, but he passes it to Carter instead. "Why don't you get a turn?" I hold up my hand, confused.

"My days alternate with both of yours. I take whatever is left over, and those are usually our non-travel days," he explains. "But I also get to switch off with one of you if we need to in case our travel schedule needs adjusting."

"All right. Here comes the hard part—cooking. Are you allergic to anything? Have a special diet? Tell us what you can and can't do in the kitchen."

"Can't we just cook our own food?" Four large, round eyes blink rapidly back at me at my suggestion. I guess I hit them where it hurts, their stomachs.

"I make a tasty Linguine with Shrimp Scampi. You don't wanna miss it. You know what I mean?" he teases in his best Godfather impersonation and pinches his thumb and two fingers together kissing them, letting the kiss go out into the air between us.

"I'm trying to eat healthier. You know, more vegetables, less carbs. You may not like the things I cook. Richie never did, so I ate alone most of the time."

They both look at each other for an extended minute before Carter pulls the cap off the fat green marker and puts an X under my name for Monday. "We'll have meatless Mondays. How does that sound to you, Derek?"

"Sounds great to me. I love vegetarian food. Man, what I wouldn't give for some of Uva's vegan gnocchi right now. That creamy lemon, garlic butter sauce is to die for."

Carter marks an X on Wednesday and Saturday for himself.

"Wait. Why do you get to choose two in a row?" I reach across the table and swipe my thumb through his Wednesday mark, completely erasing it from existence. "I thought this was a democratic splitting of chores."

Derek bursts out laughing, but not at me. He points at Carter with one hand and high-fives me with the other. "Thank you, Teddy, for calling him out on his shit. It doesn't happen often, but I'm always thrilled when I get to witness it."

"All right, all right. This is a fair process," Carter concedes, handing me the marker. "Here, choose your day since I assigned the other one to you."

I take it from his hand, ignoring the burst of electricity that shoots up my arm when our fingers touch. I tap the end of the pen on the table as I think. "I don't want two nights in a row, but if I go too far out, that still makes it too many healthy meals close to each other. Hmmm." I circle the tip of the marker over Wednesday, debating on whether or not to take it from him. On a whim, I quickly draw my X on Thursday, making it thick and bold.

Carter's mouth falls open. "Why didn't you take Wednesday? What was all that fuss about then?"

I ignore his incredulous squawking and slide toward Derek. He stands to let me pass by and out of the seating area.

I approach Carter from behind and run my hands over his broad shoulders and down his thick biceps, teasing him. "Darling, Carter," I speak softly in his ear, but loud enough for Derek to hear. My lips graze the tender flesh of his lobe as I speak, "Most women don't like their decisions made for them. You took away my choice when you gave me Meatless Monday and then again when you chose two days in a row for yourself. This may be your RV and your vacation while I'm a simple hitchhiker on this journey, but it's still my life, my time, and my body."

I walk down the hallway and into my room but whistle for Molly to come before I shut the door. I have to get him out of my sight before my brain lets me do something I'll regret.

DIARY

*D*ay 14

    New Orleans. Yes, I'm saying it in my mind with a long Cajun drawl to it—Nawlens is how it sounds bouncing around in this thick skull. The Big Easy...or the Crescent City. By either name, I love it. We've been here for no less than four hours, and the electricity pulsing in its air hums through me. I'm shaking with uncontrolled excitement. The music, the atmosphere, the French Quarter and Jackson Square...I've had a full experience, and it's only been one day. There are ten more things on my list to do tomorrow. For as much as I'd like to stay here longer, I'd like to make it to the Pacific Ocean at some point.

    I will say one thing though—damn, it's fucking hot here. This is the kind of heat that steals your breath from you. But then again, maybe it's Teddy in that tank top and those shorty shorts she's wearing. Temptation is an evil thing sometimes, especially when it comes in the form of powdered sugar on soft lips at the Café du Monde eating beignets. We're sitting here waiting for our walking tour to begin, and damn, she's beautiful when she's messy. She wipes her dusty hands across the ass of her shorts, and that faded handprint is going to tease me for the rest of the day.

Derek seems to love it here too. He takes a picture of something or someone every few inches. I'm amazed we've seen as much as we have already. This city is amazing, and this tour guide, Luis, is said to be the best. I wonder if he gives other tours for the rest of the city or just the French Quarter. Guess we'll find out when this one is over.

ELEVEN

CARTER

I think I might die of blue balls long before this brain tumor does me in. It's been a few days, and there's no relief in sight. Yesterday I sported a hard-on all day as I walked around behind Teddy. And when she whispered the word "darling" in my ear the night we divvied up chores, I thought I was going to bust a hole in the crotch of my khakis. I'm pretty sure death by blue balls is a thing.

Add to that my longing to pull her into my arms and show her how a real man treats his woman after hearing about how Richie made her eat all alone—I'm a goner. But then I remind myself that I'm still on karma recovery from my previous *Carter 1.0* life, so I decide to leave it alone. I'm more fucked up than she is. If she knew about my past, she wouldn't have stepped inside this bus.

Teddy is the purest form of temptation to a recovering womanizer and an all out chauvinist pig.

I wonder how she'd take me demanding that she erase *him* from her thoughts completely—like he was never there and doesn't exist beyond Nashville.

Today, all I can do is lie here. My head is fucked up, and the pills aren't helping. I feel really fucking old right now. My hands are trembling so damn badly, I can't even text Derek to bring me some water. I crawl out of bed and go to the bathroom and get it myself.

Derek lowers the newspaper he's reading when he hears my door open and looks directly at my drawn and tired face. The drop of his shoulders tells me he knows it's a bad day. He'll take care of everything. I won't have to worry about a thing. Derek always has my back.

Molly follows me back into my room and lies on the bed, curling into me. "What a good girl you are." I pet her in long, even strokes, and she rolls sideways to give me more access to her belly. "You knew I didn't feel good, and I didn't have to say a word. You instinctually honed-in on it and came to share the love. Good girl."

We both fall asleep, snuggled up in the blankets.

I wake up to the deep bass of Black Velvet thumping through the RV. It's coming from the kitchen with a sweet melodic voice humming along. The door to my room is slightly ajar, and Molly is missing. My headache is gone, for now, anyway.

I hate missing whole days sleeping, but lately it's becoming more and more the norm for me. I roll over and sit up, feeling slightly nauseous and woozy from the sudden movement. I need to eat. Guess it's time to go out and join the world today.

The man in the mirror staring back at me is frighteningly pale. A smudge of darkness colors the skin under my eyes, but it blends in well though with the five o'clock shadow spreading across my jawline. It's time to feed this ugly ass mug.

I slide the door back into the wall just in time for the second chorus. Teddy stands at the stove, drizzling olive oil into a pan. Her torn jeans hang low on her waist, showing just a hint of her flat belly as she moves. The curve of her ass and hips tease me. I want to touch her so fucking badly, but knowing Teddy she'll take my head off with one swift punch.

She pushes a mound of chopped vegetables into the pan from the cutting board and picks up a wooden spoon to stir it with but uses it as a microphone instead. Her raw, gritty voice scrubs my soul clean.

My knees buckle slightly with the emotion pouring from her during the final notes. It must be one of her favorites, because she starts dancing around lost in the music. The chorus fades into the final verses of the song, and she goes back to humming it until it ends.

I lean against the wall and clap proudly, startling her. She quickly turns away from me, placing the knife and cutting board in the sink and goes through the motions of washing and drying them.

I take a seat at the table and lean back against the wall. "Do you only give solo concerts or is this a special occasion?" Silence passes between us. Her back is straight as a board, but her hands clench the kitchen towel tightly. "C'mon, Teddy. Talk to me. I don't bite. We can be friends. I promise."

She finishes drying the cutting board and places it in the cabinet. Her back is still turned to me.

"Teddy," I say softly.

I get up and stand beside her. Her breath shudders as I stroke her cheek with my fingers and turn her face to me. She refuses to look at me, focusing on an unknown spot on the wall behind me. "I know he hurt you. I don't know for how long or how deep the scars go, but I want you to know you're safe here. I won't let anyone hurt you. You can stay with me as long as you want."

Her green eyes darken when she finally looks into my eyes. "You'll change your mind as soon as you get to know me. I always manage to screw things up." She turns and stirs the veggies, bumping me so that her back is facing me again.

"Stop it. OK?" I take a seat at the table again. "I'm not easy to know either, just ask Derek. I can be an asshole. Everyone can be given the right circumstances. I judge people on how they treat me over time, because moments are just that…a small place in time, and each has its own special circumstances surrounding it. A good moment to you may be exceptionally bad to me. Everyone deserves to be given a chance or as many chances as it takes for others to see the good inside. Just because one person, or a set of people, didn't like you doesn't mean others won't find you amazing and talented. Just like they say, beauty is in the eye of the beholder. And I just happen to think you're the most beautiful woman I've ever seen."

She places the lid on the pan and turns down the flame before turning to face me. "I know who you are, Carter George," she says, clenching her hands at her sides, completely ignoring my feeble attempt at being sweet. "You take down the lives and vitality of those around you, like a common criminal. You're a monster. Will the *real* ruthless New York real estate billionaire please stand up?"

I drop my head into my hands and rub my fingers in circles over my temples. My headache is returning in full force. I fucking hate Page Six and Google.

The door opens, and Derek walks in with grocery bags hanging from his arms. He sets them down on the counter and starts to empty them, whistling a tune. I don't feel like socializing anymore, so I stand. Teddy is staring at me. Sadness flickers in her eyes as I rise.

"Like I said, everyone deserves a chance to show their goodness." I head back into my room and pull the door shut. Derek calls after me, but I ignore him.

∾

I SKIP EATING. I'M NOT FEELING IT ANYMORE. INSTEAD, I LIE IN BED, my eyes focused on the ceiling.

Will I only be remembered as Carter George, the rich asshole who ruined more lives than he saved?

The idea makes my guts churn. I know deep in my heart though that if I hadn't been diagnosed with impending death, I would've never changed. Maybe I really was a monster. Doing a few nice things doesn't change a man. It just makes the man more wicked, because really, who tears the world apart then tries to brighten it with a few good deeds? That's like putting a band-aid on a self-inflicted knife wound. *What good is that?*

Maybe it's too little too late.

A soft knock pulls me from my morose thoughts. I don't even bother acknowledging it.

"Hey," Teddy's soft voice wafts to me.

My treacherous heart kicks up at the sound of her voice, but I don't look at her, wondering if maybe she'll just leave me to my self-loathing in peace. The depression that has set over me today is real.

My bed sinks down as she lies beside me, taking my same position with her hands resting on her stomach and her eyes focused on the ceiling. I imagine it's how I'll look stuffed into my casket in a few months. May as well start practicing now.

"I'm sorry for snapping at you earlier," her voice is timid, very unlike the person she is.

"You weren't wrong." I continue to stare at the ceiling.

"I was, though," she persists, rolling to her side, all her dark hair spilling around her. She leans forward so her face is partially obstructing my view of the ceiling. Her hair tickles my chin. "I shouldn't have said that. I don't even know you."

Tearing my eyes from the ceiling, I lock them on her wavering green ones. Such beautiful eyes. She keeps so much hidden inside, but those eyes. . . they tell a story. On instinct, I reach up and cup her cheek in my hand, my eyes searching her face. My thumb rubs a soft circle on her cheek. Her lips part as she stares back at me.

"Bad always overshadows the good," I whisper. "I *am* a monster. I'm only trying to be a better one, but maybe it's too late for all that now."

"It's not," she murmurs, a plea in her voice, her fingers splaying across my chest. The touch is electric. My heart rate kicks up. "Derek told me about what you did for Luke."

"One good deed doesn't change a man," I say sadly, unable to pull my touch from her.

"One good deed is a start, though. And I admire that." She grows quiet, her eyes darting to my lips. A faint flush paints her cheeks before she speaks again, "I'm a monster too. And one monster shouldn't judge another. Trust me when I say that I screw up and disappoint people more than I make them happy."

85

"Are you proposing monster solidarity?" I raise an eyebrow at her. A beautiful smile that lights up my entirely too dark fucking world spills across her lips.

"Strength in numbers, right?" She leans into me, her breath catching as my thumb moves to brush against her bottom lip.

This is your chance! Take it, Carter! You only have so many left! The moment is screaming at me. My heart somersaults in my chest like an unsteady gymnast.

Reality slaps me in the face with its giant, veiny dick.

I'm a dead man. No woman would want a dead man. What? I'd love her for a moment before leaving her broken?

Nah. I spent my life breaking women. That's not how this will go down. Not this time.

My hand falls from her face, breaking whatever spell we're under, and I sit up, breathing hard over what I'd almost done. What I so fucking desperately wanted to do. If this was a different life, I'd have loved that girl so hard.

But it isn't a different life. It's a half-life. What's left of my life.

And I'm not dragging anyone down with me.

TWELVE

TEDDY

J almost kissed Carter. If he wouldn't have pulled away from me, I know I would've. Something about him just reels me in. I can't shake him. Even after our first meeting, he was all I could think about.

Something's up with him though. I spend the better half of the morning Googling his name only to come up with information on how ruthless he is and how many women he's been through. Other than that there's nothing. No known long-term romantic relationships. No reasons for his sudden departure from his company, which is making headlines around the world. Nothing. Carter George is an enigma.

I wipe my sweaty palms down the front of my shorts, blowing out a shaky breath. The moment with Carter in his bedroom is still with me, making my heart hammer in my chest. I've never responded to a man like that before. No man has ever made my heart simultaneously skip a beat and rush to beat faster all at once. Literally a race to see which would kill me first.

"Carter come out of his cave yet?" Derek asks, popping his head into the living area of the Beastmaster.

"Oh. Uh, no. He said he needed a nap, so I left him with Molly." I glance at the closed door, my heart yearning for his touch again. *Jesus. That's a new feeling.*

"Yeah, he likes to nap sometimes." Derek's eyes shift around the room before he clears his throat. "Do you want to go for a walk and explore a bit?"

"That sounds good."

I'm on my feet, ready to get out of there before I bum rush Carter's room and straddle him, demanding he touch me again. The thought sends heat flooding between my legs, and I duck my head to keep from showcasing any of my dirty thoughts which are probably clearly written on my face.

Derek takes no notice and moves aside so I can step past him onto the pavement. He locks the door and nods for me to follow him.

He's quiet for a moment before he speaks, "You should know that Carter really *is* a good guy. Even with all the shit people say about him in the tabloids and news, deep down in his soul, he's a good man."

"I was out of line. I apologized to him," I say.

"Good."

We're quiet as we walk, me taking in all the beauty that is New Orleans—the vibrant colors, the smell of all the food, the laughter as people chat with one another outside the storefronts. We veer off and walk through City Park. It's peaceful, something I need after my morning with Carter. My heart yearns for him to be here with me, walking through the park, his hand in mine, that sexy growly voice of his in my ear—

Whoa. Teddy, girl, check yourself!

I flush again at my rampant thoughts and clear my throat.

"So, what's the deal with Carter?"

"Deal?" Derek turns his brown-eyed gaze on me.

"Yeah, why does a billionaire suddenly walk out on his company and go across country on a road trip, helping out the hordes of unfortunate?"

Derek stuffs his hands into his pockets, seemingly contemplating his answer.

"He just needed a break. He's been stressed. Doc told him to take some time away and relax," his words come out in a guilty rush. "That's all."

"A woman didn't break his heart?" I press. Maybe he kept his serious relationships quiet.

Derek lets out a laugh, shaking his head.

"No woman has ever been close enough to Carter to break his heart, except maybe his mom." Derek grimaces, casting a quick look at me about his apparent overshare.

"Don't tell Carter I said anything, OK? He's a private guy. And he's a royal pain in my ass when he's pissed."

"My lips are sealed," I promise, mocking a zipper over my lip that makes Derek grin. "He's just doing this road trip to de-stress then?"

"You could say that. Find himself and all that jazz." Derek's eyes flit to a couple walking a Labrador. "Don't be too rough on him. He's going through some shit he won't talk about."

I nod. That much was apparent.

"What's your story anyway?" he asks.

"My story?" I raise my eyebrows at him and chuckle. "Just a small-town girl living in a lonely world."

Derek laughs. "Don't quote Journey to me as an answer. A beautiful woman caught up with some douchebag in Nashville who finally breaks free is more of a Lifetime movie."

I grin back at him. "Fine. I really am from a smaller town. I was in med school, as per my father's wishes. But it wasn't my wish. I didn't make it very far before I dropped out. When I told my dad about wanting to be a musician, he told me to pack my bags and have a good life. So far, the best thing I've done is pack my bags. Life, on the other hand, hasn't been nearly as kind as good old dad was."

"Saying you have a rocky relationship with him—"

"Would be an understatement." I laugh sadly. We stop at an ice cream vendor, and Derek buys me a chocolate cone and some chocolate chip monstrosity for himself.

"No Christmas dinners with the family then?" Derek presses as we continue to walk with our cones in hand.

"Nope. My mom always begs me to come visit, but I can't. My dad would lose his shit on me. He made it clear I wasn't welcome back home unless I did something with my life." I frown down at my cone. A pang sears my heart at missing my family.

"That sucks." Derek gives me a sad look.

"It does, but this is what I wanted. I liked med school, but I didn't *love* it. And why spend your life doing something you only *like*? Doesn't make much sense to me." I lick at the chocolate that's quickly melting before continuing, "I miss my family, but I can't go home until I succeed."

"Then I think you got in the right RV," Derek proclaims, bumping shoulders with me.

I grin back at him, my heart swelling in my chest at the thought of Carter.

"I think I did too."

DIARY

Day 16

I feel like shit. I spent all of yesterday in bed, moping about my shitty remaining existence. What made it worse was laying in the dark listening as Teddy's soft laughter wafted down the hall to me as she and Derek talked. I couldn't hear what they said, but my heart jumped in my chest every time I heard her laugh and him murmur again.

OK. So, I'm a moping, dying, jealous asshole now.

I'm a big enough man to admit that I'm feeling not only a little ashamed of my pouting, but also like I want to break my best friend's face for talking to the girl I like. This isn't high school, and I need to pull my head out of my ass.

Do I really want to spend my remaining days in bed? Fuck no.

But lying here, replaying the memory of Teddy over me makes my dick hard. All I had to do was take the moment. I'd probably be kissing on her right now if I wouldn't have chickened out yesterday.

Today is a new day. Even if I've convinced myself that I can't be with her, there's still this tiny part of me telling me one kiss won't hurt. One touch. One...night.

Every dying man has a wish. I thought mine was to live longer.

Instead, I'm beginning to realize it might just be to have a moment with her wrapped in my arms.

THIRTEEN

CARTER

*M*y dick is harder than a fucking lead pipe. It's been that way for hours. I've resisted doing anything about it because, really, aside from jerking myself raw, the only other thing I want to do is bury myself so deeply inside Teddy that the rest of the world could go fuck itself.

The sun is just starting to rise. I've missed too much time because I've been moping around. Derek's snoring is coming at me in waves. I need to get up, medicate, and maybe go for a run. Deciding that's the best course of action, I go to the bathroom and start a shower.

It should be a cold shower because my dick is still hard. I close my eyes, breathing out as I rest my forearms against the wall of the shower.

Fuck. I need her.

No woman has ever had this effect on me. If I don't do something about it, my dick will be hard the rest of the day. I can't fight it any longer. Taking my cock in hand, I begin stroking it, all my thoughts on Teddy. Her long, dark hair. The way her lips part when she looks at me. How her green eyes sparkle.

I imagine the way she'd taste as I kiss her lips before proceeding south to dip my tongue in the promised land. I imagine how my name would slip from her mouth as I bury myself deep inside of her, lost in everything that is her.

I pump my dick harder, my eyes squeeze shut, as my breathing comes in sharp gasps.

"Teddy," I moan softly, breathlessly. Her name is a fucking prayer to me. The only one that can release me from the torture.

I let out a groan as my orgasm spills hot and heavy over my hand, my body quivering in the aftermath. I have to lean against the wall to steady myself, my vision dotted with sparkles at what has to have been one of the best orgasms I've ever had in my life.

After my moment of recovery, I wash and dry myself, feeling somewhat relieved. I forgot to bring clothes in with me, so I wrap a towel around my midsection and slide the door open to find Teddy standing there, her green eyes wide.

"I-I'm so sorry. I thought I heard my name—" her eyes sweep over me in my towel, pink staining her cheeks as her eyes linger on the area the towel covers. She tugs her bottom lip between her teeth as her breathing changes.

My dick is getting hard again.

"You did." I smirk down at her as her eyes take in the hard planes of my chest, before trailing over the muscles I've spent years defining.

Down, boy. I silently plead with the gods of chaos for my dick to behave.

"I-I did?" Confusion covers her face before comprehension replaces it. "Oh! Oh, wow."

I expect her to back away from me. In fact, she does for a moment, but then she draws in a deep breath and leans into me, that sweet summery scent of hers that's been lingering on my pillow since she lay beside me yesterday envelopes my senses.

"If you need me, ask for me," her soft voice shakes a bit in my ear, sending a thrill of goosebumps through me. I close my eyes, the heat from her body blanketing me. Her t-shirt clad breasts press against my bare chest. "I'll help you next time."

Jesus fucking Christ.

Her fingers gently brush against the top of my towel before she moves away from me, those luscious hips swaying in her tiny, pink shorts. She doesn't look back.

She knows what she's doing. I grin at the game she wants to play, shaking away all my prior thoughts.

Fuck cancer. *This* woman is going to be the death of me.

AFTER TAKING A FEW MOMENTS TO CALM MYSELF, I COME OUT OF MY bedroom fully medicated and dressed, my dick on his best behavior in my khakis.

Derek is awake and sitting at the table with his back to me. Teddy is across from him, a cup of coffee in hand. Her eyes land on me the moment I come into the room, a tiny smirk on those lips. If she's ashamed of her actions from earlier, she certainly doesn't act like it. And it only makes me want her more. I love a woman who wants to play dirty. I've already had "the talk" with myself, promising that I won't act on anything. We can be flirtatious friends. Hell, it'll be more of a steady relationship than I've ever had in my life. Nothing can happen past that.

I move to go to the coffee pot, but Teddy's voice calls out to me.

"I already made you a cup."

I glance at her as she nods to my cup on the table. She slides over, daring me to sit next to her. I do so without hesitation.

"Good morning, Teddy. *Again*," I say, casting a smile at her. Her lips quirk up higher, her green eyes sparkling.

"Morning, Carter."

Derek lifts a brow and looks between us. "Did I miss something?"

"Nothing you'd want to see," I retort, remembering how I'd heard him making her laugh the previous night.

Calm down, you jealous bastard.

Derek shrugs before going back to his bagel.

"What did you guys do yesterday?" I grunt, taking the bagel Teddy hands me. Her fingers brush against mine, causing me to pause so I can relish in her warmth. She wiggles in her seat beneath my stare, a playful smile still on her lips.

"We walked through City Park, ate some ice cream, and Derek told me all about your trip."

My hands twitch, my gaze landing on Derek whose eyes widen.

"Relax." Teddy chuckles, releasing my bagel. "He didn't tell me your deep, dark secret. He said you needed to de-stress, and this is how you're doing it."

The tension rolls out of me, and I relax in my seat.

"Yeah, work can be a bitch," I say, taking a bite of my bagel.

"Sure can," Derek mumbles, breathing out a whoosh of air and sinking back into his chair.

For a moment, I feel awful about my jealousy, then I realize it's *Teddy*. The woman of my dreams. And I'm *dying*. I can be a jealous prick here and there if I want to.

"Anything you want to do today?" I ask Teddy.

She cocks her head at me and smirks. "You're the one who needs to de-stress. Is there anything *you'd* like to do today?"

"I'd like to eat some gumbo," I say thoughtfully. "Never had it before. Maybe hit up Bourbon Street after. Have some drinks. Look at everyone living their best life."

"Let's do it." Derek grins. "I could use some good food and drink."

"I'm game," Teddy agrees, wiggling in her seat again. Her fingers brush against my leg as she brings her hand off the table to rest on her lap.

"Sorry," she says immediately.

But everything in those green orbs suggests she's anything but sorry.

FOURTEEN

TEDDY

I order us a Lyft and off we go to Marie Laveau's House of Voodoo. Not that I'm into that particular sort of thing, but being in the medical field has made me acknowledge that this world contains all kinds of weird shit. So, yes, I believe ghosts roam the world, looking to match their bodies back to their souls, and I believe in miracle cures. I also believe in higher powers at play in this world which is why I want to see the Voodoo Museum and get my palm read.

"Tell me again why we are going to the House of Voodoo?" Derek says nervously as we exit our ride. He takes a picture of the sign hanging over the front entrance. When he peeks inside, he says, "There are skeletons handing from the ceiling...umm, I think I'll wait out here."

"Oh, c'mon Derek. She just wants to get a voodoo doll of Richie and curse him to the seven circles of hell but while he's here on Earth. Right?" Carter says, elbowing him as we all laugh.

Little does he know, that's not a bad idea.

"I actually want to get my palm read or future told, whatever they may do here. This seems like the perfect place to see what lies ahead for me. Hopefully it's not too expensive. I'm on a budget."

"I'm sure I can wheel and deal them into a two for one deal. Then

I'll get mine done too and pay," Carter says matter-of-factly, placing his hand on the small of my back to escort me inside. Derek follows closely behind.

"Hey, check this out. A shrunken head on a string," Carter exclaims, picking it up and moving its jaw while he laughs eerily.

Derek takes it from him and hangs it back up.

"No." Carter smacks at his arm and takes the skull off the post it was hanging on again. "I want that. We need an RV mascot. It'll look great hanging from the rearview mirror."

"I'm *not* driving with that thing swaying back and forth hexing me. If you want it, then you can drive."

Carter places his mascot into our basket and moves along, picking up different items and commenting while Derek ignores him. We enter another room toward the back, and I see the sign for readings. Ten dollars.

"Yay! I can afford this. Not sure how much of my future is worth that price, but maybe she can get me through the month. Be right back," I say. I hear Carter grumble about wanting to pay for me, but I ignore him.

I approach the half-open curtain. A young woman with bright red, curly hair sits inside, shuffling cards at a small table, and blowing bubbles with her chewing gum.

She looks up and pops a bubble to speak, "You want a reading?" Her southern drawl is cheery and welcoming.

I nod and take a seat, laying my ten-dollar bill on the table.

"Don't be nervous. Relax. This'll be fun. I'm Roya, by the way." She swipes her deep purple fingernails in the air at me as she closes the curtain behind me.

"I'm Teddy," I say, my voice quivers as the little curtained room we're in grows darker and smaller.

"For ten dollars you get a tarot card reading, for fifteen dollars a palm reading, and for twenty dollars an aura evaluation. So which one are we going with?"

I slide the ten closer to her. "Tarot," I confirm. It's cheaper and will probably yield the same results as a palm reading.

"And which aspect of your life are we reading today?"

I look at her wildly. *Shit. What do I want to know?* "My love life."

Amusement glints in her eyes. "Very well."

She sets the cards down in front of me. "Touch them please."

I do as she asks.

She shuffles the cards again and aligns them neatly before setting them in front of me again.

"Please touch them again." she requests, and I do.

She shuffles them a third time and fans them out in a large display across the table. "Please run your fingertip from one end of the cards to the other, touching each one." As I touch the cards, she whispers something I can't understand and stops when I lift my hand from the table.

She picks the cards back up, shuffling them one last time and spreads them across the table again. "Pick three cards and hand them to me."

Without hesitation, I pick the three cards in the center of the pile. No sense in ruminating over it too long. If it's truly my future, taking different cards from the spread isn't going to change it any.

She picks up the rest of the cards with ease, like a dealer playing blackjack at the casino. "Hmmm, these are interesting." She shakes her head, her curls bouncing.

She turns the first card over and pushes it toward me with her fingertips. "This is the Reversed Emperor card. It signifies dominance and rigidity in thinking, suggesting an abuse of authoritative power. It could be from a lover, a boss, or even a father or father-like figure in your life. Does someone hold power over you? Or maybe you hold their thoughts or opinions in such high regard that it's invisible power over you."

"So this card means I have *daddy* issues?" A mocking laugh escapes my lips. My dad would show up in my tarot reading. He's smothering my life like a giant squid.

"Possibly." She pops a small bubble in her chewing gum before continuing, "You need to consider how much power you give others over your life. Are you trying to please them too much? There are many ways to make others happy without giving up control or taking their power from them. Lead from a place where your personal power is the strongest."

"I have no idea what that means." I sigh heavily. I'm convinced I just wasted ten precious dollars.

"Find what you're good at...what you excel at, what makes you happy, and work to live your best life using *that* power."

She flips over the second card and pushes it toward me. It's an angel. "This is the Upright Temperance card. It's the card of balance. See where one foot is in the water and the other is on dry land?"

I nod.

"The foot in the water represents the subconscious mind. The foot on land represents the material world." She clicks her long amethyst painted nail on the symbol of the sun on the angel's forehead. "This means illumination. This card suggests compromise between extremes to maintain a balance, to take the middle road. It shows that we need to balance the ups and down in life with inner and outer awareness."

That's what Carter says I do. I take the middle road. Maybe Roya knows what she's talking about. A line of worry forms between her eyebrows as she studies the next card. She flips it over to face me and sets it on the table.

"This is the Upright Fool card." She slides it forward on the table.

"Oh, shit. I chose the joker. That's just perfect," I say, shaking my head in annoyance.

"The Fool card is numbered zero in the tarot stack, meaning it has infinite potential. It's the beginning, if you want to think of it that way. It's like a blank slate or a new start. He's an optimist and views each day as a new adventure. He believes anything can happen in life and opportunities are around every corner."

I sit forward in my seat, studying the card. "But he's getting ready to walk off a cliff. See?" I point to the little white dog on the card. "The dog here is barking, trying to warn him."

"Teddy, you're a pessimist. You see the negative in this picture, but this isn't the *Reverse* Fool card. This card is trying to tell you not to worry about what is or isn't coming in the future. It suggests that you take one day at a time and enjoy the journey."

"That's easier said than done." I blow out a long breath thinking. "So the overall picture here is that I need to stop pleasing everyone else. Work on my happiness and enjoy the journey while balancing it with smart decisions."

"You're quick. Believe, Teddy. Have a little faith in the higher powers that place opportunities in front of you." She pops one final large bubble with her gum before making it snap and pop sharply against her smiling lips.

"So, the moral of the reading is that things happen for a reason, and I have no control over it. And most of my frustration is because I'm trying to control it. Good to know." I stand and step toward the curtain.

"Teddy," she says softly, and I turn slightly to look at her over my shoulder. "I think the moral of the reading is that you have a new start coming. Take the opportunity to live in *that* moment. Consider all options before you take action. And realize what it is that *YOU* want. Once you know that, life should get easier and be more fulfilling."

I slide the curtain back and step out into the brightly lit shop. Carter's sobering handsome face is looking directly at me from across the room. "Hey, where's Derek?"

"This place was giving him the heebie jeebies, so he stepped outside. Are you OK?"

"Yeah, sure. Why do you ask?" I turn sideways from him, picking up a simple doll made of sackcloth from under a sign that reads *'Voodoo Dolls'*. I shake it at him and smile.

"No reason. You just had a worried look on your face when you came out."

"No, it was good. Roya is good, really good actually. You should give it a go. She read tarot cards for my love life."

"And did you get the burning heart of love card?" he jokes, elbowing my side teasingly.

"Stop it. There's no such card. Here, give me your shrunken head." I take it and roll my eyes over why he wants this ugly thing. "I'll hold it while you get your reading. I'm going to go look at the crystals upstairs." I point to the sign above the staircase showing him where I'll be.

FIFTEEN

CARTER

*T*eddy's been quiet ever since we left the voodoo shop. Her fortune must have hit deeper and been more on target than she expected. I don't even want to think about my reading. My recent state of being in a bad mood is getting deeper and darker the longer this vacation goes on.

"I want to go see the Backstreet Cultural Museum," Derek chimes into my thoughts, pointing to an advertisement for it taped inside a shop on Magazine Street.

"Please tell me it's not a museum for the Backstreet Boys." Teddy and I both groan. Glad I'm not the only one not happy about that idea.

"Hell no," he exclaims, shaking his head at us like we're ridiculous. "Why would I want to see that? Google says it's this little family run museum showcasing the unique and quirky traditions of New Orleans. The reviews say it's pretty cool."

Derek plugs in the address into his phone for walking directions, and we're not too far away. When we arrive, we're greeted by the owner himself who gives us the full-blown tour of everything New Orleans and makes great suggestions for our gumbo dinner. My stomach is already growling just thinking about it.

"Man, I feel like I've lived here my whole life after that tour,"

Derek says excitedly. He's flipping through the pictures he took on his phone already re-living the memories.

"I'm glad you like it, but I need to sit down." I throw Derek a mercy look. "My feet are burning with all the walking we've done today."

Derek opens up his pedometer app showing us the screen. "We've walked just over 29,000 steps today. That's insane."

"Yeah, I think that calls for a seat, a beer, and some gumbo," I announce, punching a few buttons on my Lyft app because I can't take another step. "Lyft will be here in five minutes."

I take a seat on a bench just outside Louis Armstrong Jazz Park and wait, while Teddy and Derek walk over to the street corner and watch some kids beat on a mix of household items like drums for money. It sounds really good, but my head is starting to throb to their beat.

It's nearly 5:00 PM. The uncontrollable shaking of my hands only reminds me I need to eat and take my meds. The heat is fucking adding on to my misery and foul mood since we left the voodoo place. Fucking Roya and her Card of Death. When I close my eyes, I'm back in that dark room…

At first, all I see when she flips over the first card is the white knight and people falling at his feet. They look so happy. Maybe he's their savior. Hmmm. Maybe I'm on the right path, trying to help those I'm encountering on this journey. I can be their white knight.

I lean forward and look more closely. Fuck. *I home-in on the knight's face—an aging yellow skull, and I know it isn't good.*

I peek up at Roya, and her cheerful smile and pink color are fading quickly from her face. She nervously tries to play it off. "Um… that card can mean positivity and um… ah… being like a white knight."

I know better. Like Teddy said, I have a monster's soul and I know a kindred spirit when I see one. Fucking Knight of Death.

Roya hastily moves on with the next card. It's a backwards seven of swords or something. It's kind of cool with an ordinary looking dude carrying a bunch of swords. Maybe it symbolizes I'm fighting for my life, and I'm going to crush the knight's skull.

"This card means deception. He's stealing the swords. See the *smug look on his face, it shows his victory. Getting this card may mean that you have the opportunity for some sort of renewal of conscience."*

I can half buy-in to that train of thought. I mean, I am out here on this adventure doing my best to undo some of my dirty deeds. Apparently, the tarot cards see right through me. I'm nothing but a fraud. God's going to put my ass on the express elevator to Hades as soon as the Book of Good Deeds is opened, and He only finds one thing under my name...Luke. One's got to be better than none. Right?

Church bells ring in the distance, and my phone buzzes in my hand, drawing me out of my mental reverie. I swipe across the screen to see our ride is here as a white Chevy Trailblazer pulls up to the corner. "Teddy, Derek," I call their names and point toward the street. They toss a few dollars at the boys and head to the car.

We decide mid-ride to head back to the RV before dinner. Per our driver, the best gumbo in town is Arnaud's, and Teddy isn't exactly dressed for the experience. Granted, I like her white, cut-off shorts with the long strings swaying to the motion of her hips. It's mesmerizing. And her red-striped half shirt just begs me to see if my hands will span the width of her waist, but I'd like to take her somewhere nice to eat while I still can.

"Let's get changed to fit the Arnaud's atmosphere. Dinner is on me tonight," I announce. Teddy and Derek high-five each other, and that little prick of jealousy I have toward my best friend flicks me in the heart. *Motherfucker, it hurts too.*

Within the hour, I call out in the silence of the RV. My voice reverberates off the closed doors back at me. "C'mon, let's go. I'm wasting away as we speak."

Derek's door opens first, and he's sporting a nice blue, button-down shirt with a navy paisley tie to match. His blue blazer is lying over his arm.

"Did you order our ride yet?" he asks, digging in the cabinet. "Because I need to feed Molly."

"I already fed her and took her out. She's sleeping in my room."

"Poor girl. She deserves a whole day at the park, but we should be hitting the road tomorrow. Maybe I'll take her out in the morning for a long run."

Teddy's door slides open, and she steps out into the hallway facing me. Derek's back is to her, but he turns when he hears me catch my breath.

She's fucking gorgeous.

She has on a wine-colored halter dress which clings to her long legs. I assume it's backless from the shape of the front and sides. Jesus Christ, there's no way she's wearing a bra under that. A devilish smile spreads across my face, as I step toward her and hold my arm out.

Her wide eyes bounce back and forth between me and Derek, trying to gauge our opinions.

"You look beautiful," I say.

Derek just whistles, and I smack him on the chest as I pass him to take her arm.

"Is it too much? It's the nicest dress I own now since Richie ruined everything else. It's my graduation slash wedding slash fancy dinner dress."

"It's perfect."

She pats her hair, making sure it's still up and in place where she twisted it.

"Stop fiddling. You look amazing. Now let's go eat," I tell her.

With perfect timing, my phone buzzes indicating our ride is here.

God, I wish we were taking the Mercedes out, but it's a two-seater. Maybe we'll go for a ride tomorrow while Derek is out with Molly. I'd love to see the outer parishes of the city...just the two of us.

SIXTEEN

TEDDY

I don't *need* to have my arm wrapped around Carter's, but I can't seem to let go, my want for this enigmatic man growing by the second. Maybe it's because he pulls me in only to push me back. Maybe I'm a damn glutton for punishment, always wanting the man who's emotionally unavailable. Everything about Carter's Google history tells me he doesn't do relationships.

But then he looks at me, his full lips curving up into that teasing smile, and I find that I don't give a damn. I want to experience whatever Carter George is willing to give me.

Carter helps me into the car, sitting between me and Derek. The warmth from his body causes a shiver to rush through me.

"Are you comfortable?" he asks, quirking an eyebrow up at me.

I'd be better if I was on your lap!

My face heats at the thought, but I manage to smile at him like I'm not having the world's dirtiest thoughts.

"I'm fine. Thanks," I say, going breathless as he reaches over me to latch my seatbelt.

"Safety first." He casts a playful wink at me, the back of his hand brushing gently over my breasts. I'm not sure if it's an accident or on purpose, but my mind demands I believe he wanted to do that because the alternative upsets me.

With all of us safely buckled in, we make our way to the restaurant.

"I hope they have chicken tenders," Derek says as we pull up, his dark eyes narrow at the posh building.

Carter snorts at him, and even I chuckle. Secretly, I'm hoping they do too. The idea of eating anything that resembles an insect has anxiety uncoiling in my chest.

The moment we're out of the car, Carter holds his arm out for me to take. I do so without hesitation, casting a smile up at him. He wastes no time returning it, which only jolts the butterflies to life in my stomach.

"Right this way, please" a host greets us and takes us to our table. Carter pulls my chair out for me and runs his fingers between my shoulder blades as he pulls his own chair out to sit. The teasing look in his eyes makes a shiver run the length of my spine.

We're left with menus, and Derek is quick to breathe a sigh of relief at finding something he'll eat.

"I'm not picky," he argues as Carter points it out to him. "I just know what I like and prefer to stick to it. My stomach doesn't always take kindly to new dishes."

"It's a shame because this is going to be amazing," Carter insists, breathing in deeply.

I have to admit it does smell divine in here. His gaze rests on me. "How about you, Teddy? What are you having?"

I scan the menu quickly and glance at Derek who grins at me.

"She wants chicken tenders too," he says.

"Come on, Teddy!" Carter rolls his eyes. "We're traveling the country. We're experiencing what this great city has to offer. Don't deny the adventure."

"I'm not denying it," I defend myself, lifting my brows at him. His hand comes to rest over mine. I bite back the whimper that rises inside me at his warm touch.

"Live a little, Teddy Bear," he says softly, his thumb tracing a tender circle on my skin. "Live with me in this moment. You won't regret it."

How the hell can I say no to that? If his words and tender nickname don't capture me, the look in his eyes does.

"OK." I nod, letting out the breath I'm holding. A wide smile spreads over Carter's face that has me grinning.

"Don't let him do that to you," Derek groans.

"Do what?" Carter asks innocently, removing his touch from my hand.

"You know what! All you have to do is look at a woman, and she swoons. Add to it *your moves,* and they don't stand a chance."

Carter lets out a loud laugh at Derek. I frown.

Did he seriously just play me?

"Did you just trick me?" I demand.

Carter stops laughing, his eyes filled with warmth as they come to focus on me.

"I'm just looking for a little adventure, sweetheart. Thought you were too. That's all."

Well, two can play that game.

I move my hand to rest on Carter's thigh. He tenses beneath my touch, obviously surprised at this turn of events. I pop a brow at him, my hand moving higher. He shifts beneath my touch, but not away. *Oh no, not Carter George.* If anything, he's enjoying the game we're playing with one another.

I rub his thigh gently, discretely, as Derek tries to engage Carter in a conversation about the next place we're going once we leave New Orleans.

"I'm thinking the Grand Canyon," Carter says with a shrug. "Unless there's somewhere Teddy wants to see. How about it, Teddy?" His eyes are hooded as he focuses them on me, my hand rubbing the junction of where his thigh meets his groin.

Oh yeah. I'm going there.

"What do you want?" he murmurs at me, the question loaded.

"I want what you want," I answer, hoping we're on the same page.

A tiny smirk cuts across his handsome face.

"I think we're in the same state of mind." His hand reaches down and takes mine before full on placing it over the very large erection he's sporting beneath the table. He gives me a wink before releasing my hand. My face heats at his boldness and the fact that for once in my life, I don't know how to react.

Carter George just upped the ante.

SEVENTEEN

CARTER

*T*eddy has me so hot. I have a hard time focusing through dinner. I know what I said. I *know* I said I wouldn't pursue anything, but damnit, I want what I want.

There's nothing wrong with just playing. Maybe she'll get bored of the games.

But God, I don't want her to.

She's all I can concentrate on at dinner, missing the warmth from her hand as it's now holding her spoon. Her cute nose is turned up as she stares down at the meal I know she's nervous about.

"All you have to do is open your mouth and put it in," I say to her in a husky voice, something other than food on my mind.

Her cheeks flush pink, and I imagine that's the color her sexy ass would be if I could just turn her over my knee and give her the spanking she's earned for giving my dick a bit of hope.

She does as I suggest, a soft moan leaving her lips as she chews.

Fuck. She's so sexy it should be a sin.

I grin, digging into my own gumbo.

Derek gives us a look that suggests we might be crazy. I shrug it off. Fuck it. Food is good. Company is even better. I'm living for it.

"There are some good clubs down on Bourbon," Derek says, taking a sip of water. "We should hit one up, or as many as we want. I was checking out some really cool places on my phone before we left."

"Sounds good. Teddy?" I glance over at her.

"Sure." She shrugs, winking at me. "Let's do it."

"Let's do it." I smirk back.

"Wow!" Teddy laughs, leaning in so I can hear her.

The club music is so loud it makes me wince. It's creating a dull ache in my head that I'm praying doesn't trigger one of my headaches. Her hair brushes my cheek, and I'm instantly hard as steel again with thoughts of running my tongue over her sensuous neck.

She points in the direction of Derek who's dancing up on two females. They seem rather excited by his nearness since they're touching him back.

"I didn't know Derek was like that!" Teddy continues, shaking her head in shock. "Look at his moves!" And she's right. Derek can dance.

"Like I said, we're all on an adventure," I reply, smiling as Derek is sandwiched between the two women, a grin plastered from ear to ear across his face.

"Do you want to dance?" She motions to the dance floor.

There's a painful spasm in my head, and I grimace. The smile on Teddy's lips falters as she takes it to mean no.

Fucking tumors.

"Why don't you go dance? I could use a drink," I say, my heart deflating. I want nothing more than to dance with her. I've been sporting a semi-hard-on since dinner just being near her.

She gives me a smile that doesn't reach her eyes and nods. "OK."

And with that, she sashays away. Her luscious ass is all I can focus on until my hands twitch.

"Fuck," I hiss, giving them a shake.

My head is starting to pound. Maybe this wasn't such a good idea. I make my way to the bathroom where I splash cold water on my face. The image in the mirror looks a little gaunt. I'm a built guy, having honed every muscle to perfection, but as I stare at myself in the overly bright mirror, all I see are dark circles, cheeks that are starting to sink in, and pants that are too loose from losing weight.

I grip the sink tightly, hauling in a few deep, calming breaths before I pull my bottle of pain pills from my pocket and swallow one down in the hopes of maybe one more night of normalcy. Just one more fucking night. It's all I ever wish for.

I GRAB A DRINK AT THE BAR. THEN ANOTHER ONE. DEREK AND TEDDY are dancing together. I hate that. She throws her head back and laughs as he makes some weird move against her, a grin on his face. I should be grateful they're getting along, but I'm not. I'm jealous that he's enjoying her company while I continue to throw back drinks in the hopes of drowning my pitiful reality.

I watch them dance through three more songs before some guy cuts in. Derek steps away and turns to some other girl and dances with her. I throw back another drink as one song ends and another begins. The new guy is getting too close to her. She's starting to look uncomfortable as his hands rest on her ass.

I finish my drink and make my way over to her.

I decide to let the alcohol do my talking.

"Hey, baby," I coo in her ear, wrapping my arms around her waist from behind and tugging her against me and away from the shithead who thinks he can touch her. She turns around, her arms encircling my neck as she presses herself against me.

"Thank you," she says in my ear as I lean down to hear her. "I was about to commit a crime."

I chuckle softly, enjoying the fact she hasn't told me to remove my hands from her ass. Her arms are still around me, and she moves against me to the music.

Restraint, Carter.

I'm trying, but it's a helluva struggle.

She spins so her ass grinds against my cock. I let out a low hiss, my hands shaking on her waist. Her arms are around my neck again, pulling my face to her neck. My hands travel lower, exploring the way she feels tucked against me. My fingers dance along the hem of her short dress, her cleavage in my line of sight.

And oh what a glorious sight it is. What I wouldn't give to taste her on my tongue. On my lips.

Fuck.

My dick aches with need as she grinds against me. Teddy could probably get me off just by dancing on me. In fact, if we don't slow it down, I'll be spilling my raging want of her in my damn pants.

Her hair is falling down in dark tendrils around her. It's making my need grow.

"Teddy," I growl against her ear.

Her answer is to bend over before slowly moving up, her eyes focused on me over her shoulder.

I really am a dead man.

Hastily, I tug her back against me, letting her ass continue its torture against my cock. Teddy isn't innocent, something I find extremely attractive. Most women want to play sweet, but not Teddy. She gives it how it is, even if I don't like it. And even if I fucking love it.

She spins to face me, her arms back to resting casually around my neck like they've been there a thousand times. There's a twinkle in her eye that makes me smile. I lean down and let myself slip for just a minute, my lips skimming across the soft skin of her neck.

She smells like fucking freedom. A place I want to get lost in. A future I never cared about until she came along.

But I'm Carter George, and the only future I have will be carved on a piece of granite in a cemetery no one will ever visit.

I tighten my hold on her, living in this one blissful moment. These are the moments I've been searching for. The moments that make my shit hole of a life finally worth something.

I want her so badly my heart physically aches. I pull away and give her a smile she returns, no questions asked.

This is the first time in my life I've wanted something and couldn't have it.

And it fucking sucks. She's not a million-dollar deal. I can't claim her then rip her apart like Carter 1.0 would have done.

Or I could but at the cost of her heart.

DIARY

Day 17

Last night, I went to bed with blue balls. I didn't make a move past that slip of a kiss on her neck. She didn't push me. But Teddy likes to hit me with surprises. It's something that fuels my fire. And I don't mean to just "get her". This is about more than that. It makes me want to get up every morning. It terrifies me at night as I think about leaving the world without her.

Not that I want to kill her and take her with me. I'm not a psycho. I just mean being alone for eternity. If we're talking about believing in a higher power, I believe that while I'm roasting marshmallows in Hell, Teddy will eventually get married, have children, make some other man happy.

Am I a prick for not wanting her to have that with someone unless that someone is me?

This is the torturous shit that's been plaguing me since she came into my life.

Fuck it. Maybe I should just ask a higher power.

Dear Diary, how the hell do I get the girl and beat this disease?

Send help.

-Carter.

EIGHTEEN

TEDDY

I've been battling the sun shining through the window for an hour now. The thin white curtain does little to shield me from the sunlight.

I squint at the material. It reminds me of one of my grandmother's old curtains. The sides of her curtains were worn thin from years of constantly checking the driveway, waiting for my grandfather to come home from the war. *'Til death do they part.*

I'm not sure I'd have the strength to wait that long for someone. Their love ran deeper than the time of their separation. *Sigh.*

I know deep down inside Grandmother Bruce would be happy I'm out here fighting for my own place in this world without my dad, but I'm running pretty low on fighting fuel at the moment.

Carter used it all up last night. We parted ways on the dance floor; me to go to the restroom and him to sit down. He kept rubbing his temples like another headache was stealing him from me. Even after we separated, I could still feel his lips on my throat like they branded a tattoo on my skin.

He was the last thought on my mind before I drifted off to sleep, and then during my restlessness all through the night. Bits and pieces of us dining, dancing, and his warm lips on my skin kept passing through my dreams. He'd be with me, then he'd disappear, and just when I got frustrated, he'd appear again.

Molly barks in the kitchen a few times. I throw the sheet off me and let my feet dangle off the loft bed. She must be hungry. I push myself to sit up when there's a knock at my door.

"Yes," I say with a yawn. "It's not locked. You can come in." I rub the sleep from my eyes and am surprised when my eyes open to find Carter standing in the doorway.

"Do you want to take a ride with me?" A smile spreads across his face.

"To where?"

"Just out and about. Nowhere in particular. I feel like driving today." He shrugs.

My eyebrows knit in confusion. "Can you drive this big thing? What does Derek call it...the Beastmaster?"

His eyes crinkle with amusement. "Nooooo. I can't drive this thing. We have my car with us, but you didn't know that, did you? C'mon then. You're in for a surprise."

"I need a shower. Give me thirty?" I jump down from the bed and grab my robe off the hook. With him standing in my room, it suddenly feels smaller and intensely hot.

He turns sideways to let me pass through the door. "Hurry up, buttercup," he teases, swatting my ass as I squeeze between him and the door.

～

WITHIN TWENTY MINUTES, WE'RE STANDING AT THE REAR OF THE BUS, waiting for the back hatch to lower. My eyes are fixed on the door as it slowly reveals the 'surprise' awaiting me. "Wow, Carter. Look at her. She's beautiful. May I back her out?"

His Adam's apple bobs up and down with uncertainty, but he's a brave man because he dangles the keys in my face. "Sure. Why not?"

I take the keys from his fingers and stand on my tiptoes, kissing him quickly on the cheek. "Thank you. I promise, I'm a good driver." I race up the ramp and slide into the driver's seat. I adjust it for my long legs and angle all of the mirrors for my height before pressing the ignition button. "Oh, baby. She purrs like a lover being stroked," I say as he joins me in the passenger seat.

"Yes, that would be the appropriate analogy." He laughs loudly.

I back her out nice and gentle, despite the temptation rushing through me to floor the gas pedal and open her up. We pull up next to the RV, and I regretfully place her back in park.

"Chinese fire drill?" I ask, feeling my cheeks redden with my bold challenge.

"You're on, sister." He throws open the door and bolts toward the front as I dart around the back. We both slide into the other's seat and shut the doors at the same time. "Looks like it was a tie."

"That's OK. It's early in the trip. I'm sure there'll be plenty of other times to beat you coming up."

He throws his head back and laughs loudly. He's still laughing as we drive out of the RV park and into the morning rush hour traffic.

As we wait to enter the highway, he lets the top down and a hot wind blows across my face.

"We're heading to the Grand Canyon next. Does that excite you?" he asks, glancing over at me.

"I've been there before. My family took me when I was ten. I was bored the whole time." I unwrap the hair tie from my wrist and throw my hair up into a messy bun. Sweat is already trickling down my temple, and it's not even 9:00 AM yet.

"Bored? I can't imagine being bored at the Grand Canyon."

"We didn't do anything special. I wanted to go rafting, maybe ride a horse down to the basin, or do one of those plane rides, but *no*. My dad would only take us to the horseshoe overhang. I was so scared I couldn't go out on it. If I remember correctly, I peed my pants when he tried to drag me out onto the overlook."

"He *dragged* you? I don't know your dad, but that's a dick move."

We get on the highway and see a sign for Lake Pontchartrain. I point to it, and he changes lanes for the causeway.

"Then you do know him. My dad isn't Ward Cleaver. He's a doctor.

One of the best in neurosurgery. And he's a teaching doctor at that. He pushes his students hard, and I was no exception since he was paying for my private education." I lower the seat back and let the warm sun shine on my face.

I close my eyes and see my father's stern face. "He used to quiz me the night before tests until I could answer every one of the questions he made up from my books. Even if I fell asleep, he'd shake me awake and continue on. My father is a hard man, but a great doctor. I'm his greatest disappointment."

We enter onto the Lake Pontchartrain Causeway and drive over the open expanse of water. After a few minutes, I can't see the shoreline. I'd hate to be on this during a storm.

"I take it singing isn't something he supports?"

"The entertainment business isn't a noble profession in his eyes... saving lives and getting the chance to play God every now and again is."

We leave the causeway and get off onto a regular street, just passing through the neighborhoods. Many of them look to be still recovering from Hurricane Katrina.

"Did you follow in your dad's footsteps or forge your own path?" I squint at him in the bright sunlight.

"I took over my father's business when he passed a few years back. This apple didn't fall far from the tree," he replies, sighing loudly. "My dad was also a ruthless son-of-a-bitch. I learned from the best then added my own twisted endings. From his deathbed, he warned me to change my ways, but like any son at the peak of his career, I was too stubborn to listen."

"And so now you're listening? Jaunting out across the country performing good deeds for those in need—what changed?"

A quick smile plays about his lips. A slight dimple appears in his cheek when he twists his lips a certain way. "What do you mean? Nothing happened. The stress of my last big deal started weighing on me. I developed headaches. Derek suggested a vacation to relax and here we are. End of story."

"I don't believe you. It's too easy and clean."

"Fine. You win," he answered with a soft laugh. "I'm a few weeks from dying, and this is my last adventure. My last hurrah, if you will. I've traveled all over the world but not this country, and it seemed like a great idea."

"And now you try to bullshit me? I'm disappointed if that was the best story you could come up with."

We stop at a red light. "I promise you, no bullshit. It is what it is. I'm sorry if it's not glamorous enough for you. I really am de-stressing. The New York real estate market is a beast. I've conquered it for years, but it's taken a toll on me." He turns slightly toward me and takes my hand in his. "I'm ready to slow down. Find someone of my own who doesn't want just my money and my penthouse on Fifth Avenue. This is me clearing my head and leaving the asshole behind. I call it the rebirth of Carter George, 2.0."

The light turns green, and he shifts facing forward again, slowly releasing my hand like it's the last thing he wants to do. We enter back onto Interstate 55 South.

"OK. I'm sorry I doubted you," I say, my apology heavy in my throat. "The Carter George I've read about doesn't match up with the Carter George I know. That's all."

He flashes a quick smirk in my direction. "Well good. My re-birth is working then."

My eyebrows draw together in confusion. "Is this all a PR strategy to clean up your image?"

"Nah, I don't give a damn about public relations. You take me at face value or don't take me at all. I really don't care."

I glance at the steering wheel and watch his hands tremble. He's not telling the whole truth, but that's OK. I'm a stranger invading his vacation. We've got plenty of time to figure each other out because the one thing I know is that I'm not going anywhere without him.

NINETEEN

CARTER

*M*y phone buzzes in the console with a text. "That's probably Derek. Can you reply to him?"

Teddy picks up my phone and swipes across the screen to wake it up. "Oh my God, Carter," she shrieks in disbelief. "You have 481 text messages. Aren't you going to respond to them?"

"The only messages I reply to are from Derek. He's all that matters to me right now."

"Yep. It's Derek. He says we're fueled up and ready to roll when you are."

"Text back and let him know we're almost there. Maybe another thirty minutes or so."

I exit the interstate and merge onto Highway 18 which winds along the Mississippi River. The muddy waters churn with barges. Teddy's face is flushed red from the heat and sun, so I raise the roof and turn the air conditioning back on.

We drive in silence for a while, enjoying the view until she sighs loudly.

"Are you OK?" I lean over and put my hand over hers.

She rolls her head to look at me. "I'm fine. Why do you ask?"

"Well, for starters, that was the saddest sigh I think I've ever heard.

Secondly, you've been quiet for a while. I thought you were just loving the ride, but that sigh tells a different story. Are you all right?"

"I'm worrying about things I have no business worrying about. That sigh was my mental pep talk to let it go."

"Tell me what you're worrying about. Maybe I'll have some insight into your troubles."

"If you really want to know, I was worrying about you or your business, to be honest. Aren't *you* worried about your company? Or your employees? Is it falling apart at the hands of whoever you put in charge? I mean 481 text messages tell me something is wrong."

"Teddy, my company will be fine. If they run it to the ground then they're the ones out of a job."

"How can you be so laissez-faire about it? Don't you care about your people? They have mortgages, children to support, and bills to pay."

I don't even know how to respond to that. *Why does she care? She doesn't know me or my business, much less any of the people I have under my care.* I ruthlessly choke the throat of the businesses I take over for my people. That's why I poke and prod every last cent out of them in every deal I barter.

So I can fund the secret savings account each and every employee has with my company. My dad knew living in New York was expensive. He knew most of our employees lived paycheck to paycheck to fund taxes they had no voice in creating. We pay them well, but emergencies happen. So Dad started to stipend a secret savings account for them. They each get $500 per quarter with compounded interest. Hell, most of our older, loyal employees are millionaires and don't even know it. They find out when they quit or retire.

I slam the steering wheel with the base of my palm. "I care. Trust me. I care too damn much. But the real question here is why do *you* care? Are you worried about my billions in hopes that you'll be granted some the minute I give in and taste that sweet pussy you keep prancing in front of me?"

"Fuck you. Fuck you to hell and back, Carter George." She turns her shoulder away from me, her back acting as a wall between us.

She's shutting me out.

A few minutes later, I pull over into an empty parking lot off the side of the road. "Hey, listen. I'm sorry. I don't know why I said that."

She removes her seatbelt and jumps out of the car, walking away from me.

"Teddy Bear. Don't walk away."

She flips her middle finger in the air at me as her hips sway, taking her farther and farther away from me in the warm Louisiana morning.

Damn it.

I run after her, wrapping my arms around her when I finally get to her. "You're a runner," I whisper in her ear. "I know this now, and you're not running away this time."

I hold her tightly as she squirms to be set free.

"You're hurting me, Carter."

I loosen my grip just a little bit and turn her around to face me.

"Teddy, sweetheart. Look at me."

Her jaw tightens as I lift her chin with my index finger.

"You drive me crazy. Do you know that?"

She shakes her head. Her stormy green eyes look everywhere but into mine.

"My head swims when you're within a foot of me. My heart pounds against my chest, sometimes so hard, I swear it's going to crack my ribs. I want to do everything possible to make you happy, but I have no fucking clue what that would be."

"I don't need your money to be happy. I grew up rich and spoiled. I already know that's not where happiness is found."

The dejected look on her face cracks my heart. A tear breaks free from the corner of her eye and slowly rolls down her cheek. *Jesus Christ.*

I pull her into me, cradling her face in my hands. My thumb swipes over the trail where that one tear fell. I can't fucking stand the ache any longer. I can't stand the constant warring in my head when I think about wanting her and hurting her when she learns our forever is only six months tops. All I know is that I *need* her. Every single delicious part of her. Fuck death and fuck the greedy bastard within me.

It's now or never, and never can't happen when it comes to her.

Our lips burn hot when they collide, our tongues rolling over each other in a long, anticipated dance. Her hands dig and claw into my back, holding me to her as I take our kiss deeper. God, I've wanted her for so long. I've been waiting for this moment my whole life.

We sway into each other as we pull away to catch our breaths, the momentum of our frenzied kiss throwing us both off balance. I cup her cheek tenderly in my hand.

"I'm so sorry I was harsh earlier. I need you to know I never cared enough before, but with you, I feel things I've never felt. I care about things I've never cared about. I want to experience everything with you, but at the same time, do absolutely nothing but spend the rest of my life with you. Is that crazy?"

"It's not crazy. I feel the same way. I'm drawn to you. From the first moment I saw you at the bar, I've been pulled in your direction. I never strayed far from the RV in Nashville. I watched you for days come and go, wanting to go to you but not wanting to *need* you. It seems we're being thrown together." She presses her cheek to my chest and hugs me tightly.

"We're being thrown together, and for whatever reason, we need to stop fighting it. I want you here with me. I want to get to know you. I want to experience your good days and bad ones, learn what makes you cry and what makes you laugh so hard you cry. We're going to falter and say the wrong things at times. It's the growing pains of getting to know each other, but we can't run. Promise me no more running?"

Her eyes search mine and soften a little. She cups my face with her delicate hands and presses her lips to mine with a kiss that speaks volumes of promises to come. "No more running," she affirms. "C'mon. Let's get back."

"Do you want to drive us back into the city?"

A smile spreads across her pretty face. It brightens my whole world.

"Are you kidding me? Hell yes."

I hand her the key fob.

"Can I open her up and see if she'll do eighty?" Her eyes dance in anticipation of my response.

"Can you pay the speeding ticket?" I chuckle under my breath.

Those perfect pouty lips turn me on. "All right then. I guess we'll go the speed limit."

TWENTY

TEDDY

*W*hen we get back from our drive, we leave New Orleans. Carter kisses me gently and goes to take a nap. I help Derek navigate the next leg of our trip. We end up driving into Texas. When we're on the outskirts of Houston, we finally stop for sleep.

I wake up feeling giddy. I can't wait to see Carter. I don't want to be *that* girl—the one who's clingy and needy—but I seriously *need* this man. Like, he makes me feel…alive. It's the only word I can think of to describe it.

I get out of bed, eager to see Carter, but he's not in the living area.

"Derek, is Carter still sleeping?" I ask, sliding into the seat across from him at the table with a cup of coffee. He pushes a box of muffins at me.

"Yeah. He was up for a bit but went back to bed."

I frown, a niggling feeling that something isn't right with him.

"Is everything OK with him?" I press, worry settling in my guts.

Derek shrugs, his eyes focused on the muffin he's picking apart. "He's just stressed."

"You guys keep talking about this *stress*, and I totally understand why he should be, but when we were out yesterday, I looked at his phone. He had over four hundred missed texts. Don't get me started on

131

the missed phone calls. Is he in trouble or something?" I lean forward and plead with my eyes for Derek to tell me anything.

"It's stress. He's not in any sort of trouble other than that. If he wants to tell you about it, he will," Derek says gently, peering into his coffee mug. "Carter is a complicated man. Don't push him on it. When he wants to talk to you about his troubles, he will."

"You just said he's not in trouble—"

"He's not. It's stress."

I scoff, hating that word. Fine. Carter is stressed. Maybe he needs un-stressing. I don't touch my coffee. Instead, I get to my feet and go to his room and tap on the door gently. He doesn't answer, so I slide it open and peer at him. He has little dots of sweat on his forehead, and his t-shirt clad chest is heaving as he pulls in ragged breaths. His hand is clenched on his blanket. A whimper comes from his mouth. Molly lets out a whine as she curls against him, her nose nuzzling him, trying to wake him.

Immediately, I'm at his side. He's dreaming something bad.

"Carter," I murmur, cupping his damp cheek. "Carter. Hey. Wake up."

His long lashes flutter, his eyes unfocused for a minute as he stares at me, confusion evident on his face. He looks lost and scared. Vulnerable. Nothing like the strong man I know he is. It's a look that breaks my heart.

"Teddy Bear," he murmurs, coming to. His lips brush against mine as he pulls me to him, his arms a vice around me. His kiss is fire on my lips. I moan against him as his hand finds my breast over my tank top, giving it a tender squeeze.

Molly jumps from the bed, her nails clicking as she retreats to Derek.

"The door is open," I whisper against Carter's lips as he rolls me onto my back, his body leveled over mine.

Derek calls out to Molly, then the door to the RV opens and closes, signaling he's taken her out.

"It won't be a problem," he whispers, his lips skimming a trail along my jaw.

I respond by twining my fingers through his hair, drawing his face closer to mine. His tongue sweeps against mine, leaving me breathless. I'm desperate to have him, my hips lifting up to meet the grind of his hard length against my thin pajama shorts.

He trails kisses down my neck to my collarbone before he tugs my tank top off, taking my bra with it. With nimble fingers, my shorts and panties come off next, tossed to the floor.

His eyes are locked on mine as I breathe hard.

"What do you want, Teddy Bear," he growls, his eyes sweeping over my body. I can see the massive bulge straining against his pajama bottoms.

"I want you," I manage to breathe out. "All of you."

His mouth captures mine again, and his fingers tangle in my hair briefly then trail down to squeeze my bare breasts. Hot lips make haste following his hands and finding a pebbled bud. He pulls it into his mouth, causing a gasp to fall from my lips as he suckles. His fingers slide through my slick folds like a man on a mission.

"Oh God," I gasp as a finger finds the warm bundle of nerves. He rubs me, and I shamelessly buck into his hand as he strokes me gently before he inserts a finger into my slick canal. He curls his finger up and hits all the right places. He adds another one which causes my eyes to roll back in my head as the pressure grows, the tingling making me whimper.

"Give it to me," he commands with a rasp, his fingers moving faster, bringing me to new heights.

I'm so delirious with pleasure that a garble of words exits my mouth as my pussy clenches around his fingers, drenching the sheets and his hand.

He buries is face in my neck, his fingers slowing as I come crashing back down to Earth.

"Good girl," he murmurs in my ear. "My good girl."

TWENTY-ONE

CARTER

*T*eddy's breaths come in short, sharp gasps as her orgasm crashes down around her. There's something about being the one to give it to her that sends a thrill of satisfaction through me.

I let out a low hiss as she finds the waistband of my pajama bottoms and wraps her fingers around my aching cock. Her eyes meet mine in a silent plea, and I'd be a fool not to let her have what she wants.

She strokes me, my eyes rolling back in my head at the euphoria her warm touch brings. I push my pants down to give her better access. Her green eyes widen as she takes all of me in. I can't help the smirk that crowds my lips.

Yeah, baby. It's all for you.

A pink flush covers her cheeks and bare breasts, making my heart jackknife in my chest. I've never been with such a beautiful woman before. Sure, I've tapped some hot chicks in my day, but not one of them excites me like Teddy does.

My mouth meets hers in a desperate plea for release as her hand moves faster on my dick. I'm so fucking close to release. I can't stand it. The tingling builds in my lower spine. My hand finds hers and helps her pump me.

"*Fuck*," I hiss, my toes curling into the mattress as I find release. My whole body feels electric, the current of euphoria flowing through me. I'm breathing heavy, my vision still dotted from the incredible orgasm delivered by her hand.

"I'll be right back," her voice is soft as her lips brush against mine. A moment later, my bed is empty except for me, her distance making me ache. Water flows in the bathroom for a moment before she pads back to me, her naked body crawling up the bed and her dark hair a wild mess around her.

"You're beautiful," I whisper in awe of her. "Come here."

She does as I command, cuddling beneath the blanket, her warm, bare body curled up against mine. My arms wrap around her in a hold she'll never be able to break away from.

"That was fun," she giggles softly, her head resting against my chest.

"Most fun I've ever had," I say, giving her a tender squeeze.

She wiggles against me, making me bite back a groan. "Carter?"

"Teddy?" I look down at her. Her hand moves to rest on my abdomen.

"Did it help?"

"Did what help, sweetheart?"

"What we did, did it help with your stress?"

I let out a soft chuckle and tilt her chin up so I can plant a sweet kiss on her lips.

"It's stressing me out to know that I want you even more if that's possible—all of you."

"You can have me—"

"And I will, Teddy Bear, but I want it to be perfect just like you." I kiss her again.

"Aw, are you saving yourself, Carter George?" she teases, grinning at me.

I let out a soft laugh. "Baby, the best parts of me were meant for you."

~

"THIS SUN IS KILLING ME," I MUTTER, PUSHING MY AVIATORS ONTO MY face. I'm sitting in the front of the Beastmaster with Derek as we drive to San Antonio, Texas—home of the Alamo. Teddy is resting, worn out from our morning tryst in my bed.

"You take your meds?" Derek asks, glancing over at me.

I nod, hating those fucking pills.

We're quiet for a moment before Derek talks again, "Have you considered experimental treatments, Carter? I was looking online last night and saw there's a doctor in Baltimore who's studying your disease. It sounds like he's close to a breakthrough.

Had he asked me that a few weeks ago, I'd have blown him off. Now my mind wanders to Teddy. I can't leave her. On the other hand, I know our time is limited. I don't want her to see me fucking wither away on my deathbed.

"I don't know," I mutter, leaning my head back against the seat. "Doc says it's a lost cause. Plus, doing it will take away from all of this." I gesture to the open road. "What if I do it and die anyway? Then I'll miss out on the last fucking trip I'll ever take, unless you count the one down to hell."

Derek rolls his eyes at me. "You're a dead man if you don't. Trying it might buy you a little more time. Not only for your trip if you recover, but for her."

I snap my head in his direction, my eyes narrowing. "What are you talking about?"

"Don't play dumb with me, Carter. I know you and Teddy are messing around." His head tilts as his lips twist and frown as he sees me open my mouth. "Don't even try to deny that shit. I *heard* you. Why the hell do you think I took Molly out?"

I smirk at him, knowing I'm caught. "Fine. You win. There's something going on between us. And yeah, I want to stick around for her." I swallow hard and let out a deep breath. "I think she's *the one*, you know?"

I let out a yip as Derek nearly drives off the road, his eyes wide with shock.

"Don't kill us, damnit!" I say, relaxing as he gets control of the Beastmaster.

"Sorry, but are you saying you've *fallen* for her?"

I let out a soft chuckle, shaking my head. "Yeah, guess I have or am. I don't know. It's my first time doing this shit."

"A little word of advice," Derek says, glancing at me before continuing, "figure out what your plan is. If you're just going to go back to New York to die in your high-rise, then you need to let her go before this really starts. If you plan on trying to fix this, then you need to let her know what's going on. She's been asking. She's a smart girl. You won't fool her for long."

"I tried to tell her during the car ride, but she didn't believe me." I snort. "Hell, I can't even believe it, and the shit is inside me, ruining my life." I grow quiet for a moment. "I'll tell her. Just not yet. I want to enjoy being normal for a little bit."

"Fine. I get it." Derek nods. "But don't wait until the last minute to do something about this. And by this, I mean telling her and seeking out this possible treatment."

I don't say anything. Instead, I pet Molly's head as she sidles up next to me. She's always there when I start to feel down.

This might be the lowest I've felt in a long time though. There's only one thing that'll make it better, and she's asleep in my bed.

TWENTY-TWO

TEDDY

"I love all this traveling, but this heat sucks," I say as we step out into the near hundred-degree weather of San Antonio. We've done nothing but lounge around in the Beastmaster for the past twenty-four hours while we try to catch up on sleep.

Carter smirks at me, his hand landing on my waist. "You could wear less clothes," he murmurs in my ear. Despite the heat of the day, his words send a torrent of shivers through me.

"So could you," I say, planting a kiss on his cheek.

He grins down at me, his eyes bright. Despite the dark circles around his eyes, he looks happy.

"Hey, guys," Derek calls out, jogging over to us.

Carter doesn't seem to care if Derek knows we've grown closer. He pulls me to him and presses a kiss to the top of my head.

"What's up?" Carter asks.

"There's going to be a flash music mob in the park down the street. I think we should go to it. Sounds like fun. Teddy can play her guitar and sing."

"That *does* sound like fun," I say, looking to Carter, really hoping he's on board with the idea.

"I'm game." He smiles down at me. "Get your guitar, Teddy Bear."

I spin to go back to the RV but stop and turn back to the guys. "I'll only do it if you guys do it too."

Carter and Derek look at each other, eyebrows raised.

"Baby, I can't sing for shit," Carter starts as Derek shakes his head.

"So? Do it for the adventure," I argue, challenging them. "When will you ever get a chance to do something like this again in your life?"

Carter blows out a breath and nods. "You're right. I might not ever get another chance like this again. I'm in. Derek?"

"Damnit," he groans as I plant a hand on my hip and tap my foot. "Fine. I'll do it. If we get kicked out, you just remember it was your idea." He points a finger at me for emphasis.

I grin at him before flouncing away to the RV to grab my guitar.

When I return, it's to see Carter and Derek in deep discussion, both peering down at Derek's phone. I figure Derek is just showing him our next adventure. When I reach them, Derek darkens his screen before stuffing it into his pocket.

"Ready?" Carter asks.

"Ready," I say, suspicious of what they're up to. If either of them takes notice, they make no mention of it. Instead, Carter wraps his arm promptly around my waist after he takes my guitar from me.

"Have we thought any more about camping?" Derek asks as we make our way to the park.

"Like in tents?" I wrinkle my nose at the thought.

"Aw, does my princess not like the outdoors?" Carter teases me.

I chuckle. "More like I hate mosquitoes."

Derek nods. "I hate them too, but it's so much fun to be in the middle of nowhere."

"I like nowhere," Carter says, squeezing my hip with his fingers. "And didn't you say you wanted to get lost, Teddy Bear? This seems like the perfect opportunity to do that."

"I *did* say that," I muse, impressed with him remembering. "But I also don't want to get eaten."

"No?" Carter gives me a wolfish grin that has me flushing.

"You know what I mean." I bump my hip against him, causing him to hold me closer.

"I think we're here," Derek calls out.

He's right. There are hundreds of people gathered around with their instruments. My heart lurches in my chest like it does every time I prepare to perform. It's the rush. The excitement.

"You're so beautiful when you smile," Carter murmurs in my ear, pulling me out of my thoughts.

His words only make me grin wider.

"Here. I'll go find who's in charge." He hands me my guitar before placing a kiss on my lips that makes the butterflies dance in my belly.

"You really like him," Derek says when Carter is out of sight.

"I do," I admit, biting my bottom lip. "He's everything I've ever dream of, actually."

Derek nods thoughtfully. "Get him to talk, Teddy. He needs you. You'll save him. I'm not supposed to talk to you about this stuff, but Carter needs someone to love. I can see he's falling hard for you. I'm hoping you're what he needs to help him get through the… stress he's under."

"Save him?" My breath catches.

"Yeah." Derek swallows and gives me a sad smile. "He's stressed and not well. He doesn't listen to me. Maybe he'll listen to you."

"I'll see what I can do," I murmur, worry setting in. It doesn't take a genius to know Carter is going through something that he doesn't talk about.

He'll tell me once he's more comfortable.

"We can set up over here," Carter calls out, waving us over. I push my worries away, my heart skipping as I take in how happy he looks as he smiles at me. He doesn't let his touch stray far from me. The moment I'm near him, his hands are touching me, holding me, letting me know I'm the only one he has eyes for, despite the women in the crowd eyeing him.

I've never been with anyone quite like him. Deep in my heart, something tells me we might just save each other.

TWENTY-THREE

CARTER

*T*eddy's grin is infectious. We're in the middle of a hundred musicians, but she's the only one I want to hear. When the music starts, she opens her mouth, belting out the lyrics to Journey's "Don't Stop Believing".

Derek sings along uncomfortably before backing up to snap some photos. I grin at him as I bellow into the mic. I'm not a terrible singer. I'm nowhere near Teddy or Luke in terms of pipes, but I can hold my own. My mom always wanted me to sing. She even had me take lessons until Dad found out.

Teddy grins at me throughout the song. I sing like my life depends on it. I dance, causing Teddy to laugh, her fingers still strumming her guitar as her green eyes sparkle. Derek snaps photo after photo, smiling right along with us. It's some of the most fun I've ever had.

It's just hundreds of people, enjoying the music. There are photographers from local stations snapping photos even. Usually, I shy away from the cameras, hating being in the papers. This time doesn't feel like it'll be so bad. At least it's not a scandal or me tearing apart someone's livelihood.

Ten points awarded for my charisma, I guess.

By the time the afternoon is over, we've sung and danced ourselves out.

"Hungry?" I ask Teddy as she sags against me.

"Mhmm," she mumbles.

I chuckle and nod to Derek. "Food?"

"Hell yeah," he says with a grin. "Let's get some Mexican. I've been craving it since we hit Houston."

"Teddy Bear, Mexican good with you?"

"Tacos are life." She cuddles against me as we walk.

I let out a contented sigh. *This* is what life is supposed to be like. I wish I'd have known sooner.

When we make it back to the Beastmaster, Derek takes Molly out after she practically tackles us at the door in excitement over our return. Derek casts me a knowing smirk before he leaves me with Teddy.

"You were incredible today," I say, pulling her to me and kissing her gently. She smiles against my lips.

"Thank you, but I was there. I heard *you* sing. You've been holding out on us, Mr. George."

"Mm, maybe a bit," I murmur in a husky voice, my mouth finding hers again. "Teddy Bear, I want you."

"You have me," she breathes out, her fingers tangling in my hair. Her head lolls to the side as I kiss her neck.

"Do I?" My hot breath on her neck causes her to shiver against me.

"Carter," she moans, her hand rubbing my hard cock through my pants.

"Tell me what you want," I say as I move the strap of her tank top aside to kiss her collarbone.

"I want you. Please," she pleads, unzipping my pants.

"Baby, we don't have enough time before Derek comes back for me to do all the things to you that I want to do." I chuckle. "But maybe I can help alleviate some *pressure.*"

Without another word, I lift her up. Her legs wrap around me, and I walk her to my room where I slide the door closed and lay her on the bed. In moments, I have her skirt pulled up and her panties down.

I trail my hands between her legs, pushing them apart to reveal her pretty, pink, glistening pussy to me.

Eyes filled with wanting lock on mine as I move my face between her legs. I plant a chaste kiss on her moist lips before darting my tongue out to taste her. Her back arcs as she lets out a whimper.

"Fuck, baby, you taste like my kind of heaven." I plunge in, face first, like a man starving. She lets out the sexiest moan I've ever heard in my life as I flick my tongue over her hot center. Her fingers are in my hair, pulling my face closer. I grip her hips tight, devouring her.

Her breathing kicks up as I work my tongue against her. My girl is about to burst. I insert a finger inside her, and she moans again. Deciding I want to go for more, I insert another finger, my mouth never leaving her sweetness.

She bucks against my face, whimpering my name and calling out to God as her pussy tightens around me. I lick like a greedy bastard, not wanting to waste one drop of her. Only when her movements still and her breathing slows do I come up for air.

"Carter," she says, her voice hoarse. "Let me do you—"

"No." I shake my head at her. "We don't have time, Teddy Bear. We can worry about me later."

She pulls me up to her, and I take her in my arms and hold her.

"Are you sure? I don't mind sucking your—"

"Teddy, I swear if you finish that sentence, I'll come undone right in my pants," I growl, nipping her bottom lip. She giggles beneath me. The door to the Beastmaster opens with a creak.

"Times up, beautiful." I kiss the tip of her nose. "Let's get some food then maybe when we get back you can help me relieve some stress."

Her eyes sparkle as she stares back at me.

"OK," she agrees.

I move off the bed and slap her bare ass, leaving a handprint before I rub it gently and drop a kiss on the redness. She practically purrs beneath me.

Oh, my sweet, sexy girl.

"Don't wear your panties," I whisper in her ear before backing away from her. Her lips part, but judging by the look in her eyes, I know she won't fight me on it.

~

THE LITTLE MEXICAN RESTAURANT WE FIND IS DIVINE. DEREK AND HIS Google abilities. He and Teddy could probably join forces and start a private investigation firm with their combined search skills.

I ask for a booth in the back, and we're escorted to a quaint table in the far corner, my hand sliding down to feel Teddy's ass through her thin, floral skirt as we walk.

"What would you like to drink?" the waitress asks in a thick Spanish accent.

"Water for me," Derek says.

"Same," Teddy chimes in, "and a margarita."

"Same for me," I say, winking at Teddy.

The waitress nods and hands us menus before leaving.

"This place smells fantastic," Derek says, settling back in his seat, his eyes glued to the menu. "I want to eat everything. Oh shit, there's even a salsa bar. I'm in."

"Me too," I whisper in Teddy's ear.

She giggles for me, her hand resting high on my thigh. I'm grinning like a fool. I probably look like a maniac sitting there. I don't think I've ever smiled so much in my entire life.

"I think I'm going to have tacos," Derek says, pulling me away from Teddy for a moment. "No, enchiladas." He grows quiet for a moment. "Shit. I want a burrito too."

I laugh at him.

"Get it all. We'll take the leftovers with us."

Derek doesn't need telling twice. I take a moment to eye my menu. I trail my fingers up Teddy's bare thigh and beneath her skirt. She spreads her legs for me without me telling her to.

Perfect.

I skim my fingers against her silken pussy, feeling how wet she is.

My eyes are still on the menu, but I chance a glance at her to see her biting her lip and her breathing growing heavier.

"What's wrong?" I ask, leaning in to speak into her ear, my finger skimming against her slick entrance.

"N-nothing," she stammers back.

I smirk at her, enjoying the way she feels against my fingers. I tease her just enough to get her hot and bothered, knowing it'll make our night that much more fun.

I don't stop when the waitress comes back with our drinks and asks for our order.

Derek orders everything he talked about, including chimichangas. I go with enchiladas. Then the waitress turns to Teddy. Her cheeks are flushed.

I grin at her.

"She'll take the taco dinner. Add an extra order of tacos on there as well as another order of enchiladas," I say, my fingers still rubbing Teddy, not missing a beat. Derek looks at me questioningly for ordering for her before seeming to not care. He folds his menu and hands it back to the waitress with mine and Teddy's.

I play the game with her for a few minutes until I knew she's ready to burst. Then I pull away. She lets out a soft cry of protest which she quickly covers with a cough.

"More water?" I ask, raising an eyebrow at her.

"Yes, please," she answers.

Derek is too busy watching the mariachi band play to notice us. I kiss her gently before moving to whisper in her ear, "I'll finish this when we get back, Teddy Bear."

Her green eyes peer back at me with all the answer I need.

TWENTY-FOUR

TEDDY

*C*arter nearly kills me at dinner. By the time we get back, I'm barely keeping myself together.

"I'm going to bed," Derek proclaims, rubbing his belly after putting our massive amount of takeout in the fridge. "That food was delicious, but it's sitting heavy."

We bid him goodnight as we sit on the sofa.

"Did you have a good night?" Carter asks, trailing a finger down my arm.

"I did. Up until you stopped," I say, challenging him.

Please say we'll finish what you started!

He lets out a soft chuckle. "Teddy, if you want something from me, just say so."

His hand stops its trek, a tremor going through it. I crinkle my eyebrows down at his shaking hand then look back at him. He's wearing a scowl, but quickly rights it into an impassive look.

"Carter, are you O—"

I'm silenced as his mouth meets mine in a hot kiss. All coherent thought leaves my mind as his tongue tangles with mine, his hand up my skirt again.

"I want you," I breathe out between kisses. "Please, Carter."

He growls against my mouth. Derek's soft snores sound in the background. *Good. He's sleeping.*

Without our mouths disconnecting, Carter lifts me up and hauls me to his bedroom, my legs wrapped around his waist. He places me on the bed. But this time when he tries to press me to my back, I sit up straight and unzip his pants. He smirks down at me.

"Whatcha got there, pretty girl?" he asks as I push his pants and boxers down to reveal his incredible length.

I've been dying to feel its velvety smoothness since the last time I struggled to wrap my fingers around it. This time, I want my mouth around him.

I respond by running my tongue down his cock, causing a low, hissing breath to leave him. Carter is a big guy. As intimidated as I am by his size, I know it's something I want to conquer.

I lick the head of his cock, slowly pulling him into my mouth until he's hitting the back of my throat.

"Fuck," he groans as I move him in and out.

Both his hands tangle in my hair as he moans softly. I love how salty sweet he is. I suck harder, wanting to taste more of him.

"Baby, if you keep doing that, it's going to severely impact our evening," he says in a husky voice.

He gently removes his dick from my mouth before pushing me onto my back, situating himself between my legs. The heat between us makes me pant. His cock brushes my entrance, teasing me.

"Please don't make me wait," I beg, rocking myself beneath him.

"Greedy little thing," he murmurs, kissing me.

His cock torments me until I'm shamelessly rubbing my pussy against him. We're both panting, our mouths hot on one another's.

"I don't have a condom," he whispers, slowing down. "Fuck, baby. I'm sorry."

"It's OK. It's fine," I assure him, breathless. "I'm on the pill." Even if I wasn't, I've reached the point of wanting him so much that damn everything else. He pushes forward, bringing with him a pinch of fire as he enters me.

"Oh, my god," I whimper as he fills me completely.

He grunts his approval before moving in and out slowly. My nails dig in his back, urging him to give me more. He obliges by rocking hard into me. His hands cradle my breasts, caressing, kneading and teasing them with his fingers. When he slows and removes himself from me, I stutter out a whimper that makes him chuckle softly.

With a sly, teasing smile, he bends forward and licks a warm path from my navel to each nipple, taking them one by one into his mouth.

"Carter," I breathe out, the burning need in my core growing with each tongue twirl he does on my nipples.

"Patience, baby," he murmurs as his hot mouth moves lower until his tongue is darting out at the apex of my thighs. A moan of ecstasy leaves his lips as he delves into my folds face first, licking and sucking at all the places that make my toes curl.

My vision darkens as the tingles come.

"Carter." I can barely breathe as the orgasm overtakes me, causing my body to tremble as the pleasure ebbs and flows through me.

With a final lick, Carter withdraws his face from between my legs and gives me a teasing smile.

"Good things *come* to those who wait." He laughs softly, planting a kiss on the inside of my thigh.

I smile dazedly at him, still lost in the fog of how incredible he is. His lips trail back up until they're pressed to my mouth again, his cock rubbing against my sensitive pussy.

I let out a squeal of surprise when his hands press against my hips, and he tugs me onto him. He inches forward into me more, my legs bent, riding higher on his thighs. He moves into me, going deeper and deeper with each thrust. A small twinge of pain teases the edge of my pleasure.

I want to call out as the pressure tingles and builds within me, but I remember Derek and bite my lip, locking the moans in their warm prison.

I wrap my legs around him, never wanting him to stop whatever magic he's working on me. My hands grip and twist the sheets as he picks up speed. My back arches as my orgasm sends me spiraling over the edge. A moment later, he comes with me, letting out a low groan against my neck.

He balances himself over me on his arms, both of us sweaty and breathless.

"You're amazing," he whispers, kissing me gently. "I wish I'd have met you earlier, Teddy Bear."

His voice is soft and sad, making my heart clench.

"You have me now though, Carter."

He kisses me again, his words on my lips.

"And you have me. Always."

I wake up to Carter planting soft kisses on my skin, following the hollow along my left hip. He must have started near my feet, because there's a cool trail of wetness rising from my ankles. His fingers trail first then kisses follow. When he gets to the soft indentation by my belly, I raise my arm above my head.

"Did I wake you?" he murmurs softly.

"I'm dreaming of the most luxurious kisses on my skin. Please don't wake me."

"Never." He scoots himself higher up my body, his hard-on brushing against the curve of my ass, and a soft moan escapes from my lips. His body spoons mine, as he continues kissing the tender flesh of my neck. The scruff of his day-old stubble scrapes my shoulder. I lift my leg just enough for his cock to nestle into the warmth between my legs.

His arm encircles me, his fingers splaying across my belly, stopping to rest for a moment. He sighs heavily in my ear. "Exactly where I want to be."

"Mmhmm," I agree. "Exactly where I want you." Moonlight streams into the room through a small sliver of an opening in the curtains. I lift my head and see it's 3:48 am. "Why aren't you sleeping?"

"I'm making up for lost time, and I'm so far behind."

"So far behind at what? Work?" I roll onto my back to look at his face, concern filling my mind from his cryptic words.

"No," he whispers against my shoulder. "Far behind in loving you. Now, shhhh. Let me get back to my work." He pushes me back onto my side, and trails kisses down my spine. As he moves further down my body, he positions me on my stomach, and lays his cheek against the rump of my ass like a pillow, snuggling into it. His thumb gently massages the tender flesh of my inner thigh.

His fingers inch closer and closer to my wet core while he draws invisible circles on my skin. His face is still resting on my butt cheeks. I look over my shoulder at him. His eyes are closed. "What are you doing back there?"

"Shhhhh. I'm dreaming of all the ways to make your ass mine."

"Just my ass? There are other parts that might like you to own them too."

"Oh, really?" He pulls himself up onto his knees, spreading my legs wide. He crawls closer to me, lifting my thighs so that I'm slightly on my knees, waiting. "You're not going to…" I stop to swallow the nervous knot in my throat. I've never done *that* before. Not that I'm not curious. If I were to give it to anyone, Carter George would be the man I'd choose. I almost say so, but he speaks again.

"Relax, Teddy Bear. I won't do that to you unless you ask me to. For now, I want to feel you from a different angle."

He reaches forward with his fingers and strokes my clit, teasing my folds with his thumb. I rock back and forth, moving up onto my elbows and arching my back, preparing to take him deeper. "Carter, I need you. I need hard and fast," I say panting.

He pushes into me, filling me up with his length. His tight grip on my hips is hot and steady, pulling me onto him faster and faster, over and over.

The scruff of his facial hair brushes against my shoulders as he leans in to kiss my heated skin.

A broken moan escapes my lips, and I bury my face in the pillow to keep from screaming my pleasure. His palm moves to my lower back holding me steady as he swivels and thrusts, penetrating me deeper.

Sweat beads on my forehead, and my hair sticks to my face. When I raise up slightly on my knees to brush the hair from my face, my new position causes my orgasm to race forth. "Carter?"

"Yes, baby?" he says breathlessly.

"Keep moving just like that. Don't shift." My legs go numb and start to shake. My knees won't hold me up anymore, and I stumble forward, bracing my hand against the wall. He continues to pound into me and releases his own orgasm as I climax.

He falls forward, his sweaty forehead resting against my back.

"Jesus, baby. You're going to kill an old man." He rolls off me, spreading himself across the entire length of the bed.

"Stop it. You're not old." I swat at him, as I crawl off the bed, giving him space.

"I've lived a lot of life in my thirty-two years, but none of it has been as exciting as you." His eyes hold so much adoration in them as he stares back at me. I lean down and press my lips against his in a soft, sweet kiss.

"I'll be right back," I murmur against his lips as I break the kiss off. If I don't leave now, I won't ever leave.

I step into the bathroom and wet a wash cloth, wiping the sweat and sex from my body. I wet another one and take it into him. I straddle his legs and wipe him clean, cooling down his body too. The heavy scent of sex fills the air.

He scoots over and makes room for me. When I slide against him, my bare hip hits the wet spot. "Damn it. I'm in the wet spot."

He laughs quietly. "You mean spots, because I'm lying in one too. Hold on." He jumps out of bed and fumbles around in his mini closet before pulling out a huge beach towel and folding it in half. I stand and help him lay it across the mattress. "There. That should work."

We snuggle back together, pulling a sheet over us. I fall asleep smelling suntan lotion and coconuts.

DIARY

Day 22

Day 21? No 22. I didn't write yesterday. Or the day before. Hell, I don't even think I wrote before that. Shit. I've already messed up this journal. So just know if you're reading this after I'm gone, it's not written in real time because my fucked-up brain has no actual clue what day this is.

I did something last night I've never done in my life. I had sex with the same woman twice. **Twice.**

Holy fuck. I fucked her. Twice. I know you're probably thinking I sound like as ass because I keep referring to having sex with Teddy as 'fucking her', but I got lost in her the minute I entered her heavenly body.

Mind you, that wasn't my intention, but that's what happened, and I cannot tell a lie.

It was hard and fast and glorious.

The way she shivers and quakes when she comes, holy fucking hotness, Batman. I want that kind of sex every fucking day for the rest of this life. It may sound shallow, but it's my highest compliment. This woman has a rockin' body, knows her own mind, has a keen intelligence, and a sassy mouth. She's perfect. And I think I'm in love.

TWENTY-FIVE

TEDDY

"*Hey*, Derek. We're near the Alamo. Can we check it out? It's almost lunch."

"You want to see The Alamo? I thought it was just a boring building," he says, scrunching up his nose. "But if you want to go, I guess we can. It's not like we have any real schedule we need to keep." The screen on his phone brightens as he begins searching for walking directions.

"I'll go wake up sleepyhead."

I climb out of the front captain chair and step over Molly. I slide Carter's bedroom door open and watch him sleep. He looks so peaceful. His dark brown hair is spiked up from sleep, and he's hugging the pillow I slept on. I tug on the pillow.

"Hey, babe. Time to wake up."

His eyes flutter open.

"W-wha-what—" He shakes his head with frustration and closes his eyes, taking a deep breath before forcing the rest of his sentence out. "—time is it?"

I sit on the edge of the bed while he sits up and wipes the sleep from his eyes. His fingers massage the creases in his forehead.

"Are you all right? I've never heard you stutter before."

A look of concern flashes across his face but it disappears into a soft smile.

"I've never stuttered before. See? I'm not doing it now. Maybe my mouth tried to work before my brain was awake. I need some coffee," he says, shrugging his shoulders. He stands up and appears coherent and steady.

"We're going to the Alamo."

"Why?" he says, his mouth faintly mocking.

"Wow. You and Derek are both down on the Alamo. I'll have you know it's an important part of Texas history, and without Davie Crockett and Sam Houston, we'd be ordering our ribs, barbecue, and tacos in Spanish."

"Well, I don't know any Spanish, so we'll stop by and pay our respects to the men who allow me to order my food in English in this state." He swats me on the rear end as we head to the kitchen.

"So, this is it, huh?" Derek says as he takes a few more pictures of the board of rusted weapons found after the battle of the Alamo.

"Yeah, there's not much to it, but now you can say you've seen it the next time you order your Mexican food in English," Carter says with sarcasm as he winks at me.

I roll my eyes at him and let out a giggle as he gives my side a tickle.

We head back to the RV in the parking lot, and Carter decides to take Molly for a walk before hitting the road again. I boil water for pasta. Might as well eat before our next long trek up the road.

Carter and Molly arrive back as the penne with alfredo sauce is ready. I place the large salad bowl and vinaigrette dressing on the table as the boys dig in.

"It's roughly sixteen hours to the Grand Canyon from here. That doesn't include stopping for sleep and checking out any nearby places. It'll take us a few days to get there. Have we decided if we're going to the northern or southern rim?" Derek looks back and forth between Carter and me.

"Ssssss-southern rim," Carter spits the words out, not looking at either of us.

I swallow the pasta I'm chewing. "First your hands shake, and now you're stuttering. What's going on Carter? Are you sick?"

"He's just..." Derek starts, but I interrupt.

"I know, he's stressed out. Stress doesn't cause stuttering. It only aggravates it. Neurogenic malfunctions cause stuttering. Are you an epileptic? Have you had a traumatic brain injury? Do-do you have MS?"

"No. Nothing like that. I get bad headaches. Migraines actually." Carter begins to rub his temples in his familiar habit.

"Like I said, he suffers from excessive stress," Derek chimes in, glancing nervously at Carter. "He also gets excited at times, and I have to calm him down. It's the little things that get him worked up. We have to keep him grounded and neutral—"

"I want to take Teddy rafting down the Colorado River," Carter states, cutting Derek off. "That should be relaxing."

"Um, have you ever been rafting, Carter? It's not relaxing. It looks stressful. Maybe we shouldn't do that." I grab his hand and encircle it with mine, worried that he's not telling me everything. "We could just go horseback riding. That's peaceful."

"No!" he spits out. His eyes are bright and pleading as they lock on mine. "I want to give you the Grand Canyon trip you wanted. Hell, we may do both, but we are *not* going to sit here and discuss my health. It is what it is. I'm stressed out from leading a selfish life. End of story. Let me have my adventures with my lady and best friend. That's all I want."

I nod, swallowing down the lump which has formed in my throat. Call it intuition, but it has to be more than stress. But the desperate, pleading look in his sad eyes has me agreeing to anything he wants. He lets out a breath, a tiny smile gracing his lips as he gives my hand a squeeze. His hand quivers slightly over mine before he pulls it away and gets to his feet, his plate in hand.

With lunch over, Carter and Derek take the realm of driving and navigating while I clean up the lunch dishes. Once everything is put away, I start Googling all of the symptoms I know about Carter and apply it to my knowledge gained at Columbia University plus listening to my father's conversations over the years. He could have multiple sclerosis and wants to travel before it becomes too difficult. I just wish he'd tell me. I can't shake the idea that something else is going on, and I have a feeling he needs me more than he knows.

DIARY

Day 35

Yes, Day 35. Derek helped me count our days away from NYC so I can straighten out my journal. If only I could go back and add in the missed days, but they're long gone at this point. Suffice it to say, I either slept through them or laughed my way through them, because I've been in nothing but pure heaven since Teddy joined us.

She's been a little standoffish since my stuttering moments a few days ago. I haven't done it since but trying to convince her that what's wrong with me is just stress is getting harder and harder. The woman can see right through me, I swear.

Doctor Aarons and I are messaging back and forth. He's not happy with me, but he called in a new prescription at some pharmacy in Flagstaff for me that Derek retrieved. Not sure it's doing anything new or special from the old medicine, except make me sweat more. We'll see how I feel in a few more days.

I don't want to admit it to myself, let alone Derek, and especially not Teddy, but I'm starting to feel different. I had trouble tying my shoes this morning. Even fastening the buttons on my shirt was a fiasco, which explains why today I'm wearing a twenty-dollar t-shirt from the Alamo gift shop that says, 'Remember the Alamo'. I was worried before. Stressed before. But it's getting worse. It's coming. I don't know how long I have. I've been praying for my six months, but at the rate I'm going, I might only have three.

I'm trying not to draw into myself. I'm trying to enjoy the woman I'm falling for. I'm trying to enjoy all the moments, but every fucking time my hand shakes or the words falter, I'm reminded that I'm a ticking time bomb and the minutes are blinking faster.

I know. Shut the hell up about it. And I should. I need to stop focusing on my disease and focus on the positives. But even those are turning to negatives because I'll be leaving them soon.

Anyway, enough of my boo-hooing.

We're off to ride the trails down to the Colorado River on horse-back then to whatever we decide our next adventure will be. Derek booked us on the gentle course, but we were warned the river is up, so it could be a little more adventurous than we bargained for. I'm all in. I just want to see Teddy laugh and have a good time. She's all I care about.

We're going to pitch a tent too. We have two, so I'll have some privacy with Teddy. I plan on making use of our time together.

If the tent is a rockin', don't bother knocking. If it's not doing anything, best check on me. I could be dead.

TWENTY-SIX

CARTER

"Fuck," I hiss, fumbling with the button on my cargo shorts. I panic, craning my neck to see if Teddy is coming. She's been riding my ass lately about me telling her what's going on. Asking me if I want to talk to relieve some stress. I've been making up lies, telling her that work texts have me exhausted. I'm not sure how much longer I can hold her off. I mean, I can't even button my damn pants this morning.

I try again, but my fingers can't seem to follow the instructions I'm giving them.

"Come on," I whimper, my fingers slipping once more. I sink onto the bed, my face in my hands. My cheeks are wet. I'm crying.

"Damn it," I sniffle.

"Carter," Teddy calls out, popping her head into the room. I look up at her, my heart warming as her bright smile greets me. It falters on her lips.

"What's wrong?" She's at my side in moments, thumbing the wetness on my cheeks away.

"I'm having a bad day, sweetheart. Headaches." I give her the feeble lie, hating myself for it. I don't know why I don't tell her the

163

truth. Maybe because I know it'll crush her, and I can't bear to see her hurt.

Imagine her pain if you die on her, you dumb ass.

"Is there anything I can do?" she asks, brushing her lips across my jaw. "I heard that sex can help alleviate stress and headaches."

I chuckle softly, loving how ready she always is. "Mm, baby, I should be the most stress-free man in the world if that's the case. All I've been doing is burying myself in you." My lips find hers in a sweet kiss which has my cock growing three sizes in my unbuttoned shorts.

"Then what's one more day?" she purrs against my lips.

I tug at her tank top, desperate to get it off her so I can feel her warmth against me. I need to forget about all this bullshit. She's what matters to me. Not my goddamn pants. In moments, we're both naked. She's straddling my lap, and her large breasts are pushed against my face. I let out a groan as I bury my face in them, sucking and kissing the sweet mounds.

Her wet center slides down on my aching cock, causing my eyes to roll back in my head. She rides me like a cowgirl, her head thrown back in ecstasy, my fingers tangled in her dark locks. My Teddy Bear can sure move. She has my toes curling in moments, her pussy spasming along my cock as we peak together.

It's hot and fast. And perfect since we're supposed to be meeting Derek outside.

"I'll never get tired of this," she breathes out against my lips.

"M-me either, b-baby," I reply with a stutter, kissing her tenderly. Her forehead rests against mine.

"Carter, I'm worried about you."

I'm silent, internally screaming at myself to just tell her what's wrong.

"I-I-I'm fine. J-just h-h-h-headaches," I manage to choke out. My heart pounds harder in my chest. I feel dizzy and weak. I close my eyes for a moment as she runs her fingers through my hair, grounding me.

"You're not. You need to tell me—"

"We n-need to get d-dressed. D-Derek is w-waiting. Let him know

I'll be there in a m-moment," I stammer out, lifting her off my lap and pulling my boxers back up with shaking hands.

I need water. And my medicine. I'm sweating like a damn horse. She gives me a frown before putting her clothes back on.

"Call me if you need me," she says, grimacing slightly before planting a sweet kiss on my lips as I sit on the bed in my boxers. Her words are innocent enough, but her eyes say everything she's thinking. She knows I'm sick. I just need to confirm it.

The moment she's gone, I let out the breath I'm holding and bend to reach for my shorts. A wave of vertigo takes hold, and I slide off the bed, hitting my head on the door of the closet.

A groan of pain leaves me, and I lie on the floor, stuck between the bed and wall, staring up at the ceiling. My heart hammers painfully in my chest. My vision is dotted with dark sparkles. Tingles rocket through my body.

I can't get up. I know I can't. So, I lay there, praying this isn't the end.

"Carter?" Derek calls out, coming into the Beastmaster after the minutes race by. "Carter!"

"I-In h-here," I manage weakly. "Help."

Derek's footsteps thunder toward me. In moments, he's beside me, worry in his dark eyes.

"I seem to have fallen," I say, wincing.

"You should go to the hospit—"

"No," I say sharply. "No."

"Carter—"

"Damnit, Derek, just listen to me! Please," I plead, my voice choked. "The end is coming. P-please. I just need more time. T-teddy...I don't want to go. I just want to have these last m-moments."

"What if you can get help?" Derek murmurs, helping me to sit up. "What if there's something that can be done?"

He assists me to my feet, and I sway, his hands steadying me.

"I'm a dead man walking," I sigh, rubbing my eyes.

At least, I'm not as dizzy anymore. When I open my eyes, it's to see Derek staring at me, a frown on his face. "Don't tell Teddy."

"She needs to know, Carter. What the hell am I supposed to do if you don't wake up one day? Or if you stroke out or something? Did you know her dad is a brain surgeon?"

I scowl at the information. She'd mentioned something like that to me, but I'd been so eager just to be near her that I hadn't paid much attention.

"I'm not sure why that matters. She doesn't even talk to her family anymore."

"It matters because from what I've learned from her, he's one of the best in the country. Probably the entire world. Maybe he can help you."

I shake my head, my heart hurting. No one can help me. Doctor Aarons said there's no cure. That's why we're on this trip. One last hurrah.

"Please. Don't tell her. Promise me?"

A muscle in Derek's jaw pops, but he gives me a curt nod anyway.

"Also, do you have pants without buttons?"

Derek sighs and backs out of the room. I pull my t-shirt back on with shaking hands. It's not long until Derek's back, holding out a pair of gray basketball shorts. I eagerly take them and tug them on.

"How do I look?" I ask.

"Like you're living the dream, man."

I nod. "Good. That's the look I'm going for."

DEREK SETS OUR TENTS UP AT THE GRAND CANYON NATIONAL PARK. I'm feeling slightly fuzzy but loads better than I was earlier. I drink in the sight of Teddy in her tiny tank top and barely-there shorts. My girl looks amazing as she bustles around our campsite, her long, dark ponytail swinging behind her.

I can't help myself. I wrap my arms around her waist from behind and inhale the lavender scent she's wearing.

"Baby, you smell good," I say, grateful I'm no longer stuttering.

She turns in my arms, her breasts pressed against my chest. Her lips find mine, giving me a deep kiss which I eagerly eat up.

When we break apart, her eyes are locked on mine.

"Are you feeling better?" she asks, the worry evident on her face. It breaks my heart.

I force out a smile. "Yes, Teddy Bear." I kiss the tip of her nose. "I'm fine."

"Carter, you really had me worried this morning. I-I've never seen you like that before. Migraines don't cause that—"

"Mine do. OK?" I brush a stray piece of hair away from her face. "Don't worry about me. I'm fine. I feel better already." I force a smile onto my face.

She bites her bottom lip before nodding at me, uncertainty in her eyes.

"Carter, if you're lying to me—"

"Then I'll let you spank me." I give her a playful wink, making a grin dance onto her plump lips.

"If you want rough, I can do rough," she teases.

I grab her pert ass cheeks and tug her so close there isn't any air between us.

"Oh, I want rough, Teddy Bear." I nip at her ear. She shivers against me, her breath hitching. "Someday, I'm going to bury myself in your sweet, little ass and conquer all of you."

"I want that," she whispers in a choked voice.

I chuckle softly. "Me too."

Before I can lead her away to do just that, because hey, I'm on borrowed time, Derek calls out to me, "Carter, you have a phone call."

I pull away from Teddy and pat my pockets, looking for my phone. I thought I had it with me. I glance up to see Derek lifting it from the folding chair I'd been sitting in.

"Who is it?"

"Aarons," Derek says, glancing from the screen to me.

I peek down at Teddy. She's staring at Derek with narrowed eyes. *Damn her and her intuition.*

I shrug at Derek. "Let it go to voicemail."

"But—"

"Voicemail, Derek. I doubt he has anything I need to listen to."

Derek puts my phone down and grumbles before going back to setting up a portable grill.

"Want to see the inside of my tent?" I murmur in Teddy's ear, picking up my thoughts where I left off.

She giggles, her hand rubbing against the front of my basketball shorts where my bulge is growing. "Aren't you tired? We just had sex a few hours ago."

"Teddy," I admonish in mock shock. "You dirty girl. I asked if you wanted to see my tent not fuck me."

She throws her head back, her exquisite neck on display, as a loud laugh falls from her lips. I grin at her reaction.

"You think you're so clever, Carter George. You know if you take me back to your tent what's going to happen."

"Mm, maybe you should enlighten me," I say, grinning wider. I like where this is going.

My phone rings again, interrupting us.

"I think you need to answer your phone."

"I think you need to answer me." I raise a brow at her. My phone stops ringing.

"I'm going to bend over and let you conquer *all* of me. That's what will happen," her voice is a low purr which has my heart thrashing madly in my chest.

"Promise?" I growl.

"Yes."

My phone rings again.

"Damn it," I hiss, drawing away from her. I haul in a few deep breaths to calm my dick as she laughs knowingly. I don't really want to go over where Derek is working on the grill with a raging boner.

The phone stops ringing as I pick it up. I move to silence the damn thing when it jingles once more, Doctor Aarons's name flashing across the screen. I cast a hasty glance at Teddy who's gone to help Derek put burgers on the grill. Taking it as my opportunity to see what the hell he wants, I answer it, moving away from the campsite for privacy.

"You're really ruining my day—" I start.

"Carter, I have news," Doctor Aarons plows on. "Do you have a moment?"

I frown and peek at Teddy and Derek. Molly is dancing around them as Derek tries to get her to roll over for a hot dog. Teddy is laughing, not paying attention to me.

"Yeah, make it quick," I say, moving further away from the campsite.

"I was at a conference over the weekend. Are you sitting down?"

"No." I move deeper into the woods, my heart rate kicking up. "But if you don't tell me what you called for, the anxiety you're putting me under might put me on my ass."

"There's a treatment option," he bursts out, breathless. My breath catches in my throat.

"What?"

"For your condition. I know I should've waited to talk to you about it, but I've already forwarded your medical records to this facility. I think you've got a shot, Carter."

I run my shaking fingers through my hair. The idea of more time causes butterflies to take flight in my gut. "T-Tell m-me more."

"A doctor with wild ideas and a shit ton of talent is heading the research team for it. The man is a genius, Carter. I listened to his seminar. The things he's proposing sound impossible, but I think he can safely remove the larger tumors then shrink the rest with a drug his team has been studying."

"H-How do I get this s-started?" I ask, closing my eyes and willing the stuttering to stop. "What are t-the numbers for s-survival?"

Doctor Aarons quiets on the line for so long I think I've lost him. "Phil?"

"Sorry, Carter." Doctor Aarons sighs. "I can't tell you the numbers."

"Why not?" I demand.

"Because there are none. He's never done it before."

"What?" I hiss. "Then why the hell are you calling me about it?"

"It's a chance, Carter. The way I see it, you're a dead man. You've got maybe five months tops, and that's if we're being optimistic. You're losing control of your speech. The last time we spoke, you said you were experiencing numbness and loss of coordination in your hands and feet. Plus with your headaches and dizziness—"

"Yeah, well if his miracle operation kills me—"

"You're *already* dead, Carter. Get it through your head. Don't look at this as a risk. Look at it as a chance."

"But if it doesn't work…," my voice trails off.

"Then you die anyway. Not to sound harsh, Carter, but I'd much rather die under anesthesia than waste away in a bed in my high-rise, begging for death to take me, and worrying for when it will."

I blow out a shaky breath and gather my bearings before I speak again. "Does he have *any* information on recovery?"

"It could be hard. It could be easy. I suppose it depends on what things look like once they've gotten a better look inside and how the surgery goes." He pauses before clearing his throat. "I think you're an excellent candidate, Carter. I wouldn't be calling if I didn't think you had a shot at this. Your cancer hasn't spread to the rest of your organs. It was contained when we last checked. But we need to work fast. I don't know what sort of window we have here."

"You know I can't decide this right now, Phil—"

"Christ, Carter, you could be dead in a month."

I blow out a breath and look in the direction of Derek and Teddy. As if sensing me, Teddy's eyes find mine. My heart aches as I see the affection in her eyes. As I realize I have to let go. As I realize our future together is close to expiring. *Can I put her through the pain?* My heart tells me no. But another part screams it's too late. I've already tugged her into the grave with me.

I need to tell her the truth. She needs to know our future together is unlikely. If I do the surgery, I could die sooner rather than later. If I wait, I'll have a bit more time with the woman I'm falling head over heels in love with. But the quality of that time is unknown. I don't want to waste away in a bed like my father. And I don't want her to watch it happen.

"How long do I have before I need to decide?" I ask softly, my eyes locked on Teddy who's cocked her head at me, concern on her face.

"The sooner the better. When I get the call back, I'll need to be able to give them an answer."

I nod.

"OK. I'll be in touch, Phil. I have a lot to think a-about," I say, breaking my gaze from Teddy.

"OK, son," he addresses me softly. Affectionately. "Maybe sit and talk it out with someone. Maybe your mom."

"Right," I mutter, squeezing my eyes closed. I still haven't told her I'm dying. But to her, I'm probably already dead. Can't really miss what you never bother to see and all that.

"Take care, Carter. I hope we speak again soon." His words carry more weight than I care to think about.

"Goodbye, Phil."

TWENTY-SEVEN

TEDDY

"*J* can't believe you've never roasted a marshmallow." I giggle at Carter as he sits frowning at his burned 'mallow around our small contained campfire.

"Ain't a lot of wood and wilderness back home," Derek says around a mouthful of s'more.

"But still." I glance at Carter. He's been acting odd ever since his phone call. Quieter. Withdrawn. "Didn't you do it on your roof or something?"

"No, sweetheart," Carter murmurs distractedly. I follow his eyes to the full moon hanging over us. "You can do a lot of things on a roof in New York City. Starting a fire isn't one of them."

I shrug before resting my head on his shoulder. Laughter from further down the campsite makes Molly whine.

"Carter, is everything OK?" I ask softly as Derek gives Molly one of her treats.

"Of course, baby," Carter says, moving his arm so I can tuck up beneath it. His body is warm, yet he's trembling slightly. He looks exhausted beneath the moonlight. Dark circles create a halo around his dull eyes. He's slimmer than when we first met.

"Do you want to go to the tent?"

His full lips quirk up into a small smile. "Are you propositioning me, Teddy Bear?"

I smile back. "Maybe. But we can just sleep if you want."

He shakes his head at me, a frown now replacing his smile. "I'll sleep when I'm dead. Tonight, I want all of you."

My breath catches in my lungs, and I nod at him. I've been thinking about it all day long. Having Carter George conquer all of me sounds delicious and dirty. "I want that too."

"Derek, we're going to the tent." Carter doesn't hesitate and gets to his feet, hauling me with him. Derek's eyes dart between us, a sly smile on his face.

"I get it. That's cool. I'll go check out that other campsite and make some friends. Try to keep it down. I don't want to have to explain what the hell you two are doing in there."

"Don't worry. It'll be self-explanatory." Carter grins at Derek.

Heat floods my face as Derek winks at me. Without another word, Carter leads me to our tent and motions for me to go in. I'm grateful it's a big tent. Something tells me we're going to need the space.

Carter moves past me once he's inside and doesn't waste time removing his clothes. I giggle as he lies on our air mattress and looks up at me.

"Strip for me, baby," he says in a husky voice, his eyes hooded. "Slowly. I want to savor this."

I bite my bottom lip. "I've never stripped for anyone before."

"Don't be shy. It's me," his voice is soft, almost pleading with me.

I don't need him to beg. I want it as much as he does. I'm just nervous.

I swallow down the nerves and breathe out, slowly pulling off my tank top. Carter lets out an appreciative growl, his eyes drinking me in. Heat and desire flood my core as he takes his cock in hand and begins stroking it.

I take my time removing my shorts, leaving my lace panties in place. I'm completely naked except for them. Without overthinking it, I give my breast a squeeze. My hand travels down my abdomen and inside the waistband of my panties until my fingers are sliding through my slick folds, seeking out the sensitive bud that's begging to be touched.

Carter's hand moves faster on his cock, his breathing growing heavier. I can't help myself. The look of pure ecstasy on his face has me dipping my fingers into my own warmth and playing a game I've never played with someone before.

I glide my fingers in and out in time to Carter's rhythm, my breathing shallow and fast. It isn't long before I'm whimpering, the euphoria of release blanketing me, turned on beyond belief as Carter and I watch each other.

"Do it, baby," Carter growls, his hand slowing on his cock as he stares at me.

The look of awe in his eyes urges me on. I climb the peak until I'm spiraling over the edge, moaning out his name as my body shakes and trembles.

"You're so fucking beautiful," he whispers in a thick voice as I fall slowly from my high. "Take those panties off and come here."

Following his commands, I do as he says. I straddle his thighs, grinding against him in a lap dance. His hands land on my waist, his breathing rough and ragged.

"Teddy Bear, you don't know what you do to me," he chokes out as I swivel my hips on him. "I've never…" his voice trails off as he closes his eyes and leans back.

I place a kiss on his mouth which he eagerly returns, his grip tightening on me.

In a flash, I'm beneath him, his lips on my neck, peppering my skin with his warm kisses. He trails them lower until his lips wrap around my nipple. His hand kneads the other one.

"Carter," I moan. My fingers sink in his hair as he nips at a peaked bud before continuing his voyage south. His tongue sliding between my folds has me whimpering, my back arched. He lifts my legs onto his shoulders as his tongue works me over. I squirm as my orgasm builds, his fingers twisting inside of me, hitting all the areas that bring me joy.

"Don't stop," I whine.

His tongue moves faster on my swollen bud until I'm rocketing out of my mind as an intense orgasm racks my body. He slides his fingers out, his tongue lapping at my wetness. He plants a tender kiss on my overly sensitive area before he's spreading my legs apart, his cock poised at my entrance.

"Teddy Bear," he groans, pushing into me.

Our bodies tangle together, our soft moans filling the tent as we make love. Carter is tender and loving as he touches my face, kisses my lips, whispers my name like a prayer. After taking me to heaven and back again, he pulls out and stares down at me.

He doesn't need to say anything. I roll over and get on my hands and knees. He digs through his bag for a moment and pulls out a small bottle. He drizzles the lube along the cleft of my ass. Goosebumps erupt along my skin as his fingers trail down my spine before they find my puckered hole. He plays and teases it for a moment, slowly inching in and out, spreading the lubricant before positioning the head of his slippery cock at my back entrance. My breathing picks up as my body tenses.

"Relax, baby. I'll take care of you," Carter's deep voice calls out softly.

I relax at the sound. The first pinch of pain causes me to whimper. He's slow and careful as he continues to push into me. I grit my teeth, close my eyes, and collapse onto my forearms, angling my ass higher. He pushes further in, groaning. He fills me completely, stretching me, making my body tremble.

"You're so fucking amazing," he whispers against my ear. His lips meet my shoulder, kissing it before he moves away and slowly pulls out a fraction before pushing back into me.

My fingers twist in our blankets as I let out a hiss of air. He moves more. In and out. I let out a whimper.

"You OK?" he manages to rasp.

"Y-yes. More."

That's all he needs to hear before he's moving faster. There are so many emotions and sensations flooding my body I can't contain them all. I moan his name loudly, a signal for him to give it to me harder and faster.

He senses it and does just that, his hands tightening on my hips, his cock buried deep inside of me. A feeling unlike any I've ever had before surfaces. It's a tingle that blossoms, growing into a sensation which has me howling in ecstasy. An orgasm erupts so powerful my entire body quakes and twitches beneath Carter's.

"Fuck," he hisses, moving faster. "Teddy!"

I'm still whimpering and trembling when I feel Carter's dick twitch inside of me, signaling his release. His movements slow before his lips press to my temple. We're both still for a moment, our intense breathing filling the air, before he withdraws from me. I don't move. I'm trembling too much.

A moment later, he wipes me clean and tugs me into his strong arms.

"You're shaking," he murmurs, tucking me against him. He pulls the light blanket over us.

"You just made me feel really good," I admit in a quivering voice. "I've never done that before."

"Me either," he says, planting a sweet kiss on my forehead. "You took my virginity."

I let out a snort, causing him to laugh. Snuggling up against him, I feel like maybe I finally have things figured out. Being with Carter feels right.

"I've been thinking," Carter says, planting a tender kiss on the top of my head.

"Hmm?"

"You said you don't talk to your parents much. That you have a rocky relationship with your dad."

I move up to my elbow and stare into Carter's face, wondering what he's getting at.

He reaches out and twists a lock of my hair around his finger.

"I think you should call your dad."

"What?" I crinkle my brows at him. "Why?"

"It's just…I was never close to my dad. Hell, I wasn't even close to my mother. I never really got the opportunity for normal family dynamics. I want you to have the things I never had. The way you've spoken about your family, I know you miss them—"

"Carter, my dad wants *his* life for me. And I want my own life—"

"Teddy Bear," he murmurs, his brown eyes glittering in the dim tent. "I think your dad wants your happiness. He pushed because he loves you. Not because he wants your misery."

I bite my bottom lip. *Damn Carter George and his reasoning.*

"Make me a promise?"

"What's that?" I ask softly, taking in how incredibly sad and worn out he looks. A pang of worry shoots through me.

"That you'll call your dad and talk to him. I don't want you to be alone."

My heart bangs painfully against my chest. "Why would I be alone? I have you."

"You do have me, baby. You'll always have me. But you're going to need your family soon. I want you to be able to have that. So for me, please call them?" he pleads softly, his voice cracking.

I can't argue with him. I don't know if it's the way he's looking at me or the realization of how much I miss my family that has me nodding wordlessly, willing to give this man anything I can just to see him smile.

"Say it," he commands in a low, intense growl. "Promise me."

"I promise. I'll call them tomorrow."

A slow, content smile graces his lips, and he relaxes against his pillow, tugging me closer to him. I breathe out in relief. Carter is fierce in everything he does. I wonder how my dad will take me calling him. My calls are usually to my mom, my older brother, or younger sister, and even those aren't coming along as often as they once did. My father and my stubbornness have really put a wedge in our family dynamics. Growing up was tough with my dad pushing us so hard, but he always was a good dad, albeit a bit rigid. Carter is right, though. I need my family. Sitting there thinking about it makes me ache inside, the hollowness of always being alone making me swallow down tears.

"Teddy?" Carter's voice is soft and tentative as he pulls me away from my morose thoughts.

"Mm?"

"What's wrong, baby? Did I upset you?"

"No," I answer, placing a tender kiss on his lips. "You're right. I do miss my family. But I'm afraid."

"Of what?" His warm fingertips trace circles on my skin, making goosebumps erupt.

"I don't know. I guess that maybe I waited too long."

"As long as there is a breath to breathe, there's still time, sweetheart. I promise you that. Just don't wait while you're holding your last one. Trust me. I missed out on a lot with my own family because I waited too long."

"Your parents loved you too, Carter."

"In their own way, I'm sure," he murmurs. "I probably could've made things better with my old man, but he was a stubborn old coot. I'm my dad's son, that's for sure." A soft chuckle escapes him.

"And your mom?"

"My mom was a good mom while she was around. I mean, I didn't get hugged a lot as I grew older or praised, but she made sure I had someone there to feed me and go to my school functions."

I wrinkle my nose at his words.

"I don't even know what to say to that, Carter."

"There's nothing to say. My dad was cold to her too. Her parents the same. She gave me the love she knew." He shrugs and looks down as he twines his fingers with mine. "I always thought I was a product of my environment. That I'm the way I am because of them."

"You are," I say, squeezing his hand.

His eyes widen as he takes me in, clearly not expecting my response.

"Have you ever thought that maybe you're as wonderful as you are because of them?"

He scoffs at my words. "I'm not wonderful, Teddy. I'm a monster. If you knew me, the man I was b-before—"

"*I know the man you are now*. You've always been that man,

Carter. I know it in my heart. So, don't tell me any different. I won't believe it of you. Ever."

"You're so amazing, Teddy Bear." His lips find mine, his kiss deep and fierce, taking my breath away. When he breaks away, we're both left breathing hard.

"I want you to know you've changed my entire world. Thank you."

I look up at him. His eyes are shining, his lips parted.

"You're welcome, Carter, but you changed mine too." I cup his cheek, searching his face for any sort of answer he's willing to give me about what's really going on with him.

A smile touches his lips.

"I'll die a happy man then."

His words send a current of fear through me.

"Carter, don't say that."

"Say what, baby?"

"Please, tell me what's wrong. I know you're sick."

He tenses against me, confirming my suspicions.

"I'm so worried about you—"

"Don't be. Let's just enjoy our time together."

"How much time do we have?" I whisper through the silence.

He thumbs my bottom lip, his brows knit.

"I don't know," his voice shakes. "But I want you to know you're the best thing that's ever happened to me, Teddy. I'd have married you so hard."

He wipes at a tear that slips from my eye.

"I love you, Carter." I don't hesitate with the words. I've loved him since the moment I saw him. When you find your special someone, time doesn't matter. We haven't spent twenty years together, but every moment has been a lifetime. In my heart I know we're meant to be. A smile graces his lips as he closes his eyes. A moment later, he opens them.

"I love you too, Teddy Bear."

DIARY

Day...40? 41? 45?

Damn it. I don't remember how long it's been. I guess it doesn't matter.

I've been thinking a lot about what Phil said. After last night with Teddy, I've decided I'm going to let go. I'm going to die. I'm not going to seek the treatment. I'm here right now. I want to take advantage of it. I want to be with Teddy. I know, I'm a damn fool. But I keep thinking if I take the chance on this surgery, it might ruin my remaining days. I might die faster. I don't want that.

But I need to come clean with her. I think I did a bit last night. I chickened out when I saw the heartbreak on her face. God, what is she going to do when I'm gone? Who will take care of her?

The thought has kept me up most of the night, watching her sleep, my mind on overdrive with how I can set her up so she can play her music without worrying about bills and money. I'm going to talk to Derek about looking after her when I'm gone. I know they've grown close. I know he'll make sure she isn't alone when the time comes.

So, let this be my testament:

I hereby declare that Teddy is to receive my estates, the contents, all my property: cars, boats, summer homes, bank accounts, safety deposit boxes, everything with my name on it. It's hers. I trust her with my life and leave her with the power to decide my fate.

I'll be sure to make this final with my lawyers later today.

Did I mention I don't want to die?

I'm also not ready to leave our campsite. I want to stay here with my Teddy Bear, Molly, and Derek. I want to watch the sun set a few more times with my girl in my arms, my best friend at my side, and Molly wagging her tail. I'm going to tell everyone we'll put off our rafting trip for another day or two.

The end is near for Carter Anthony George. I can feel it.

TWENTY-EIGHT

CARTER

*T*he early morning desert chill makes me want to crawl back into the tent and cuddle with Teddy, but the vague dream I had about my mother has me up at 6:18 AM, tossing my phone back and forth from one hand to another. I've scrolled to her name a dozen times. *Laura.*

After spending a chunk of time last night preaching to Teddy about family, I don't feel good about continuing to ignore the only family I have.

I run the pad of my thumb over the screen, debating on calling. It's 9:18 AM in Boston. *Fuck it.*

I press dial and wait for a response.

"Carter?" Mom's voice lilts upward in surprise.

"Mom," my voice cracks into a whimper. I forgot how angelic her voice is.

"What's wrong? Is everything OK?"

I blink back the flood of tears rushing the borders of my eyelids. I hadn't expected the conversation to turn into a damn blubber fest so early in the game. "I'm sick, Mom. I've got what Dad had." She doesn't respond. I look at the phone and make sure I didn't lose her because of the weak connection in this park. "Mom, did you hear me?"

"Carter," she chokes out.

Another long silence extends between us, but her ragged breathing still puffs into the phone.

"Carter, there are some things you should sugarcoat in life, especially to your mother, and there are other times when the plain truth is required. This is a plain truth moment. So tell me, how much longer do you have?"

I swallow the hard lump of sugarcoated words down my throat and give her exactly what she asks for. "I don't know. Three months. Maybe four. I'm feeling worse by the day. Could be only a few weeks at this point." I spare her the ugly details of my speech, weight loss, and loss of coordination.

She sighs heavily on the other end of the line. "How long have you known?"

"I found out a few months ago and—"

"I'm taking the first train I can get. I should be there by noon."

"No, Mom. I w-w-w-went on a crazy adventure across the country to try and l-l-l-live some of the life I've been denying myself…I'm n-not there."

Her spoon rattles against her tea cup. I can picture her stirring it like during the snowstorm when I was seven and she had me read to her to distract me.

"I don't want you to worry about me. That's not why I called."

"You can't tell a mother not to worry about her child. It's what we do from the minute we learn of our babies growing inside us. Of course, you won't know that until you become…never mind. That was insensitive of me. Darling, tell me why you called then."

I swallow. "There's a procedure, an experimental one, they want me to undergo. I'd be the first ever, and maybe the last if it doesn't work, to have it done." I don't know why I'm telling her this. I've already made my decision. Maybe some tiny part of me is desperate to hear her tell me I'll be OK just one more time. Like she used to when I was a kid with a bellyache.

"And what have you decided?"

"I don't want to die, but I'm worried it'll eliminate what little time I do have left. I'm not going to do it."

"Carter Anthony—"

"I've found someone. I want to be here for her as long as I can be. She has my whole heart, and if I don't survive the procedure, our time ends the minute they cut into my skull," I explain, watching Teddy step out of the tent.

Her messy hair hangs in strands. She's holding her wrinkled t-shirt close to her body as she tiptoes across the grounds to the RV for the bathroom. Her beautiful sleepy doe-eyes look at me, and a smile softens her face. *Yep. She owns my whole heart.*

"Carter, you've always been an intelligent, but head-strong boy. I know I've been absent for the past decade of your life, but I love you so very much and worry for you. Those are characteristics that don't go away, no matter the time or distance between us. Tell me you are going through with this procedure. Please. I-I always thought I had time to make things right—"

"Mom, things were never *wrong* between us. You're you. I'm me. And I don't harbor ill feelings because of who we are. I love you. I always will. I guess I just wanted you to know that. You know, just in case."

"Oh, Carter," she sniffles, her voice choked. "I love you too, sweetheart. Just please, reconsider the treatment. If you love this girl, fight for her. Fight for yourself. You deserve so much happiness."

I swallow down a sob and wipe hastily at my damp eyes. "I'll think about it, OK? I'll let you know what I decide soon. I promise. Now, I've got to go. We're planning a rafting trip down the Colorado River. I want to tell them we should hold off for a few days. I'm feeling a bit weak," I admit.

"Jesus Christ, Carter. Don't do this. Come home. Let's explore all the options. Together. Let me take care of you like I should have—"

"Mom, it's my life. This is my adventure, and I made a promise to someone that I fully intend to keep. I'll call you when I've made up my mind."

She sniffles into the phone, and my heart suddenly aches for the woman I no longer know.

"You're all I have left," she murmurs into the phone.

"That's why I called, Mom. We'll talk. Soon. I promise. I-I love you."

"I love you too."

I hang up the phone and drop it into my lap not wanting to say goodbye past that. I slump forward, resting my head in my hands.

Delicate hands massage my shoulders, making me moan and release the tension I'm holding in them. "Is everything all right?"

"Yes, everything is just" —I grab one of her hands and pull her around into my lap— "perfect. Like it's supposed to be."

"Who was that on the phone this early?" The concerned look on her face pulls at my heartstrings.

"It was my mom. I called to let her know we're OK."

"Oh," she gasps in surprise. "I'm glad you did that. How was it?"

"We aren't on regular speaking terms, but she's my mom," I say, shrugging my shoulders. "Parents worry about their kids."

I brush her bangs aside and tilt her chin up, looking directly into her eyes. "You're going to call your family today, right? I can't stand the thought of you going through life without a family connection. Do it for me. Please?"

"I promised I would. I'll call. I can't guarantee they'll answer, but I *will* make an attempt." She kisses me, making me swallow down a moan of pleasure. The woman knows how to work her mouth, that's for sure.

"I'm making coffee," she says against my lips. "It should be ready now. We're going horseback riding today. Remember?" Without another word, she stands and pulls me up, lacing her fingers with mine as we walk.

"That's exactly what I need to get me up onto a horse this early in the morning."

~

THE THREE-HOUR RIDE DOWN INTO THE BASIN OF THE CANYON IS daunting, and so spectacular no one would believe me without seeing it for themselves.

The canyon walls shimmer with ribbons of bronze and copper when the sunlight hits them. It's breathtaking.

Not to mention the company I'm in. There are moments where I'm a little too busy taking pics of Teddy majestically sitting on her horse, so I miss guiding mine around some sagebrush and have to be fished out by our guides.

"City slicker," Derek calls out, shaking his head in disbelief at my distracted mind, a smirk plastered to his face. I grin back at him.

The heat of the desert is rising as the sun finds its ways into the cracks and crevices of the environment. The air is stifling at many points even though we're mostly riding in shadow. There isn't any breeze blowing.

My hands twitch, and I let out a low growl.

Not right now. Let me have these moments.

We finally round a long bend of canyon wall, and the river comes into view.

"Amazing," Teddy says, beaming the widest smile I've ever seen on her.

I walk my horse right up to hers, and we sit side-by-side silently taking in the view. I hope it's better than anything she ever imagined it to be. "It's beautiful, but not as beautiful as you are," I lean over and murmur in her ear, placing a kiss on her cheek.

"I love you endlessly," her voice is heavy with emotion.

Ever since saying the words to each other last night, we don't miss a chance to repeat them. I've spent my life thinking that things like love and loyalty don't exist. Teddy is proving me wrong on all accounts. The words aren't heavy, making me want to run. Well, maybe they make me want to run, but not away. Never away. To her, more accurately.

"And I love you back, Teddy Bear." Right then, my horse nickers as Derek approaches, so I back off.

"The river looks to be higher in its bed than I imagined it, but it's not running wild like I also pictured it from the few rafting movies I've seen. I didn't realize it was such a long way across or as narrow as some of these canyons are we just came through," Derek says, his face ashen with anxiety.

"Sounds like someone is nervous. Who's the city slicker now?" I tease, swaying forward as his fist draws back taking a swing at my bicep.

I twist away from him and follow the trail guides to the makeshift tents to let the horses rest for a bit. Teddy and Derek finally catch up to us, and we lead the horses to the water troughs. After some much-needed time on solid ground in the shade of the tents, the guides start checking the horses.

"Ready to head back?" Alan, our lead guide, asks, rubbing the scruff of his dark beard.

I glance at Teddy who's admiring her horse as she coos to it. A smile touches my lips as I shake my head at Alan.

"Would you mind giving us a few more minutes?" I ask.

"No problem."

I hand my phone to Derek.

"Will you take some pictures for me?"

"Sure," Derek says, starting the camera on my phone and following me to Teddy. I sweep her up in my arms. Amid her gasp of surprise, I press my mouth to hers in a delicious, deep kiss. When we break apart, we're both breathless, our foreheads pressed against one another.

"Smile for the camera," I instruct, turning my face to Derek who wastes no time snapping our photo a few times. When Derek is done, I take the phone from him and snap a selfie of the two of us before getting all of us in the shot.

I want to print these off and give the images to them, so they'll remember this day.

"I think I was blinking," Teddy whines as I pocket the phone.

"I'm sure it's fine, baby," I assure her, helping her onto her horse. "You're beautiful both with and without your eyes open."

A pretty pink flush warms her cheeks causing me to grin like a lovestruck fool. I turn to get back on my horse, but before I do, a wave of nausea and dizziness rushes over me. Falling isn't my intention, but I go down to my knees, a headache blasting me full force.

"Carter!" Teddy shouts.

Derek is at my side as I hear the guide call out, asking if I'm OK.

"Carter, talk to me," Derek urges, shaking my shoulders as I slump forward.

"J-just a-a-a-a l-lit-a-a-little diz-dizzi-n-ness," I manage to force out. "G-gimme a m-minute."

Derek lets out a yelp and falls sideways as I retch onto the ground in front of me.

"It's OK," Teddy murmurs over and over, her warm hand rubbing my back, her voice cracking. I never heard her get off her horse.

Alan hands me a bottle of water, which I take gratefully, sloshing more of it down my front than in my mouth, but it brings some relief.

"I-I can go. Let's go," I say.

Derek gives me an unsure look before taking my hand and pulling me to my feet.

"Carter—" Teddy starts, but I give her hand a squeeze and shake my head, wincing.

My brain feels like it's being squeezed in a vice, and my vision is spotty. For a minute, I forget where I am or why I'm there.

"Carter?" Derek calls through the fog.

I cock my head at him. Carter. Carter George. That's me. I'm in Arizona. I'm dying.

"I need to sleep," I mumble, stumbling forward. Derek steers me to the horse where he and Alan help me climb on.

"I'm not too sure about letting you ride alone," Alan says, worry etched into his young face.

"The sooner we leave, t-the better," I breathe out.

"Well, I'm just going to tie you into your saddle, Carter. Don't need you falling out and getting hurt." Alan quickly cinches me in place without a word of protest from me.

"Ready?" he asks.

I give him a tired nod before he seems satisfied and mounts his own horse, leading us away from our resting place.

"Are you OK?" Derek asks.

"No," I whisper. Or I think I whisper. Something tells me I haven't because the look on Teddy's face says it all.

TWENTY-NINE

TEDDY

*C*arter can barely hold his head up by the time we're back at camp. It takes both me and Derek plus some guidance on Molly's part, to get Carter walking on his own.

"My tent," he mumbles as we steer him to the Beastmaster.

"Carter, you need a real bed, not an inflatable one," I admonish, his large frame weighing my slight one down. I suck it up and keep balancing him.

"No," he whimpers. "No, Teddy. My tent. P-please."

I cast a glance at Derek who looks troubled. He lets out a sigh and nods to me. We turn Carter back to the tent and help him inside. He collapses onto the air mattress and begins snoring almost immediately.

"We need to talk, Derek. Now." I stomp out of the tent, the sound of Derek's reluctant shuffle behind me.

The moment we're out of the tent and away from it, I round on him and jab him with my finger in his hard chest.

"What the *hell* was that? It's like he had a damn seizure out there."

"It's just stress—"

"I swear to all that is good and holy, Derek, if you don't tell me what the hell is going on with my boyfriend, I'm going to bury you in these woods."

Derek flinches away from me, his eyes darting around the campsite as he licks his lips.

"Teddy, Carter is my best friend. I swore to him I wouldn't say anything. I can't break that promise."

I sigh and rub my eyes. "I'm afraid, Derek."

"Me too," he admits, moving forward and wrapping me in a hug. "When Carter is ready to talk about it, he will. For now, saying he's stressed isn't a lie. Let's let him rest for now. We should do the same."

I nod, sniffling, as I move away from him. I need to call my parents. I swore I would, and now seems like the perfect opportunity.

"I'm going to make some hamburgers on the grill. You want one?" Derek asks.

I nod at him and wipe my eyes. He chucks my chin and gives me a sad smile.

"Cheer up. Carter wouldn't want you to be sad. He'll be fine," his voice shakes a little.

"He'd better be," I whisper. The fear of something really bad being wrong and me losing the one thing I'd been searching my whole life for nearly overwhelms me.

That possibility isn't acceptable. I'll do whatever I have to do to prevent it from happening.

$$\backsim$$

"Mom?" I ask as the phone clicks and my mom's voice comes over the line.

"Theo? Honey, is that you?"

"Hey, Mom," I say, my eyes burning. It's been months since our last conversation.

"What's wrong?"

"N-Nothing. Well, everything."

"Oh, baby. Is it that Dick you're dating?" she asks.

I snort. "Richie, Mom. His name is—*was*—Richie."

"You broke up? Is that what's wrong? Because, honey, that boy was about as useful as tits on a bull."

"Mom!" I'm shocked at her language. My mom is usually so reserved and proper.

She laughs for a moment. "It's for the best, Theo. He wasn't good for you."

"I know, Mom. We broke up a while ago. I-I met someone else. I think he's the one."

"Really?"

"Yeah, but, um, he's sick. He gets these headaches. They're bad. He won't tell me what's wrong." I pause for a moment. "I'm worried, Mom."

"You need to talk to Dad, huh?"

"Do you think he'll talk to me?"

"Sweetheart, you're still his daughter. He's a stubborn old thing, but he loves you. He's in his study. Do you want to talk to him?"

I bite my lip before letting out a nervous sigh. "Yeah. Yeah, I do."

"One second."

The line goes silent for a moment before I hear her whispered voice then my father's deep one. I'm not even sure if he will take my call. My mom has always been optimistic. I'm surprised a moment later when my dad's deep voice comes on the line.

"Theodora."

"Hey, Dad," I breathe out. A fat tear snakes its way down my cheek at the sound of his deep voice, and I hastily wipe at it. I was always Teddy to my dad. Hearing him address me by my full name hurts.

"Do you need money?" his voice is tight. Even if I did, I know he won't give it to me.

"No. I-I called for a few reasons. None of them financial."

"I take it you're making money playing on street corners."

I haul in a deep, calming breath. "I don't play on street corners, Dad. In fact, I haven't played for money in a long time."

He's silent for a moment before speaking, "Your mom tells me you broke up with that loser you were seeing in Nashville. That guy who paraded around, pretending like he was an agent."

"I did."

"Good." There's a note of relief in his voice.

"I met someone else. I'm in love."

Dad is silent for so long I fear I've lost him.

"Dad?"

He clears his throat. "What does this man do? Music as well? Starving artist?"

"He's a businessman. Real estate, mostly. He owns his own company."

"Really?" Dad's voice lifts, relief coming out. "That's good, Teddy."

Teddy. There it was.

"He's sick, Dad. Really sick. I'm worried about him," my voice is choked again, and those damn tears are streaming down my cheeks. "I think he's dying."

"What makes you think that?"

"He has these headaches. His speech becomes slurred. He's forgetful. His coordination is going. And today, I think he may have had a slight seizure. He doesn't have a history of those things. He's on this vacation, driving across the country. Derek, his friend, says he's just stressed, but I know it's something more, Dad. I-I need your help. I can't lose him. I love him."

"Where are you? I can see him early next week. I'll have Janice move some appointments around," he's gruff, rushed. He's all business now. This is a good thing.

I breathe out in relief. My dad is a busy man. For him to do this, it warms my heart, making me think he might not hate me so much.

"We're in Arizona right now. He has this crazy idea that he wants to go whitewater rafting. I don't know if he's healthy enough for it." I fidget with the hem of my shirt while I talk.

"Get him here. I'll take a look at him. Tell him to get in touch with his doctor and have his records forwarded to me. I want them on my desk before he gets here. Understand?"

"Yes." I nod gratefully, even though he can't see me. "What do you think it is?"

"I can't say without a proper exam and records. What do *you* think it is?"

His question slams into me, reminding me of a game we played when I was growing up. He'd give me a list of symptoms, and I'd guess the illness. Seems weird, but it was one of my favorite things in the world to do.

"I-I think it's MS or-or a brain tumor. A cancer of some sort. Maybe new onset of grand mal seizures, but that's a strange thing to happen at his age. If they aren't from cancer, then idiopathic, perhaps... No head trauma as of late. It just doesn't make sense." I tick off the possibilities, wishing I'd gone to medical school longer.

"I think you're on the right track. Let's just hope not."

I sink down onto one of the camping chairs and run my fingers through my hair, thinking about all the things Carter has said to me.

"Dad?"

"Yes?"

"I-I'm sorry for disappointing you. I know I'm not like Ethan and Naomi," I say, speaking of my older brother and younger sister. "But if you can fix this, I swear I'll do anything you ask me to do. I'll go back to college and finish my medical degree—"

"Teddy," he sighs. "I'm not disappointed in you. I only ever wanted the best for you. And maybe my idea of the best didn't coincide with your idea. It doesn't mean your idea is wrong, though. So, let's not worry about it, OK? The only thing in the world that matters is that you're happy. Are you? Happy?"

"So much, Dad," I sniffle. "He's my whole world."

"Then we'll figure the rest out later. Let's get that young man feeling better first."

My heart soars at his words. While we spent the last few years not getting along, this feels like something good is about to happen.

"Thank you, Dad."

"You're welcome, Teddy."

"I'm so happy!" Mom's blubbering voice comes on the line.

"Mom?"

"I'm sorry. I was listening in. I know that's rude, but I've been so worried about you two. Your dad is right. Let's get your special someone fixed up. You guys can come to dinner after the appointment.

I'll make sure Ethan and Naomi are here. It'll be a reunion! My family together again! Oh, I'll make lasagna!"

I share a chuckle with my dad over her enthusiasm.

"I'll be there."

"I love you, sweetheart. You take care. We'll see you next week."

"Love you too, Mom," I say. Her sniffles of happiness fill my ear before the click of her hanging up leaves silence.

"Teddy, keep a log of everything. Bring it to me at his appointment. OK?"

"I will."

"I wish I could talk longer, but I'm working on this breakthrough experimental surgery. We just got the paperwork in from a patient who I think will be an excellent candidate, and I need to finish reviewing his charts."

"I understand, Dad. I'll call you when we get to the city."

"I look forward to it."

I smile. "Night, Dad."

"Night, Teddy."

LATER, I CURL UP NEXT TO CARTER. HE'S BEEN OUT FOR HOURS NOW, and it's starting to worry me.

"Why are you crying, Teddy Bear?" Carter's soft voice pulls me out of a fit of silent tears. He reaches out with shaking fingers and brushes my tears away.

"I'm worried about you—"

"No, baby, no. No worries. I'm f-fine. I'm here."

"You're not fine, Carter. I know you're not."

He presses a tender kiss to my lips to silence me. "I missed you," he says, his lips tickling against mine.

I cradle his face in my hand, the rough two-day stubble scratchy on my palm.

"My dad wants to help you."

"You talked to your family?" His lips quirk up into a small smile.

196

"I did. My dad says he'll see you early next week if we can get there. Please, Carter. *Please* agree to see him. My dad is one of the best doctors in the world. I know he can help you—"

"Is that what you want, Teddy Bear?" His eyes sweep over me in our dimly lit tent. "You want me to meet your parents, so you arranged for me to have an appointment with your dad?"

I know he's teasing me, but I'm too worked up.

"No, Carter, I want you to be OK. I'm so worried about you. Please, I'm begging you to see my dad. If you won't tell me what's wrong, tell *him*. My dad will fix you—"

"Sweetheart, I love you so fucking much," he says fiercely, his brown eyes shimmering. "The last thing I want to do is hurt you. I've thought about my issues for a long time. In fact, my own doctor is recommending me to someone for an experimental treatment. I told him no."

"No, Carter," I sob, my chest tight. "No, please! Tell him you'll see whoever it is! You can send everything to my dad too. Just, please—"

"Shh, baby."

He places his warm fingers to my lips. I can feel the slight trembling in them, and my heart breaks just a little more.

"I told him no. But my love for you knows no limits. And truth be told, I'd do anything for you, even die. I'll call my doctor tomorrow and tell him yes. I'll also have him send everything to your father's office, but only after I speak to the doctor he wants me to see. OK?"

I nod vigorously, relief flooding through me. "Thank you."

"I'll tell you everything soon. I'll meet with the other doctor first, though, OK?"

"OK," I say, knowing it's probably the best I'm going to get, but it's better than nothing. We're quiet for a moment, holding one another, before Carter speaks again.

"What about your music? I set Luke up. I can do that for you."

"Not yet. My music will still be here. I want to make sure you're fine first. Besides, I want to make it on my own. It was never about the money or being famous for me. I just love singing. It makes me feel alive. Even if I'm bussing tables and playing music in the park, I'll still be happy."

"Oh, my incredible, stubborn girl." Carter chuckles, kissing the tip of my nose. "What am I going to do with you?"

"Love me and never leave me," I whisper.

A tiny, sad smile flits across his handsome face.

"I'll love you forever and beyond, Teddy Bear. That much I can promise you."

THIRTY

CARTER

"*H*ello?" I answer my phone as it buzzes by my head, Teddy's naked body in my arms. I'm feeling better since my ordeal earlier. Almost as if it never happened. In fact, I wouldn't know it happened if my damn body wasn't so sore. Other than feeling like I hit the gym hard, I feel *almost* normal.

"Hey, Carter! It's Luke!"

"How are you?" I grin.

"Incredible. My song is getting some airtime, and it's in the Billboard Top 100."

"That's fucking awesome. I knew you could do it."

"Ah, well, it wouldn't have happened without you. I just wanted to thank you. I'll be finishing my record here in the next few weeks, and they're talking about touring. Can you believe that?"

"I sure can, man. I'm happy for-for y-you." I wince at the stutter.

"I'll have tickets for you to come see me in New York. I *know* I'll be heading there."

"I hope I'm still around. I'll definitely be there if I am."

Luke grows silent for a moment before talking again, "Is it getting worse?"

"Yeah," I say hoarsely.

"I'm sorry, Carter. Truly. You're a good man, and you don't deserve an ounce of pain."

My eyes burn at his words, and I blow out a shaky breath. "I have Derek, Teddy, and Molly here for me. I expect it won't be long now."

"Is there anything I can do?"

"Just follow your heart. Always, man. No matter what. Live your dreams and don't let anything ever hold you back."

"I can do that," he vows solemnly.

"Good," I rasp, wiping at my eyes and giving Teddy a tender squeeze with my other arm. She smiles in her sleep and snuggles closer before her lips part again, and her breathing deepens.

"How's Molly?"

"Good. Great. She looks out for us. But I think she misses you."

"I miss her too. How's Derek?"

"He's doing good. I think I'm wearing him out. He's not looking forward to our r-rafting trip coming up."

Luke lets out a laugh. I imagine he's sitting in his lavish hotel room with his guitar at his side and a mess of papers on his bed as he tries to write more music.

"And Teddy? Last I heard from you, you said you had a thing for her. How'd that turn out?"

I grin like a lunatic. My last exchange with Luke was a message that I was going to get the girl and his reply telling me he didn't doubt me one bit.

"I got the girl."

"Hell yeah, brother," Luke whoops. "Did you tell her about everything?"

The happiness subsides as I look down at her. She looks so beautiful lying in my arms, her milky white skin pressed against mine.

"I haven't told her yet. She knows I'm sick but not with what. I'm going to go see a doctor if he accepts me as his patient. It might prolong my life. Maybe cure it if the procedure they're trying doesn't kill me first."

"You'll never know if you don't try. I'll pray for you."

"Thanks, Luke," I murmur, choking on emotion. "I mean that. You're a good friend."

"You call me if you need anything. Doesn't matter when. I'm here for you."

"That means a lot to me. It really, truly does."

"You keep fighting the good fight, Carter. You're going to beat this thing. I know it."

"I hope you're right." The thought of failing makes my chest clench.

"I am. My knee has been killing me lately. Whenever that old football injury acts up and something bad is going on, I know whatever troubles are a'coming, everything will be all right."

"Your knee is psychic?" I muse.

"Ain't never been wrong yet. You'll see."

"Well, Luke Boyd, let's hope you and your psychic knee are right. If they aren't, make sure my gravestone says *Luke was wrong*."

Luke laughs loudly, causing me to grin.

For a moment, hope swells inside me at Luke's words. I have to believe it. The alternative is way too fucking painful.

"WHAT ARE YOU DOING AWAKE?" I ASK DEREK, SINKING DOWN INTO A seat around the coals of a fire that's long gone out.

"Nothing. Molly and I are looking at the stars," he answers, his eyes focusing on me. Molly whines and comes to sit beside me, her head on my lap. I give her a good scratching that has her eyes closing, a deep, contented breath leaving her.

"Are you feeling better?"

"Yeah. That was fucking brutal."

Derek gets to his feet and spears a hot dog then brings it over to me.

"Eat. Those coals should still be warm enough."

I take the speared hot dog from him and roast it over the fire for a few minutes before placing it in a bun. Derek hands me some toppings, and I place them on top. Then I take a bite. It's delicious. I'm suddenly starving.

"You need to tell Teddy. This is killing her," his voice is low and urgent.

I swallow my bite and look to the ground.

"I know."

"*When* are you going to do it? You said you were going to. You're getting worse, Carter."

"I'm calling Doctor Aarons tomorrow. I'm agreeing to see the doctor he heard about if he'll take me as a patient. I'm going to do the procedure. Teddy called her dad tonight, and he says he'll see me too. After I see where the hell I stand, I'll tell her. I just want to do it with maybe some good news to follow up the shitty news with."

Derek nods, looking satisfied. "Good. I'm glad you're going to tell her soon. She scares me sometimes. She threatened to bury me out here if I didn't tell her. I believe her, too! Girl is fierce."

"Yeah, she is," I say fondly. "Derek?"

"Yeah?"

"If none of this works out, will you take care of her? Make sure she's safe and happy."

"Carter—"

"No other words. Just your promise. I'm so fucking in love with that woman. I need to know that if shit goes below ground, she'll have people around her to take care of her. Promise me."

"I promise," Derek sighs. "But you better promise me that you'll fight as long and as hard as you can. No pussying out."

He holds his hand out to me, and I grin at him.

"Deal."

DIARY

Day one million ten (Or that's what it feels like.)

My body hurts. My muscles scream at me as something as simple as breathing begins to cause me tremendous pain. I'm tired. But I'm happy. The happiest I've ever been in my entire life. Funny, it took dying to learn how to live.

We're holding off on the rafting trip for another day. Two tops. I'm calling Phil later to tell him I'll do the procedure if chosen. I'm fucking scared.

Scared of death. Scared of living like this. Scared of telling Teddy that I'm dying. Scared of losing her forever.

It's too much to write today. I can't.

I really only came here to say one thing anyway.

Teddy Bear, if I'm gone when you wake up, I love you.

THIRTY-ONE

CARTER

*M*y lips work their way up her bare leg, scattering tender kisses on her warm skin. I'm feeling better and know that Teddy is stressed because of me. If there's one thing I need to do, it's make my girl feel good.

She lets out a soft moan as I reach the apex of her thighs. I place a tender kiss in the place I long to taste.

"Carter," she whispers, her voice filled with sleep.

Her fingers thread through my hair, nails raking against my scalp, making me want to full on purr beneath her loving touch.

"Teddy Bear," I growl before spreading her legs apart.

A sigh of contentment falls from her lips as I dip my tongue into her sweet center and feast on her. It doesn't take long for her back to arch. She tugs fiercely on my hair, pulling my face into her warm, wet core. She's a savage beauty so close to treating me to what I'm so desperate to see. To hear. To taste.

One final flick of my tongue sends her spiraling over the edge, her breathing shallow, her moans of pleasure making my hard cock ache with want.

I kiss my way up to her breasts, taking care to lick and suckle on each of them. She whimpers as I nibble, her body writhing beneath mine. My mouth finds hers, kissing her deeply. I swallow her moan as my cock slides against her slick folds.

"Are you sure?" she manages breathlessly as I tease her.

"I've never been so sure of anything before," I murmur against her lips as I push my throbbing cock into her.

Her breath hitches as I drill deeper in until I'm buried to the hilt, her tight heat making my dick ache even more with want. I move in and out, pushing the niggling ache in my head away. I close my eyes, my forehead against hers, as I make love to her.

It doesn't take my girl long to explode in a magnitude of gasps and moans around me, milking me for all I'm worth. I spiral with her, both of us breathless by the end.

I don't withdraw. Instead, I stay nestled within her warm confines. My own personal heaven.

"You're shaking," she whispers. "We shouldn't have—"

"Shh, baby," I say in a hoarse voice. "I *needed* this. I needed to feel you. I needed to be inside of you. You're my happy place."

"Oh, Carter," her voice trembles, a tear slipping from her eye. "I love you so much. I'm so worried about you."

I kiss her tears away. "I'm going to be OK. I promise." My words are fierce. "I'd do anything for you, Teddy Bear. And that includes being OK. Do you believe me?"

Her lips meet mine in a tender kiss, her hand cradling my face.

"Yes, I believe you."

That's all I need to hear. I don't know how I'm going to do it, but I *am* going to beat this thing. I have to. I can't be without her. Not now. Not ever. I said it before. This girl is my heaven. There's no need to die when I'm already where I'm supposed to be.

"PHIL, IT'S CARTER," I SAY INTO THE PHONE THE FOLLOWING MORNING.

"Carter, how are you feeling?" Doctor Aarons greets me, his voice painted with relief.

"Like hell," I admit, fidgeting with the drawstring on my basketball shorts. "Coordination is going to shit. I'm dizzy. Tired. Weak. My speech is slurred sometimes. I've probably lost twenty pounds. My head is killing me most of the time," I rattle off a list of my current ailments, leaving off my heartbreak and the anxiety over the possibility of not making it out of my current predicament alive.

"Unfortunately, those are things we expect," Phil says. "But I have good news. You've been accepted as a candidate for the procedure. The team has already secured a room in a hospital in the city for when you return. You'll meet with the lead doctor beforehand to sort out any concerns. It's sounds like they want to start immediately. The doctors on this team think you have a shot. That is, if you're willing to take it."

I bite my bottom lip and look at Teddy across the campsite. While still beautiful, she looks tired. Stricken. Sad. I hate that I'm putting her through it. I need to find an end to this shit. Either I die and leave her with some semblance of a future, or I kick this disease and spend my life with her. Even though I've promised myself that I'm going to beat this, I still made the plans with my attorneys to set her up, along with Derek. Even if I'm gone, Teddy will be taken care of. I've made sure of it.

"I'm going to do it," I say, tearing my gaze from Teddy as she gives Molly a good scratching. "When do I need to meet with the team?"

"I'm so glad to hear it," Phil exclaims, his voice filled with relief. "I'm going to email you the paperwork. All you need to do is give your digital signature, and we can get things rolling immediately. The lead doctor thinks we need to get on this sooner rather than later. And I gotta tell you, Carter. I'm with him."

I nod. "I understand. Did h-he say the l-l-likelihood of success?" I grind my teeth at the pain in my head and the stutter.

"Well," Phil sighs. "It's experimental, Carter. You understand that. It's not a one hundred percent know-all win."

"I know," I murmur. "I just want to know if I should be saying my last goodbyes anytime soon."

"That's up to you, Son. I think at this point, it might not hurt," Phil's voice is gentle, but I get it.

There are no guarantees. I might be dead this time next week. I peek at Teddy again. She's smiling at Derek as he tries to juggle some jumbo marshmallows.

"I have to try. Even if it can't save me, it might save someone else. It'll be my magnum opus."

"For what it's worth, I think you have a fair shot. If nothing else, it could buy you some time if—"

"If it doesn't kill me first. I get it. It's fucking scary, but I get it. And I'm all in. Send the paperwork over."

"I'm doing it as we speak," Phil confirms. The tippy-type of his computer keyboard fills the background. He pauses. "Carter?"

"Yes?"

"What made you change your mind?"

I chuckle softly and lock eyes on Teddy who gives me a sweet smile which warms every facet of my being.

"I'm in love. I want to get married."

Phil is silent for a moment before answering, his voice shaking, "Then let's get to work, shall we?"

"Let's fucking do it."

THIRTY-TWO

TEDDY

"We don't need to do this, Carter," I say as Carter brushes his soft lips against mine. His body shakes, his eyes unfocused as we break apart. Even with the extra few days of rest he looks rough. "Let's just get you home. You can see your new doctor."

Knowing he has it set up has given me a few moments of relief. The way he's looking today though has my heart in a vice. He's pale and quivering with dark circles under his brown eyes.

"We came here to raft, baby doll. And we aren't leaving until I conquer that water." He gives me a sad, sweet, tired smile. If there's one thing I'm learning about Carter George, it's that he's stubborn as hell.

"Stop w-worrying, sweetheart. I've already promised Derek that the moment my feet touch solid ground, we'll head back to New York. Besides, I can fly back if I need to. No worries. Promise."

"OK," I pout with a sigh.

He grins, the dullness in his eyes fading away. My heart flutters. *God, this man…*

"You ready?" Derek shouts. "Our ride is here to take us down to the launch site."

I reluctantly pull away from Carter and grab the last of our bags. Carter snatches them from me before I can protest and loads them into the Beastmaster.

I give Molly a kiss on her head as we depart. Carter, the sweetheart that he is, looked up dog sitters and managed to find someone on short notice to come sit in the air-conditioned Beastmaster with Molly while we're gone for a few hours. Waving goodbye to Greta, the college-aged dog sitter, we climb into the waiting SUV, Carter and Derek sandwiching me in the backseat.

"Are you excited?" Derek asks me was we bump along the road to the launch site.

I cast a glance at Carter who seems even paler than before.

"No. I just want this over with. I'm worried."

Carter squeezes my hand and gives me a tired smile. "Don't worry. Everything is OK. I'm just a little tired. That's all."

Derek catches my eyes. Our eyes mirror one another's. We're both worried. Carter has never looked like this before.

The rest of the ride is silent. When we arrive at the launch site, we're greeted by a well-built guy around my age.

"I'm Bo. I'll be the guide on your adventure today," he introduces himself and shakes each of our hands.

"I'm Carter. This here is Derek, and this beauty is Teddy."

Bo gives us a smile before launching into the dos and don'ts of boating safety. Carter becomes paler as the minutes pass by, his body trembling.

"Carter, we should wait—"

"I don't have time to w-wait," he says, his voice a low hiss.

He's never spoken to me like that before, and I flinch away from him, his words creating a whirlwind of fear in my guts.

"Baby, I'm s-sorry," Carter says, reaching for my hand and clutching it. "I just really n-need to do this. Please. M-my headaches are getting worse. I may be laid up for a while. With work and all after this, I don't know when I'll get back here."

He's lying. I *know* he is. This isn't about work and stress. There's so much more he isn't telling me. I know arguing with his stubborn ass won't change anything, so I let it go. *Again.* Getting him to my dad can't happen quickly enough.

"Fine. But if you get sick on this, I'm going to be so mad at you," I huff.

His eyes soften as he leans in and plants a tender kiss on my lips.

Before he can say anything, Bo is directing us to get into the raft. We do so quickly. Carter stumbles. Derek catches him before he falls.

"You OK?" Bo asks, looking from Carter to me. "You look sick. No offense, but we haven't even started."

"Just had a late night," Carter mumbles, situating himself in the raft. He gives me a tired smile and pats the spot next to him. I sit in it, immediately reaching out to clasp his hand. He takes it and gives it a trembling squeeze. Within the half-hour, we're settled into the raft and ready to begin our journey from the western edge of the canyon into Hualapai tribal lands.

"The river is faster than I thought it was going to be," Derek shouts.

I nod, my stomach twisting into tighter knots. Carter is smiling, laughter bubbling from his lips.

We quickly get wet, rounding the first bend where the winds whip the water. We glide over smooth rock, dipping and swaying with the swirling eddies, first left then right in semi-circles. Bo keeps a watchful eye on the river and our faces, giving us maximum adventure.

"Holy shit." Derek bursts out laughing, reaching over and gripping the rope railing of the soft cataraft. "Now, *that's* exactly what I expected."

"Well good, since we've got nine more miles of it until we hit Lake Mead," I holler out over the rushing torrent of the river, my heart pounding in my chest from that initial rush.

I'm not sure what I'm more worried about at this point—this damn wild ride or the fact that Carter's hand is shaking in my grasp.

Cold water continually splashes and drenches us as Bo maneuvers us through the harrowing turns.

"Are you all ready?" Bo yells out. We all look up, but before I can ask, he points to a small waterfall we're about to go over.

And down we go. Sideways.

"Holy shit!" we all scream, the momentum lifting us from our seats.

Bo revs the engine on impact and uses an oar to push against a rock, forcing us out of the cascading water. The water smooths out as we drift away from the faster currents.

"Whew," I say, taking my seat again after being bounced. I lean forward to catch my breath. I press my hand to my chest and look to check on Carter.

"Y-y-y-you all right, Ted-d-d-d-dy Bear-r-r-r?" his lips quiver and voice shakes from the ice-cold water soaking his clothes. At least that's what I tell myself it's from.

"Damnation, I'm fantastic. Jesus, what a ride. Now I know why my parents didn't take me rafting all those years ago. I don't think they would've survived that." I laugh, trying to lighten my mood. Carter shoots me a grin that actually reaches his eyes.

At mile five, we drift onto the shoreline for a brief hike, where we can snack and rest.

"My damn hands and feet are numb from that icy water," Carter says as we walk behind Bo.

I don't waste any time and rush up between him and Derek and hug him, rubbing my warmth into his fingers. "I'll warm you up, babe."

Carter winks at me, still playful, even though he looks like the walking dead.

"Yeah," Bo agrees. He pulls back on the rim of cloth around his ankles to show two pairs of socks. "In the early part of the season like this, the water temps and weather are unpredictable. It's definitely a shock when that first frigid splash hits your skin." He guides us to a ladder built into a hidden alcove in the rock. It leads to a summit of outcroppings where a small waterfall washes over purple and grey granite.

I gasp as I step off the ladder. "Good God, just look at that view."

Carter squeezes my hand and moves to wrap his arms around me from behind. We stare out into the wide expanse of the canyon and take in how tiny we are in this big world. He plants a sweet kiss on my cheek.

"It's almost as beautiful as you," he whispers in my ear.

Goosebumps erupt on my skin at his words. I snuggle into his arms and let out a deep breath, hoping to let my worries go for just a moment.

Derek pulls his camera from his bag and starts taking shots. "C'mon, you two. Let's get a selfie with the canyon behind us."

We get into position and smile like lunatics having the time of our lives. Bo takes a few pics for us before we finish our snack and head back down to the raft.

My socks are still sopping wet, and my shoes squish when I stomp them on the rocks.

"Damn, I hate wet feet," Carter grumbles as he joins me on a boulder jutting up from the shore as I tug my life vest back on. He sits and takes his socks off, wringing the water out of them. "Look, my feet are all pruny."

I giggle and turn my head away quickly as he tries to touch me with his toes. "No, please don't ask me to look at your feet. Feet are just ugly."

"Well, I know a certain someone who has the sexiest feet in the world. They're perfectly petite and beautifully arched. Mmmm, sensual as fuck, especially with that gold toe ring and gorgeous plum polish on them. I just might have to suck on those toes later."

I arch a high eyebrow and twist my lips in uncertainty. "I don't think so. That's kind of gross."

"You won't think it's so gross when I make you writhe with pleasure."

"You make me writhe with pleasure no matter what you do, but you will *not* stick my toes in your mouth." I grin at him, which only causes him to wink.

"We'll see about that," he says, reaching to swat my ass.

I dance out of his reach and head toward the boat, my ass swaying for him. His chuckle sounds off behind me, which only makes me wiggle my ass just a bit more for him. He seems to be feeling better, which is a relief.

At least, maybe I can breathe for a moment and enjoy the rest of this trip.

THIRTY-THREE

CARTER

I shove my socks and shoes on quickly in an effort to chase after her and her sexy swaying ass, but my fucking toes are tingling, and my hands are stiff. My head swoons with dizziness from the quick motion of getting to my feet, and I fall off the rock, landing hard on my hip. Not wanting her to know I've fallen, I push myself up to run but end up hobbling like an eighty-year-old man all the way to the raft.

Fucking pathetic.

I know she's worrying herself sick about me. I wish she wouldn't. It makes everything that much more painful.

Gingerly, I climb into the raft and sit beside her. She immediately winds her fingers through mine and smiles at me.

She's so beautiful I could cry. I'm luckier than I should be. If nothing else, if this procedure kills me later in the week, at least I can go out knowing I know what it means to love and be loved.

Who am I kidding? That only makes it worse.

"Ready?" Bo calls out as Derek settles in. He looks as sick as I feel.

"Ready," Derek says with a shaky smile.

God bless him for doing this for me. I give Bo a nod, my hand twitching in Teddy's. She slides closer to me.

"How are you feeling?"

"Baby, just enjoy this for me, OK? I'm fine." I'm a damn liar. I'm not fine. I'm dizzy. Sick. My vision is blurry, and there's this strange buzzing inside of me.

I say a silent prayer that the rafting trip ends quickly. Teddy was right. We shouldn't have gone.

We shove off the bank, and in moments, we're speeding across the water, our bodies bouncing all over. Teddy clings to me as much as I'm clinging to her. The buzzing grows louder. It's like there are a million angry bees inside my head. Cold water splashes me in the face. It doesn't do a bit of good. I blink rapidly, trying to clear my vision.

I let out a whimper as my body weakens, the twitching growing to uncontrollable levels.

"T-t-t-t-ed-d-dy," I choke out.

God no. Not like this! Not in the middle of no-fucking-where!

My gaze is locked on her as she smiles and whoops with excitement. If I'm going to die, I want her to be the last thing I see.

THIRTY-FOUR

TEDDY

"Hell fire and damnation," I holler to Carter. "Woo! That run was awesome!"

The river smooths out for a bit, and I shift so I can hug Carter. He's stiff as a board. "Carter. Carter? What's wrong?" I shake him, bile rising in my throat.

Carter's body begins to tremble, his eyes rolling back in his head. He slumps over, and I catch him, my screams for help echoing around us.

Derek turns and looks at us, his eyes wide with fright. "Bo, help!"

Bo springs into action, powering down the engine so we drift over the water. "Lie him down, slowly. I think he's having a seizure."

Derek and I flatten Carter out on the mesh floor of the cataraft. His body is cold. It violently shakes. Ugly white foam tinged with bright red blood seeps from his mouth.

"Pull a blanket out of that bin in the far corner," Bo instructs one of us. "And grab something soft to protect his head." Derek jumps up to do what he asks.

"Carter!" I beg over and over, tears streaming down my face. "Please, Carter, come back, baby."

Carter's breathing is labored, as his body continues to tremble.

217

Bo and Derek roll him onto his side to help him breathe easier.

"Is he an epileptic?" Bo asks.

"No," I choke out through my sobs. "He's not. Right, Derek?" I look to Derek for confirmation as we cover Carter's shuddering body.

"No, he's not an epileptic. He's got—" Derek swallows the words. "He's stressed out."

"Derek, please. Please. You have to tell us. He could die. Carter could die!"

Derek's eyes shoot to Carter, who's rasping on the floor of the raft, his head in my lap.

"Derek, I like you. I really do, but *please*, you have to tell us."

Derek's shoulders slump in defeat. "I swore I wouldn't. I can't tell you."

I let out a frustrated growl, ready to come across the raft and beat the answers from my friend.

"I need to know so I can treat him properly or call for help," Bo says, looking directly into Derek's eyes.

Derek hesitates, looking down at Carter. Carter's pale face makes him almost unrecognizable.

Derek's eyes volley back and forth from Bo to mine.

"Please, Derek. Please?" I beg once more. "This secret could kill him. I love him, Derek. *Please.*"

"He's got stage four IDH-wildtype glioblastomas," he blurts out.

I open and close my mouth several times in shock. I would've never guessed that. My heart sinks. It's worse than I thought. So much worse. Tears fall from my eyes and land on Carter's face. His brown eyes are fixed on my face, but he's not there. His breathing is labored and shallowed. An ugly sob rips through my body as I clutch Carter's trembling form.

"Huh? In layman's terms please," Bo says, feeling for Carter's pulse.

"He has brain cancer," I choke out at the same time Derek answers.

Bo is grim and looks at his watch. "When was the last time he gave any signs of awareness?"

"Uh, umm." I temple my fingers to my forehead trying to think.

I peer at Derek, and he shrugs his shoulders, not knowing. "He turned and smiled at me before we went down that last run," I say.

"OK, good to know." Bo glances around on both sides of the shoreline and finally sees a sign for Separation Canyon. He grabs the two-way radio, holding the button and speaks, "Mayday, Mayday, Mayday. This is Grandview Tours boat 9. Repeat. This is Grandview Tours boat 9. Again. This is Grandview Tours boat 9. Echo. Charlie. Echo. Niner. Zero. Niner. Mayday." He releases the button to listen.

"Go ahead, Grandview Tours Boat 9," a voice crackles back.

I dry the water from Carter's face. He's still shaking, just not as harshly.

"Carter, please. Come on, baby. Please," I whisper hoarsely, clinging to him.

Derek's warm hand is on my shoulder as he tries to offer me comfort. I can't believe this is happening.

Take me instead!

It's a silent plea that's on repeat in my head.

"This is Bo Ashwood requesting immediate assistance for a medical emergency."

"State your emergency," the voice requests.

"Patron is experiencing a grand mal seizure. Status is unresponsive. Current location is Separation Canyon. Request 9-1-1 call and a MediVac at Pearce Ferry. Time out is approximately seven minutes."

"Roger that. Grandview Tours boat 9. Please maintain the channel for updates." Bo powers up the engine, and I sit behind Carter, holding him close to me as we race over the water.

Tears are still running wild down my face. Let them fall. I don't care who sees them. This man—he's my whole world now. I know we've only been together a short time, but we've made it count. He's become such a deep part of who I want to be and the future I want for us. I can't lose him now. Ugly scenarios rush through my head.

I can't lose him. I only just found him! Please, God! Please!

Derek sits facing me and helps to support him as he continues to shake.

"Hey, he's going to be fine, Teddy. He's a fighter. Always has been.

I'm sorry I didn't tell you about his illness before. You did deserve to know. This past year has been rough. After his dad died, he lost sight of what he was fighting for. He's tired of being the asshole the New York City real estate market requires. I think in finding you, he's found his purpose again. He wants more."

I nod wordlessly, knowing if I open my mouth, only sobs of despair will come out. Instead, I press my hand to Carter's chest and feel the rise and fall of his shallow breathing. His eyes have drifted closed.

"Hang in there, Carter," I bend low and murmur into his ear, praying he can understand me. "Everything's going to be fine. We've-we've got help coming. I love you. I love you so fucking much."

Bo keeps peeking over his shoulder at us. I give him an unsteady thumbs up sign when I check Carter's pulse rate and find it faint but steady.

God, please bring him back to me. Give him the strength to fight this battle and all the other's coming his way. He's a good man with many faults. He's working hard to right the wrongs in his life, and just needs a second chance.

The raft takes a hard left as we round another bend and enter into the wide opening where the Colorado River runs into Lake Mead. We bounce over hard waves as Bo races to save Carter's life.

Derek fishes Carter's phone from his pocket and slides it into his.

Lights flash, and sirens blare across the rushing water at me from the distant shore. In the distance, the faint slapping of helicopter blades has my eyes searching the horizon, but I can't see anything in the bright light of day.

As we approach the landing, I can finally make out the medics waiting for us with a stretcher and bright orange medic totes. Bo revs down the motor as we approach, but we still come in a little too fast and splash a few onlookers waiting to see what the commotion is all about.

The medics rush in and load Carter onto a stretcher. It takes Derek's hand on mine to get me to release Carter from my hold. Terror courses through me as I watch them work on him. He's so pale and unresponsive. One of the medics talks to Bo, who gives him all the information we told him.

Derek and I move to the edge of the shore, giving them all the room they need. Bo joins us to ease our panic. I bury my face in Derek's shoulder as Carter begins seizing again, this time more violent.

Not good. Not good. Not good!

"Trust me. They know what they're doing. He's in good hands now," Bo shouts over the whir of helicopter blades booming through the air and the wind assaulting us as it lands. Derek's arms wrap around me tightly as my hair whips around us.

"They're taking him, Teddy. He's going to be OK," Derek repeats his words over and over in my ear, like saying them will make it true. Carter is far from OK. We both know it.

I chance a look as Carter is loaded into the waiting chopper, IVs running from his arms. He's no longer moving. They've intubated him. The ugly breathing tube protrudes from his slack mouth, causing a loud sob to rip from my lips. Derek squeezes me tighter as I weep against him.

"We're sorry to have caused all of this," Derek shouts, one arm still around me as he gestures with the other to the crowd of people, the flash of ambulance lights, and the commotion of the helicopter.

Bo shakes his head. "No one can predict this sort of thing. Just please let me know how he's doing."

I'm vaguely aware of Derek nodding. Everything seems so surreal. Fake. Like I'm walking in a cloud. This can't be happening.

One of the medics motions for us to join them.

"We will," Derek says.

"He's going to be OK," Bo promises. "We got help in time. I know it."

"We won't ever forget you," Derek assures him, giving him a handshake with his free hand. Bo's warm hand pats my back for a moment before Derek steers me to the ambulance.

"We need some information. Who can provide it?" one of the medics inquires. He's young. Maybe my age.

Derek proceeds to give them what they need for transport. The other medic joins us and takes the notes his partner has jotted down. He rushes over to the helicopter and hands off the paper to the crew.

I watch with teary eyes as the helicopter lifts off, taking everything I've ever longed for away from me.

"Come on, we'll drop you back to the launch site so you can get your vehicle," one of the medics offers.

THIRTY-FIVE

TEDDY

The impressions of my fingernails are in the palms of my hands. We've been sitting in the emergency room for hours, waiting to hear anything on Carter. Whenever I go to the desk to ask, I'm told the doctor will be out shortly.

"What's taking so long?" Derek growls, rubbing his hands over his tired face.

"I don't know," I murmur, my legs bouncing as I chew on a fingernail. I keep replaying the day in my head. His smile. His kiss. His face paling. His shaking. The blood from his mouth as he involuntarily bit his tongue and lip.

My eyes focus on the large red spot on my shorts. His blood. It's stained my clothing. It's still smeared on my thighs.

"Go clean up, Teddy," Derek's gentle voice pulls me out of my near fit of tears. "Wash yourself. I'll wait here for the doctor and will come get you if they come out."

I nod. He's right. I get to my feet on autopilot and make my way to the bathroom where I stare at myself in the mirror. My green eyes are dull, and my face is pale. There are dirty streaks on my cheeks from my tears. My hair has long since fallen out of its ponytail. I'm not even sure where I lost my rubber band. Or how.

Quickly, I wash my face and hands. Then I wipe the blood off my legs before running my fingers through my hair, fixing it the best I can. I still look like hell. I don't care. I need to get back to the waiting room.

I'm opening the bathroom door when I nearly collide with Derek.

"Teddy," his voice is choked. My heart plummets at the look on his face.

Please, God, no!

"Derek?" I whimper, reaching for him. He takes my hand in his.

"He's alive. He's alive. I'm sorry. The doctor said he's been intubated because he's having trouble breathing. He's had more seizures. They're going to keep him sedated."

I sag against Derek, sobbing.

"It's OK, Teddy. He's going to be OK."

"I'm scared, Derek." I weep into his shoulder.

"Me too. Me too."

◦◦◦

AFTER PROMISING DEREK I'M FINE ON MY OWN, HE LEAVES ME TO GO check on Molly, who's waiting in the RV in the parking lot.

A bit later, I'm staring off into space, trying to be patient.

"Mrs. George?" Doctor Barlett, Carter's assigned doctor, asks, shaking my hand. My heart lurches in my chest at being referred to as Carter's wife.

"N-no, I'm his girlfriend. Teddy. Call me Teddy."

"I'm sorry. Teddy, we have Carter sedated. We've been in touch with his primary care provider." Doctor Barlett drones on as he leads me to Carter's room. I'm barely listening. All I want is to get to him.

"It would appear that Carter had some very specific requests."

"What?" I mumble as we stop outside Carter's hospital room. I can hear the beeping and clicking of the monitors inside. Even the sound of the machine helping him breathe is loud enough for me to hear.

"Carter's doctor. . . a Doctor Aarons—" Doctor Barlett looks at the chart in his hands. "—has informed us that Carter is a candidate for a special procedure. It appears all the paperwork is in order."

"What paperwork?" I frown. Carter never told me any of this, so everything Doctor Barlett says is completely new to me.

"The paperwork Carter signed prior to his current situation. He's made you his power of attorney. You're in charge of his medical decisions. Doctor Aarons says that Carter agreed to the procedure, his signature is on file and everything is in order. The choice is yours, Teddy."

"I-what?" I squeak, looking from Carter's room to Dr. Bartlett.

"There's an experimental surgery to remove his brain tumors. Doctor Aarons says he's flying in to speak with you in person. For now, we have Carter sedated. We're going to let him rest tonight. If all goes well, we'll remove his breathing tube in the morning and see how he fares."

"H-how do you think he'll fare?"

"It's hard to say. He seized multiple times. He hasn't had one in a few hours, but that's probably due to the medication we have him on right now. We're going to lower it and observe. I'm hopeful we can get him well enough to pursue the surgery he needs."

I nod, my throat tight.

"How will he have the procedure if he's here?"

"He'll have to be flown to the medical center where it's being done. Doctor Aarons says he has all that information for you. For now, I suggest maybe try talking to Carter. Reassure him. If you need anything, just hit the red call button."

"Thank you," I say softly.

I'm overwhelmed. Carter trusts me enough to put me in charge of his life. I swallow hard and pull in a deep breath. He needs me. And I need him.

I enter the room to find him worse than I pictured. The ugly tube protrudes from his mouth. Wires connect him to a myriad of machines. He's pale and gaunt. My heart aches as I step to his side and take his hand in mine.

"C-carter," I whisper, pressing a gentle kiss to his pale cheek. "It's me. It's Teddy Bear. I'm here. I'm not leaving."

I settle in the chair next to his bed and kiss his hand.

"I'll be here when you wake up. I promise."

THIRTY-SIX

TEDDY

"*D*ad?" I say into my phone later that evening.

"Teddy? What's wrong?"

I burst into tears, the dam I've built crumbling around me. It takes me a moment to calm myself before I can speak. In a rush, I tell him what's happening.

"Carter George? *That's* who you're in love with?"

"I know. He's famous and all—"

"No, Teddy. Did you say you're his power of attorney?" Dad interrupts.

"Yes. But Dad, you're missing the point. He's sick. He had seizures—"

"I know who Carter George is. I already know his medical history."

I fall silent for a moment. "What?"

"I'm the doctor he was referred to for his surgery."

"You're the one doing the experimental surgery?" I choke out, my heart somersaulting in my chest.

"I am. He signed everything for the go-ahead a few days ago. After viewing all his records, I think he's an excellent candidate for the procedure. Teddy, why didn't you say you were seeing him?"

"I-I don't know," I whisper, feeling numb. "Do-do you think you can save him? Because it's bad, Dad."

"I won't lie to you. This is our first go at this. Aside from computer simulations, theories, and my own thoughts on the matter, it will be all new ground. The truth of the matter is, he might not wake up if things are worse than we thought once we get inside. The other side of that coin is if we're successful, we've bought him more time, probably even a lifetime. And we might buy others more time," his voice is soft. "Teddy, I *do* think Carter has a chance. Combine the surgery with the new drug, which is a combination drug and the odds go up. The meds are meant to shrink anything small that we may leave behind that's beyond our reach. Top that with the radiation therapy, he has an excellent shot at survival."

"But for how long?" I say, biting my lip.

"Years. Maybe his whole life. He might outlive you."

"But you don't know that for sure. He could also die on the operating table."

"He could," Dad says delicately. "Carter wanted this surgery. He wanted to try. Now that he's in no place to decide, it's up to you to make that decision for him. He gave you the responsibility because he knew you could handle it, and he trusts you. You probably know him better than anyone in the entire world."

I swallow a sob and nod. I feel like I'm judge and jury. If I say yes to the procedure, he could die. *Can I live with myself if that happens?*

"I already booked my ticket out there," Dad's voice hauls me back to the moment. "I'll bring a team with me so we can get him back here if you decide to do this. I daresay he's going to need another day before we can travel safely. But I'm going to need an answer soon, Teddy. I'm not telling you this because I'm trying to push you to help me try this new procedure. I'm doing it because I don't know how much longer Carter has left. Without this surgery, he will die. It's just a matter of when. With the surgery, he may have a chance."

"I-I need some time," I say, numbness taking over me.

"I understand. Just don't take too much. I'll need an answer by morning."

"OK," my voice is thick. "I'll call you in the morning."

"OK," it's Dad's turn to sound emotional, a strange thing since he's the strong, gruff type. "Be brave, Theodora. We're here if you need us. We love you."

"Thanks, Dad," I manage. "I love you guys too."

I hang up and stare down at Carter. His cheek is damp. I wipe the wetness from his cool, pale skin, my heart aching. A tear has slipped from his closed eyes.

"What do I do, Carter?" I whisper, my own tears squeezing out. I clutch his hand. "What do you want me to do?"

"I'll sit with him if you want to go to the BEASTMASTER and rest," Derek's soft voice calls out as my head lolls on the edge of Carter's mattress. My back is screaming at me. I've been hunched over his bed for hours.

"Get yourself a shower and some food," Derek continues. "I had a pizza delivered. Take a nap. You're exhausted. I'll make sure I get you if something changes."

"I can't leave him—"

"Teddy, Carter would want you to do these things. In fact, he'd steer you out of this room and make you. You know he would. So go. I've got this. I promise."

I rise to my feet and nod. He's right. Leaning down, I press a soft kiss to Carter's cool skin.

"I love you," I whisper, squeezing his hand. "I'll be back. I promise."

I let out a gasp of surprise when Carter lightly squeezes my hand. I look from him to Derek, wide-eyed.

"What's wrong?" Derek asks.

"He-he squeezed my hand," I say. "He can hear me!"

Derek smiles and looks to Carter. "Carter, you better wake your ass up in the morning. We need you, man."

Carter's hand twitches beneath mine, a slight squeeze before he stills. Tears well in my eyes.

"Baby, I'm going to leave you with Derek. I swear I'll be right back. Just please, don't...don't leave me." I kiss his forehead and back away, releasing his hand.

"What's wrong?" Derek asks as I look at him.

"I-I need to tell you something." I nod in the direction of the hall. Derek follows me out.

"What's up?"

"I-I'm Carter's power of attorney. I-I have to decide what to do."

"I know." Derek rakes his fingers through his hair and sighs. "He told me he was putting you in charge."

"That procedure? The one that could save or kill him? Remember me telling you about how good my dad is at his job?"

Derek nods.

"Well, I guess Carter's referral was to my dad. I just found out."

"Whoa," Derek murmurs. "That's nuts. Small world, huh?"

"Very," I mutter. "My dad thinks Carter is an excellent candidate for this. But there *are* risks."

"Carter would take those risks, Teddy. I've known him for a long time. If there's one thing I've learned over the years it's he doesn't back down from a challenge. This will be his biggest yet. If he signed those papers already, he was ready for it. He trusted you to finish what he started. He trusted both of us. I don't want to let him down. He's truly my best friend."

"I know," I choke out, wiping away my tears. "But he could die. In just a few days if this goes south, he'll be gone, Derek. I-I don't know how I'll live with myself if I say yes and that happens."

"Teddy," Derek says gently. "Carter is already a dead man. You won't be the one killing him. If things don't work out, it's the fucking disease. *Not* you. Do you understand?"

I nod painfully, my chest tight, my throat burning.

"Get some rest. Please."

"I will," I say as he pulls me in for a hug. "Just please, get me if—"

"I promise." Derek pulls away and gives me a sad smile. "Now go."

~

I SINK ONTO THE BED I'VE SHARED WITH CARTER THE PAST FEW WEEKS, my heart heavy. I'm not sure how I'm supposed to decide the fate of the man I love. Rolling over, I slide my hand beneath his pillow and frown. I shift the pillow and pull out a worn book.

"What's this?" I mutter, flipping it open and peering at the first page, taking in the beautiful handwriting.

I don't know why the hell I thought I'd start a diary. No. Let's call it a travel log. I guess maybe I thought it might help sort my thoughts. Perhaps after I'm gone someone can auction it off and make a few dollars. The great Carter George's innermost thoughts before his death. Yeah, I can see it becoming a bestseller now.

I snap the book closed and bite my bottom lip. This is Carter's diary. His innermost thoughts and feelings. Guilt washes over me as I finger the gold-edged pages. Carter is dying. There's no denying it. And he never told me anything about his illness or what he really wanted, but he left me in charge. Hauling in a deep breath, I open the book again.

It's better to ask for forgiveness than permission. Besides, I'm desperate for an answer to figuring out what the hell I should do. Maybe Carter's diary has the answers. I repeat it to myself before my eyes roam over the pages, taking in each and every beautiful word he penned.

By the end of it, I'm weeping. Carter loves me. Truly, deeply, this man loves me. He wants to live. He's just as afraid as I am. I can't bear losing him. God, I can't. So that's why when I pick up the phone, I say the words that will either save him or be the final nail in his coffin.

"Dad? Bring the team. We're doing the surgery."

THIRTY-SEVEN

TEDDY

"*How* long will it take?" I ask Dad as he stands before me in his blue scrubs. Derek and Phil are standing next to me. Carter was flown back to the east coast two days later. He's still on the ventilator, and they kept him in a medically induced coma. He has been here longer because it took us an extra day to get a flight back. I'm antsy because I haven't seen him.

"I can't say for certain," Dad says in a gruff voice. "It depends on what we encounter when we get inside. I'm banking on a minimum of twelve hours, though. That is, if he can make it."

The blood leaves my face, and I sag against Derek who's quick to wrap his arms around me.

"Don't tell me that," my voice is choked as I realize exactly what Dad is talking about. *Dead*. Carter could be dead in only a few hours.

"He's a fighter, Teddy. I wasn't lying when I said I think we have a shot at this."

I nod, swallowing thickly. "Can I see him?"

"Of course." Dad pats my shoulder. "I need to go over a few things with Doctor Aarons. Go see him before he's taken in."

"Come on," Derek urges, steering me forward. I feel as if I'm floating. Like I'm in a dream. No, nightmare. I can't believe this is happening.

"You go first," I whisper as we stop in front of Carter's door. "I-I need a minute."

"Are you sure?" Derek frowns at me, worry etched onto his face. I nod, unable to speak.

He gives my hand a squeeze before pushing Carter's door open and disappearing inside. I sink down onto the chair next to Carter's room, my head in my hands.

Please God. Please, let him make it. Please don't take him from me. I'll do anything!

It's a silent plea. One I've been repeating for days now.

Time seems to stand still yet passes far too quickly. Before I know it, Derek is coming out, his eyes moist.

"Your turn."

"Is it bad?" I rise to my feet, wringing my hands. I swear I've been doing it so much lately the skin is starting to peel off.

"He's sick, Teddy." Derek wipes at his eyes. "Those machines in there are helping him. Don't think about them as bad."

I tip my head, my throat tight. Derek gives me a reassuring hug as I step forward.

"I'll be right here if you need me."

I nod again, my heart thrashing around in my chest as I step through the door. My breath catches in my chest as I take in the scene. Carter is in bed with so many wires and tubes connected to him. A machine helps him breathe. The even beeping of the monitor and the *whoosh, whoosh* of the ventilator is all there is. Plus, the roar of my blood in my ears as the situation hits home.

This may be the last time I ever see him.

I repeat my prayer again as I take unsteady steps toward Carter's bed.

"Hey, baby," my voice cracks as I take his cool hand in mine. I place a kiss on his forehead, brushing his dark hair aside. "I miss you, Carter."

I stare down at him for a moment, tears trickling down my cheeks. He looks ashen. Pale. Gaunt. *Gone.*

Finally, I realize I'm sagging against the mattress, so I sit in the chair beside his bed, pushing the ugly thoughts out of my head.

"You're the best thing that's ever happened to me," I whisper, his hand still in mine. "I'm so in love with you. I-I can't do this without you. I never knew what I was missing before, but I know now it was you. It was always you, Carter. Please...come back to me. *Don't go.*"

A soft sob leaves me, the ache in my chest tearing me apart. My body shakes with my tears as I cling to his hand.

I choke on a sob as his hand twitches beneath mine. Then the slightest tender squeeze.

"Carter?" I manage to rasp out.

I'm on my feet, peering down at him, my tears splashing onto the ugly polka dot hospital gown he's in. The beeping of the monitors increases. "Can you hear me?"

His hand twitches beneath mine. It's good enough. He's still with me. Hope soars inside of me, melting away the darkness of the past few days.

"I'll wait for you," I murmur, pressing another kiss to his forehead before moving to whisper in his ear. "I'll wait forever."

THIRTY-EIGHT

TEDDY

"Your father assures me everything looks promising," Phil, Carter's doctor, says as we sit in the waiting room. Derek returns with three cups of coffee and doles them out to us.

"Carter's a fighter. He's going to make it," Derek says firmly, giving me a small smile.

I nod miserably. Despite their words and my feelings of hope from earlier, I can't shake my worry. We're approaching the sixth hour of surgery. My father has sent someone out every hour to keep us informed. So far, Carter is holding his own.

My attention is drawn to a slim, older woman dressed in a blue pantsuit. Her dark hair has streaks of gray in it and is tied in an elegant bun on her head. She peers at us for a moment before seeming to come to a decision.

Phil looks up as she approaches, recognition in his eyes.

"Laura," he greets her, getting to his feet. "It's been a long time."

"Phil," she returns, a sad smile on her lips. "We need to stop meeting like this."

Phil gives a soft chuckle before he turns to us. "This is Laura George, Carter's mother."

I widen my eyes as I take her in. The woman looks like she could command an entire nation with just the point of a finger.

"Laura, this is Derek, Carter's friend and Teddy, Carter's girlfriend."

"I've heard about you," Laura says as I stand. I'm afraid she's going to be one of those overbearing mothers who can disarm me with a single look. Instead, she leans in and gives me a gentle squeeze. "You're as beautiful as he said you were."

I'm surprised at the compliment and feel the heat rush to my cheeks.

"Thank you," I manage. "Carter means the world to me."

She nods, a sad smile on her lips. "Me too, although I'm sure he's already told you our history."

It's an awkward statement which leaves me speechless. If she notices, she doesn't seem to mind because she turns to hug Derek before taking the seat Phil has offered her.

"How long has he been under?"

"We're going on seven hours now," Phil says. She pales.

Phil rushes on. "But it's looking good. We received an update only minutes ago. They've removed two tumors successfully, which was a lot faster than we thought they'd be."

She nods, and Derek offers to get her a coffee. She agrees, and he leaves. Her gaze focuses on me again.

"How are you holding up, dear?"

"Barely," I say, my voice shaking. She pats my knee and gives me an encouraging smile.

"Carter would be proud of you. I'm sure he's going to tell you the moment he wakes up."

I breathe out and give her a smile. I appreciate that she's trying to be kind. We all need the encouragement in that moment.

"TEDDY, YOU SHOULD SLEEP," DEREK MURMURS IN MY EAR. I'VE BEEN sitting in the same spot for hours. Phil and Laura left long ago to rest.

"They haven't been out with an update in hours," I whisper, tearing my eyes away from the picture of a bowl of fruit I've been staring at for the past few hours. "He's been in surgery for fourteen hours, Derek. Something's wrong. Why haven't they come out to give us an update?"

"I don't know." Derek rubs his eyes. "But no news is good news, Teddy."

I focus my gaze back on the bowl of fruit. The hours have been long. After speaking to my mom on the phone and her consoling me for an hour, I paced the waiting room floor before focusing my attention on the fruit picture.

"Teddy, I got you a room at the hotel down the block. I even made sure you had clothes and everything waiting for you there," Derek says gently.

I tear my gaze away from the picture and look at Derek. "What?"

"Carter would kick my ass if I didn't make sure you were taken care of. And I know damn well he'd be pissed knowing that you're here hungry and exhausted. I can call you when he's out of surgery."

"No." I shake my head. "I'll wait until he's out. Once my dad gives the all clear, I'll go to the hotel."

Derek lets out a soft sigh and chuckle. "You're just like him. So damn stubborn."

I give him a sad smile. "Birds of a feather."

Derek is about to reply, but my dad comes into the waiting room. I'm on my feet and rushing to him.

"How is he?" I ask. Dad looks exhausted. His eyes are heavy, but he gives me a smile.

"It went well. I'm sorry I didn't update. We got in there, and I didn't want to stop the progress we were making."

"What happened?" I beg.

My dad grins at us. "We got all the tumors."

"*All* of them?" Derek croaks out, his eyes mirroring the disbelief in my own.

"All of them." Dad's grin widens. "He'll need a round of chemo alongside the drug we're experimenting with, but as long as it takes, I don't foresee too many issues."

"He's going to live?" Tears stream down my cheeks. My dad squeezes my hand and leads to me to sit down.

"Teddy, while the surgery was successful, Carter *will* have a lot to overcome. We're going to keep him in a medically induced coma so he can heal. This is going to be a long journey for both of you. His speech and sight might be affected, but we're hoping we can correct that as we do therapy and the medicines take hold. For now, things look promising."

"But they aren't a hundred percent," I whisper.

"Sweetheart, you know nothing in this world is. I suggest getting some rest. We all have a long road ahead of us, and Carter will need you to be rested and healthy."

"I want to see him. I want to stay with him tonight."

Dad sighs and glances at Derek.

"She's ridiculously stubborn. I've been trying to get her to go to the hotel, and she won't."

Dad chuckles. "That sounds like my girl." He gives me an affectionate squeeze. "You can stay with him tonight. These next few days are crucial to his recovery. Perhaps hearing your voice will spur him on. But tomorrow night you go to the hotel and rest in a real bed and get yourself a good meal. Got it?"

"Promise," I say, getting to my feet. "Please take me to him."

"Follow me."

THIRTY-NINE

TEDDY

I strum my fingers across the strings of my guitar and peek up at Carter. He's been in a coma for two weeks now. His chocolate eyes are still hiding from me, but the half smirk, half smile on his face lets me know he hears me singing to him.

Don't wait for me on the other side
I'm here right now
Just open your eyes
For a girl who never believed in fairy tales
You've rescued me
Oh, I've been waiting for you
To come set me free

The first Independence Day fireworks explode over the Hudson River. Their boom rattles the glass, making me jump. I set my guitar down and close my journal, tucking my pen inside. I pull the chain to roll back the blinds for Carter to have a look. Maybe the lure of bursting colors will stir him to open his eyes. I'd give anything to see his eyes again.

I push the sleeping recliner in place and angle it toward the window next to Carter's bed. Settling down into it as comfortably as possible, I take Carter's hand in mine and watch the colors erupt in the night sky.

Our first July 4th together. A sigh of relief escapes my lips as I take solace in knowing we've made it this far. He's going to be fine. If only he'd wake up. The tubes that were helping him breathe are gone. The wires and cords connecting him to life have dwindled. Carter is holding his own.

I take out my phone and snap a few pics of the brilliant view from the fifteenth floor of St. Anne's Medical Center. Then I turn the camera around to get a selfie of us together with the fireworks.

The night nurse, Chantelle, pushes her cart into the room. Quickly, I put my phone away. Must be time for vitals and medicine again.

"Oh, perfect! I timed it just right," she says, pointing to the fireworks painting the sky outside the window and winking at me. She scans Carter's wristband and proceeds to wave her magic temperature wand across Carter's forehead.

"Yes, perfect timing. They just started. Too bad you're not out there enjoying the fun."

"Girl, no. That's not fun at all. The crowds, the traffic, and all those rude people. I'm glad I'm in here where it's quiet." She adjusts Carter's blankets. "How's our patient doing tonight?"

"He's good tonight—calmer. Last week was heartbreaking to watch him struggle."

"Well, he's got his angel singing to him." She points to my guitar leaning against the window ledge. "I swear you've calmed half the patients down on this floor. If no one's told you before, you should be a singer. You've got the pipes for it." The beeping on Carter's heart monitor rises slightly for a few seconds then normalizes. "See? Even Mr. Carter agrees with me."

"Well, if Mr. Carter agrees with you, then he should wake up and tell me himself," I huff my idle threat and glare at him.

We both watch his face for a hard minute, but his eyelids only flutter, that same half-smirk, half-smile still gracing his beautiful face. My shoulders sag in defeat.

She laughs at the look on his face. "Girl, he's an alpha male. Idle threats won't scare him. Those virile eyes will open when he's good and ready. Now let's get some medicine in him, so he can come back to you sooner." She scans his ID bracelet again and pushes the medicine into his IV. "He's healing from the inside out. Give him time; he'll come back when he's ready." She winks at me and pushes her cart back through the door, leaving us alone.

Spending this time alone while he recovers—well, I've thought about every word we've ever spoken to each other...some in anger, some in friendship, but mostly in love, and he's right. I play life safe, staying in the middle lane, letting others be in charge of my dreams so I can blame them when things don't work out. I've been present but not accountable. Medical school and singing in Nashville were both my fault, and yet, I put all the blame and my anger on Dad and Richie.

What's the point of having a dream if I'm not going to own it and pursue it? My feeble attempts at my goals were simply rebellions by a young mind who didn't know what she wanted.

Well, I've grown up since leaving Nashville.

A break from music and our adventures have helped me kickstart my own passion again.

Meeting Carter is the best thing that's ever happened to me. It's fate, as cliché as that sounds. He says it's karma that led him to me.

Carter inspires me to write and sing again. He's done nothing but encourage and support me, pushing me to believe in myself.

I'm going to show him I can move into the fast lane, stepping outside my comfort zone and insecurities to be in control of my own destiny.

I open the book of notes I've been collecting from my internet research. There are clubs here in the city with open-mic nights. I *know* I can do this. I made a start once and will use my lessons learned to do things differently. I jot down a quick to-do for tomorrow and shove it back into my bag.

The barrage of the fireworks finale has started. I'll give the crowd some time to die down before making my way to the hotel for a shower and an attempt at a good night's rest. Laura asked me why I wasn't staying in Carter's penthouse. The truth is, I can't bear being in his space. I was there last week, leaving some of his clothes. While the views of Fifth Avenue and Central Park are gorgeous, his home doesn't *feel* like a home. It's cold and sterile with no signs of family or personal mementos. There's nothing there which gives me a glimpse into Carter's life, unless I count the emptiness. It's such a stark contrast to the warm and laughing man I've come to love in his black RV, the Beastmaster, as he and Derek lovingly call it. I'd give anything to be back in it with him now. Carter's dark stallion.

When I finally do stay at Carter's place, I want us to be together. We'll sleep in his bed. We'll make love. He'll whisper he loves me, and I'll giggle as he grins his boyish smirk at me. I want to wake in the morning next to him. Being there without him makes me feel like half of me is missing. Even though Derek offered me the keys to Carter's home after I complained about my noisy neighbors in the hotel, I still can't do it. It's not my place without him.

"You need to wake up soon, my love. I miss you so much," I say, my voice cracking halfway through. I swipe at a tear which threatens to roll down my cheek. *Be strong one more day, Teddy. He'll wake up tomorrow. I know it.*

Missing the man I love while he sleeps is heart-wrenching. He rescued me. He's my knight in shining armor. My muse. He's awakened the music I thought was dead.

He's the inspiration behind the song I'm working on. One random lyric popped into my head down in the cafeteria a few days ago. Then the floodgates burst open. Words rushed forth so fast, I had to write them on brown, recyclable napkins with a pen I borrowed from a nurse eating next to me.

The words feel right, and for once, I'm proud of it. Like giddy, ecstatic, uninhibited dancing kind of proud. I've been tweaking the melody and pace, and now it's perfect.

I hope Carter likes the song I wrote about him. About us.

I tuck my guitar back in its case and prop it against its designated resting place for the last few weeks. If he wakes when I'm not here, he'll see it and know I'm coming back soon. My lips touch his, and I'm happy to feel their warmth.

I whisper against them, "Tomorrow. Please wake up tomorrow. For me, baby." And stroke his head, the rough stubble from his surgery shave beneath my fingers, before dimming the lights and making my way to the elevator.

~

"TEDDY," THE NURSE SAYS QUIETLY AS SHE WHEELS IN HER CART. "I'M sorry to disturb you, but it's time to give Carter a bath. He's supposed to be prepped and ready before he goes for some additional imaging tests this morning. Could you please wait in the lounge? It shouldn't take any more than thirty minutes."

"Sure, no problem." I grab my guitar and bag, hauling my stuff down to the blue room at the end of the long hallway. It seems to be the least used waiting room on the floor and the furthest from the patient rooms. I sit in silence for a few minutes, wishing I hadn't already made my phone calls to the clubs or caught up on reading emails in the solitude of my hotel room.

I pick up my guitar and strum a few lines of "Contact High" by Caitlyn Smith and soon become lost in the vibe of the song, forgetting where I'm at. When I pluck the last notes, I sling my messy hair back over my shoulders and look up to see a younger man sitting on the far side of the room.

He claps and whistles, enjoying my free concert. "What else do you have in your set? I'd love to hear some more."

"Well, what are you in the mood for? I mostly play country, but I know lots of songs."

"You've got a bluesy vibe to your voice. The grit is so raw. I'd like to hear anything you'd like to sing."

"Thank you," I say softly as I pluck the opening chords to "I'm the Only One" by Melissa Etheridge.

A smile spreads from ear to ear as I sing, and he leans against the hard back of his chair while his toe taps to the acoustic beat. Halfway through, I speed up the chorus and go right into "Black Horse and A Cherry Tree" by KT Tunstall. He checks his watch a few times and starts to shift in his seat, so I end the concert early.

He stands and claps again when I stop the vibration of the strings with my hands. "Are you the lady who's been singing at night in Room 12?"

"Yes," I say with hesitation. I unfasten my guitar strap and let it fall to my lap. "I'm so sorry if I disturbed you or who you were visiting."

"No, please don't apologize. On the contrary, my mother enjoys your voice. It comes through the vents and she rests more soundly after you're done. So, thank you for that." His warm smile eases my mind.

"I hope she's recovering and going home soon."

"She is recovering, but..." He looks away from me for a moment and clears his throat before continuing, "She'll be moved to a rehabilitation facility first, then hopefully going home." The red rims of his eyes accentuate the hopelessness in them.

"I wish her well and a speedy recovery then." I know that feeling of hopelessness. It's a mountain you never think you're going to reach the summit of, but kind words from everyone pulling for Carter always help me make it through the day. Hopefully, I can pay it forward with my well wishes.

"I have to go. She should be back from physical therapy, and I don't want to miss a moment of our time together." He hands me a business card. "If you ever need someone like me, give me a call."

"Certainly," I reply, taking it from him. "Hey, I'll uh... stop by her room for a solo concert in the next few days. Anything to make her rest better and get home quicker." I offer up a wide smile.

"That'd be great. I appreciate it." He leaves without a word, and I tuck the card into the back pocket of my jeans without bothering to look at it.

My throat is dry from singing, so I pack up everything and make my way to the cafeteria for a drink before heading back to Carter.

My phone rings inside my bag as I step off the elevator. I dig inside and finally find it on the very bottom. I don't recognize the number, but I slide the arrow up. "Hello?"

"Hello. This is Karen, the entertainment manager at The Bitter End. I got your message."

"Thanks for calling me back. I really appreciate it."

"Open mic nights are on Tuesday by lottery. If you want to show up at 7:30 PM and get a number, then you can perform according to your ticket number. We only give out forty numbers. If they're gone when you arrive, you can't perform. If you get a number, you get five minutes on stage to do whatever you like. If the crowd likes you, then you might get an invitation to perform on Friday nights. Just see the bartender when you arrive at 7:30 for a number. OK?"

"OK."

"Any questions?"

"Nope. I got it. Thanks."

She hangs up in true New Yorker style—abruptly. Butterflies are beating inside me. I feel like something good is going to happen.

I push the door to Carter's room open to find him right where I left him. My lips meet his in a tender kiss.

"I'm back," I whisper, resting my forehead against his. His hand is in mine like always.

"I was wondering when you'd be back," his soft voice has my breath catching in my chest.

"Carter?" I'm a bumbling idiot, tears coursing down my cheeks as I pull away and stare at him in disbelief. He gives me a shaky smile, his beautiful, brown eyes bright with his own tears.

"Teddy Bear," he whispers, cupping my face tenderly. "I've missed holding you."

"Carter." I'm weeping so much I can barely breathe.

He lets out a soft chuckle. "Come here, baby."

He doesn't have to tell me twice. I'm on the bed and snuggled in his arms, sobbing like a child. His fingers thread through my hair, and he murmurs, "My sweet girl. I love you so fucking much."

"I love you too." I tilt my head up to look at him.

His head is bald because they had to shave it for the surgery. The ugly scars are a beacon to the pain he's been in. But none of that matters. Hair grows back. Scars fade. What matters is he's here now. With me. Holding me. We're together.

Before we get the chance to talk, the nurse comes back in with my dad and a few other doctors. I shift to move away from Carter, my cheeks heating. He's still weak, but he manages to pull me back for a gentle kiss that screams of more.

Before long, the room is full of people checking Carter's motor and cognitive skills. I move to the far corner of the room and give them space to make sure he's all right.

I take a few candid pics of him and send them to Derek and Doctor Aarons in a group text.

Me: He's awake. Come see for yourselves!
Derek: On my way.
Dr. A: Be there as soon as traffic allows.

WHEN I LOOK UP FROM MY PHONE IT'S TO FIND CARTER'S EYES ON ME. Everything in that look says everything I feel for that man. And more. So much more.

FORTY

TEDDY

"It's just after 8:00 PM. Go and rest, Teddy. He's probably not going to wake up until the morning with all the medication they gave him after dinner." Derek's eyes sweep over me.

I stuff my iPad and earbuds in my bag. I glance over to Carter who's been out for hours. "You're right. I promised Carter I'd go to the hotel and get some sleep. Thanks for staying with me."

"Why don't you go stay at his place? I know he's offered it."

"It wouldn't feel right without him there."

Derek gives me a sympathetic look but nods.

I pull my phone out of my back pocket to call an Uber, and a small card falls to the floor. Derek scoops it up and hands it to me. "A talent scout? Republic Records. Nice. It's about time you went after your own dreams."

"Talent Scout? What?" I snatch it out of his hands. My eyes bulge in surprise.

"You didn't know you had the business card of a talent scout in your pocket?" He laughs softly at my shock. "How is that possible?"

"He listened to me play while waiting for his mother this morning, and when he left he handed me his card and said something like "If you ever need my services…ugh. I thought he was a cable salesman or something like that."

"Teddy, that's Ed Wilcott. He signs major talent, like Grammy-award winning, multi-platinum singers for Universal Music. You *have* to call him."

I grab my case and throw open the buckles, pulling out my trusty guitar. No hesitation. Not anymore. If there's one thing I've learned from Carter, it's that we only live once so we have to take every opportunity that comes our way or risk losing it. I wrap my guitar strap around me and grab my phone. "I can do better than call him. C'mon, Derek. We have a little concert to play before bedtime." He follows me next door to Room 11.

I knock quietly, and within a few seconds, the door is pulled open. Mr. Wilcott greets us with a full smile. "You came. She's going to be so surprised."

"How's she's doing tonight?"

"Well, today's report is rough. She wasn't happy when I went to work, so she threw a fit with the nurses. But she seems to be settling down now."

"Let's see if we can relax her some more. Mr. Wilcott, I'm Teddy Bruce, and this is my friend, Derek." Derek squeezes my side excitedly.

"Please, call me Ed." He draws the curtain back as we enter the room. "Mama, we've got company."

Blue eyes open and hesitantly peer at me first then at Derek. She spots my guitar hanging around my neck, and a weak smile illuminates her pale face. Ed raises her bed to slightly sitting, as I take a seat and remove the glass pick from between the strings holding it.

"Here's a classic. It's one of the first songs I ever learned to play." I strum the opening lines to "Mama He's Crazy" by The Judds. She watches me play for a bit then closes her eyes. I can see her foot tapping to the song through the sheet, but by the end of it she's fast asleep.

I stand and grab my bag, tiptoeing to the door behind Derek who holds it open for me and Ed to walk through. I turn to him with my hand outstretched for him to shake. "Sorry that wasn't much of a concert for her but thank you for the opportunity to help her rest easily."

"She loved it, and now she's dreaming peacefully, which is exactly what she needs." He shakes my hand but doesn't let go immediately. "Teddy, I want you to call me. I'm serious. Set up an appointment with Sarah, my assistant. We'll talk. You've got a crazy talent that I can't let walk away."

"I will."

He grins and finally lets go.

"I look forward to it," he says before he turns and strides back into his mother's room.

I enter Carter's room floating on cloud nine. Derek high-fives me.

"Teddy, that was incredible. You are crazy talented."

"Thanks. Now I feel sick." My hand presses against my stomach to calm the butterflies currently going crazy within it.

"That's the adrenaline working. You just auditioned for Ed Wilcott in his mother's hospital room. How awesome and completely insane is that?"

"It's too much. All of this. Now. At once." I hold my hands out, gesturing to Carter and next door. I place my guitar back into the case and secure it.

"When things are going right, you don't question the timing. Carter is alive, your music career is about to skyrocket, and your family is back in your life. This is exactly where you belong in this moment. You're blessed. Ride the wave, because you deserve this."

I hug him tightly. "No wonder Carter loves you. You're a good man with a heart of gold and an intelligent mind. You deserve all the good things in life."

"Carter George deserves all the credit for getting that wild hair up his ass to go on an adventure," Derek blurts out. We both turn and look at him sleeping peacefully.

"Thank God for Carter George 2.0."

EPILOGUE

CARTER

Fifteen months later

S he's fidgeting in her seat as Kelsea Ballerini reads the nominees for Best New Artist. I pull her hand to my lips and kiss it. "Don't be nervous, baby. They're going to call your name. I hope you have your acceptance speech ready."

"If they do, just pray I don't throw up, pee myself, or fall in these heels, Carter."

"You're going to be fine, Teddy Bear. You're stronger than you know and more talented than you give yourself credit for. Remember the Grand Canyon? That was way worse, and you survived that."

She gives me a shaky smile. I want to kiss her worries away but know I can't since we're very much in the public eye at that moment. I settle for giving her hand a squeeze. The past year and a half have been a wild ride. Teddy and her father saved my life. Well, everyone saved my life. I'm cancer free. My hair has grown back. And my girl is achieving her dreams. Our life is hectic with her music career and me going back to my company part-time, but it's so fucking good. I travel most of the time with Teddy, doing my work remotely. She insisted I come with her, and who am I to tell her no? I'm excited for The Ultimate Roadtrip Tour. She and Luke will be touring together. I know the title of the tour will live up to its name.

The sound of the announcer's voice pulls me back to the present. I know Teddy is going to win. She's been hanging in the Billboard top slots for weeks now.

"And the Grammy-nominated Best New Artist of the Year is… Teddy Bruce."

Her song "Rescue Me" starts to play, and the camera zooms in on her reaction. Her face flashes from shock to fear to sheer joy as she jumps from her chair to kiss me. I know I'm the luckiest man alive to have the unconditional love of this amazing woman.

"Way to go, baby," I murmur in her ear as my lips brush against her soft skin. "Go get your award." I want to slap her sexy ass but refrain. Instead, I clap loudly with the rest of the audience. I'll smack her ass later.

She makes it up the wide steps and accepts her Grammy. Her voice quivers as she begins her speech—thanking the fans, her parents, and the obligatory managers and record label.

"There's one more person I need to thank because without him, I'd still be in Nashville singing at open-mic nights and probably going nowhere. Carter George, when you came into my life, I had nothing. No one. You've given me so much. Thank you for rescuing me. I love you."

The crowd cheers wildly as she exits the stage. I'm eager to get to her. I know she has to do her rounds for publicity in the back, so I sit in my seat.

"Girl has some talent," Luke whispers next to me. "We still on for later?"

"Hell yeah," I say with a grin. I have one hell of an after-party planned.

~

"I can't believe I won!" Teddy screeches as I lift her in my arms and twirl her.

"I can." I plant a kiss on her red lips which she eagerly returns. "Now let's get your sexy ass back to my place. The night's just beginning."

She grins at me without protest and lets me escort her to our waiting limo. The moment we're inside, my hands are all over her. She looks incredible in her slinky, red dress.

"Carter," she giggles and gasps as my hands find their way beneath the silky garment.

"What?" I tease, nipping at her ear as I dip my finger into her warmth. She's already wet, her breathing ragged. "I don't see much protest, Teddy Bear."

"None," she moans as I push another finger into her hot center. "I want you."

"Mm, baby, you have me," I growl, tracing hot kisses down her incredibly low neckline.

"The ride isn't long, Carter," she pleads, her fingers tangling in my dark hair.

"What are you saying?" I tease, leisurely gliding my fingers in and out of her.

"I'm saying that I want you inside of me."

That's all I need to hear. My cock is already straining against my zipper. I let it free, pushing her dress up and pulling her panties down. She straddles my lap.

"Oh God," she moans as I plunge deep into her center. "Carter."

"Teddy," I say her name like a prayer as I pump in and out of her.

She's my kind of heaven. So sweet. Hot. Wet. Her back arches, her pussy clamping around my cock. My eyes are practically rolling into the back of my head as we both find our release.

"I love you," I say, pressing a tender kiss to her lips as I rest my forehead against hers. "I want to give you so much, Teddy Bear. I promise I will."

"You already have," she whispers, angling her head up so she can kiss me again. My heart soars. This night has been incredible. And it's only just started.

~

OUR PLACE IS PACKED.

"Carter! Teddy!" Derek calls out. I grin and tug Teddy deeper into the room. People are clapping and congratulating her. Even Molly rushes up to her and gives her hand a lick. She responds by giving the dog a good scratching.

"Everything is ready," Derek murmurs to me, shoving a small, velvet box into my hands. "Luke is going to play guitar to the song you wrote. You sing it, man. Then you do your thing."

I nod, feeling breathless. It's now or never. I turn back to Teddy.

"I have a surprise for you," I say, brushing my lips along her jaw.

"Mm, I love surprises."

"Liar."

She laughs softly, and I give her a gentle squeeze.

"I'll be right back."

She kisses me again, and it takes all I have to walk away from her. But I know the outcome will be worth it. At least I hope so. I spot her parents moving toward her in the crowd. Even her brother and sister made it out. It warms my heart to see the smile on her face as she rushes to greet them.

"Sweetheart," my mother calls out to me. I turn to her. "I have my camera ready. And Ernie is here to photograph." She points in the direction of the photographer she's started dating. He's a nice guy, and I've found myself loving his work. It's just more things that scream this is meant to be.

"Are you OK?" Mom asks as I adjust my collar.

"Nervous," I laugh, running my fingers through my hair. Mom and I are close now. We visit one another often, and she adores Teddy. I couldn't ask for more. Well, I could. And that's exactly what I'm going to do.

"Don't be. She loves you." Mom kisses my cheek before moving back into the crowd. I breathe out to calm myself before finding Luke. Derek already has everything set up for Luke to play.

"Ready?" Luke grins, grabbing his guitar.

"Yes," I nod. I glance out to the crowd of partygoers and see Teddy talking with her family still. Phil and his wife have joined them. This is it.

"Good evening, everyone!" Luke's voice booms out. The room goes quiet, the excitement coursing through. Luke also took home an award tonight—Best Country Album. He's become a bit of a star.

"First off, I want to thank Carter and Teddy for having us here tonight."

The partygoers cheer loudly. Luke grins out at them.

"Second, I want to say how damn *good* it is to see Carter George cancer free and living life!"

More cheers from the guests. I grin out at them, meeting Teddy's eye. She's moved to the front and is watching me, confusion on her face.

"And last, I am *honored* to have met this man. Carter George, you changed my entire world. And I thank you for it. It's been a hell of a ride for all of us."

He nods at me. It's hard for me not to shed a tear. I wipe it away quickly and fix a shaky smile on my face.

"Now, I'm not here tonight to fanboy over Carter." The crowd laughs and even I crack a grin.

Luke continues. "I'm here tonight because Carter wrote a song for his beloved Teddy, and he wants to sing it for her. He's not as big of a songbird as she is, but let's give him this moment, shall we?"

People are murmuring and cheering. Some pull their phones out. I hadn't planned on a live stream but to hell with it. Luke strums his guitar, and I belt out the first verse of the song I wrote for her.

You say I rescued you
But baby, you rescued me
Without you in my life

This life would cease to be
I know things get hard
I know things get rough
I know things can be a bit too much
But with you by my side
this life will always be
perfect enough
I love you with everything I am
We were meant to be
Oh, Teddy Bear
Will you please marry me?

THE CROWD GASPS AS MY LAST NOTE RINGS OUT AND I GET TO ONE knee, the velvet box open and poised for her. My eyes remain locked on Teddy's, as they have been the entire time I've been singing. Derek helps her to me. Her trembling hands move to wipe her tears away as I remain kneeling in front of her, mic still in hand.

"Teddy, you're a streak of lightning that shot into my dark world. I was sick and dying and hated the man I was. You called me a monster then admitted to your own evils, and we made a pact to unite in our monsterdom. Then and there, I knew I loved you. You never left my side, and in my darkest of days, I told you I wanted to marry you. Nothing has changed. If anything, I want you more. So what do you say, Teddy Bear? Another adventure with me?"

I hold my breath, waiting for her to speak. She lets out a sob, tears rolling down her cheeks as she nods yes. I let out the breath I'm holding and push the diamond ring onto her shaking fingers before getting to my feet and pulling her in for a hug.

"I love you, baby," I say fiercely, holding her tight.

"I love you too, Carter." She giggles breathlessly, sniffling, her holding me just as tightly.

I plant a deep kiss on her tear-soaked lips as the crowd cheers in the background.

"I think we may have a number one hit." I grin down at her, breaking away.

"I couldn't agree more."

And with that, I haul her back into my arms, thanking God for a little bit of karma and a whole lot of Teddy.

Thank you for reading The Middle Road! Please consider leaving your review. We'd love to hear from you!

ABOUT K.G. REUSS

K.G Reuss is a *USA Today* and international bestselling author. Contemporary and paranormal romance with a splash of urban fantasy are her favorite genres to write.

She was born and raised in northern Michigan. She currently resides there with her husband, her children, and a few ghosts. K.G. is the author of T*he Everlasting Chronicles* series, *Emissary of the Devil* series, T*he Chronicles of Winterset* series, and *Seven Minutes in Heaven*. K.G. is also a contributing author to the Sweetest Obsessions boxed set and the Cursed Lands boxed set.

When K.G. Reuss isn't pursuing her love for reading and writing, she is working in emergency medicine.

Follow K.G Reuss:

http://www.facebook.com/kgreuss

https://www.amazon.com/K-G-Reuss/e/B01I9YU2JM

www.twitter.com/kgreuss

www.instagram.com/authorkgreuss

ABOUT C.M. LALLY

C.M. Lally is a Contemporary romance author, specializing in the Sports romance and Steamy romance sub-genres.

She has always been a bookaholic, often getting lost in the library for hours inside a good romance. She's in love with happily ever after and often combines her passion for writing with an even deeper love of music. She adores matching strong, bold, and sassy women with the men who can handle them.

She's a small town girl with big city #sassitude. She resides in Cincinnati, Ohio, where life is as unpredictable as the weather and the alpha heroes she adores. If close by, stop for a long chat, some chocolate, and a few laughs. She's always good for any or all three.

Follow CM Lally:

https://www.facebook.com/AuthorCMLally/

https://www.amazon.com/C-M-Lally/e/B01MSZ09UR

https://twitter.com/CyndyLally

www.instagram.com/cm.lally

74053637R00159

Made in the USA
Columbia, SC
11 September 2019